To Amy,
The greatest moments of my life have come with you
by my side

PRAISE FOR THE NOVELS OF CHARLIE DONLEA

THE SUICIDE HOUSE

"Gripping . . . the book's real strength is the idiosyncratic Rory, who suffers from OCD and is on the autism spectrum, a deeply developed character readers can't help rooting for. Hopefully, she'll be back soon." —*Publishers Weekly*

"Charlie Donlea is a superb psychological suspense writer . . . the book has a fast-paced plot and main characters unlike any typically found in this genre." —*Seattle Book Review*

SOME CHOOSE DARKNESS

"In Donlea's skillful hands, this story of obsession, murder, and the search for truth is both a compassionate character study and a compelling thriller." —*Kirkus Reviews*

"Part 1970s serial-killer thriller and part contemporary Chicago crime novel, this deceptively quick read has something for everyone." —*Booklist*

DON'T BELIEVE IT

"You can't blame Charlie Donlea if the ending of his novel makes your jaw drop. The title alone is fair warning that his characters are no more to be trusted than our initial impressions of them." —*The New York Times Book Review*

THE GIRL WHO WAS TAKEN

"A fast-moving page-turner. . . . Donlea skillfully maximizes suspense by juggling narrators and time all the way to the shocking final twists." —*Publishers Weekly*

SUMMIT LAKE

"With a soaring pace and teasing plot twists, Charlie Donlea's debut mystery is like a cool drink of water with a twist of lemon. It's refreshing to find a book that has such a well-developed plot and excellent writing to back it up." —*BookPage*

Books by Charlie Donlea

SUMMIT LAKE

THE GIRL WHO WAS TAKEN

DON'T BELIEVE IT

SOME CHOOSE DARKNESS

THE SUICIDE HOUSE

TWENTY YEARS LATER

Published by Kensington Publishing Corp.

SUMMIT LAKE

CHARLIE DONLEA

KENSINGTON
PUBLISHING CORP.

www.kensingtonbooks.com

KENSINGTON BOOKS are published by
Kensington Publishing Corp.
119 West 40th Street
New York, NY 10018

All Kensington titles, imprints, and distributed lines are available at special quantity discounts for bulk purchases for sales promotion, premiums, fund-raising, educational, or institutional use.

Special book excerpts or customized printings can also be created to fit specific needs. For details, write or phone the office of the Kensington Sales Manager: Attn.: Sales Department. Kensington Publishing Corp., 119 West 40th Street, New York, NY 10018. Phone: 1-800-221-2647.

The K logo is a trademark of Kensington Publishing Corp.

First Kensington Hardcover Edition: February 2016

ISBN: 978-0-7860-4142-8 (ebook)

ISBN: 978-1-4967-3699-4

First Kensington Trade Paperback Edition: April 2022

10 9 8 7 6 5 4 3 2

Printed in the United States of America

Thanks to the great people at Kensington who brought this book to life and made it exist somewhere other than my mind. To my editor, John Scognamiglio, who saw the promise in a flawed manuscript and took a chance on me. Thanks for pointing out the spot where I took a wrong turn in the story, and for helping me find my way home.

Thanks to my agent, Marlene Stringer, who pushed me over the years to keep writing when quitting was an easier option. You found this story inside of me when I wasn't sure another existed. To my sister, Mary Murphy, whose enthusiasm for my writing career sometimes rivals my own. Thanks for the foot-long texts, the brainstorming sessions and the kitchen hutch. To Chris Murphy, who reminded me how college kids talk. Thanks for taking an interest in my book while you were busy writing something yourself. And to my wife, Amy Donlea, who has an annoying habit of guessing the twist in every book she reads, including this one. Thanks for saving this story by showing me how to keep the secret a secret.

And much love and many hugs to my kids, Abby and Nolan, who never stopped asking questions about my progress on this book. Incidentally: Yes, the agent liked it. Yes, the editor "in New York" agreed to publish it. And no, you can't read it for many, many years. It's for grown-ups. But keep reading at bedtime, and keep writing your own stories—don't ever stop. One day, I'll be reading *your* books.

And if all your dreams come true
Do your memories still end up haunting you?
Is there such a thing as really breaking through
To another day and a brighter shade of blue

—Christine Kane
"She Don't Like Roses"

PART I

THE MORNING FALLS

Chapter 1

Becca Eckersley
Summit Lake
February 17, 2012
The night of her death

The winter night sucked the sky black by the time she left the cafe. She walked the dark streets of Summit Lake and pulled her scarf tight against the cold. It felt good to finally tell someone. It made it real. Spilling her secret relieved the pressure from a long-held burden, and Becca Eckersley relaxed a bit. She finally believed it would all work out.

When she reached the lake, the dock creaked under her feet until she stepped onto the wraparound deck of her parents' stilt house. Carefree and liberated after her time at Millie's Coffee House, Becca never felt his presence. Didn't notice him in the shadows, hidden under the cover of darkness. She keyed the side door to the mudroom and locked it behind her, then undraped her scarf and slipped out of her heavy coat. She set the alarm and headed to the bathroom where she climbed under the hot flow of water and let the stress drain from her body. It was a test run, her coffeehouse confession. Practice. She'd kept too many secrets over the last year, this being the biggest and most foolish of them all. The others could be blamed on youth, chalked up to inexperience. But hiding this last part of her life was pure immaturity, explained only by fear and naïveté. The relief she felt from finally telling someone confirmed her decision. Her parents needed to know. It was time.

Exhausted from law school and the frantic pace of her life, it was easy to imagine crawling under the covers and sleeping until morning. But she came to Summit Lake to get her work done. To get back on track. Sleeping was not an option. She took ten minutes to blow-dry her hair and climb into comfortable sweats and thick wool socks. At the kitchen island she turned on her iPod, pulled out her textbook, notes, and laptop, and got to work.

Earlier, the shower and hair dryer had washed out the noise of the door handle rattling from outside and the two strong shoulder thrusts testing the strength of the deadbolt. But now, after an hour of Constitutional Law, Becca heard it. A rattle or vibration at the door. She turned down the iPod and listened. A half a minute of silence passed, then a loud rap at the door. Three loud knuckle-to-wood claps that startled her. She checked her watch and froze with anticipation, knowing he wasn't supposed to arrive until tomorrow. Unless he was surprising her, which he was known to do.

Becca ran to the mudroom door and pulled the curtains to the side. What she saw confused her, and in that confusion her thoughts ran sideways. Excitement filled her gut and emotion stirred her heart, and with so much clouding her mind, no single thought shouted loud enough to give her pause. Tears welled in her eyes and a smile came to her face. She punched the code on the alarm system, bringing the red light to green, then released the deadbolt and twisted the handle. She was surprised when he forced the door open and, like built-up water against a bulkhead, pushed and slid into the mudroom. More surprising still was his aggression. Unprepared for the onslaught he threw at her, she felt her heels skid and drag across the tile floor until he slammed her against the wall. Clutching her shoulders, then a fistful of hair at the base of her skull, he wrestled her through the mudroom and into the kitchen. Panic wiped her mind blank—all the ideas and images there just seconds before, erased now—allowing her primitive instincts to take over. Becca Eckersley fought for her life.

The violent flurry continued through the kitchen, Becca grasping and kicking at anything that might help her. She saw her textbook and laptop scatter to the floor as her wool-stockinged feet struggled for traction on the cold tile. As he jerked her through the room, Becca's legs frantically scissored back and forth. A wild kick met the kitchen hutch, sending dishes shattering across the floor. With the chaos in the kitchen still settling—bowls rolling, stools bouncing—she felt the carpet of the family room under her feet. It gave her leverage and Becca used every bit of it to pull away from his grip, but her resistance only fueled her attacker's rage. He wrenched her head backward, ripping a clump of hair from her scalp and sending her into a free fall. When she landed, Becca felt her head crack against the wood frame of the couch as he heaved himself on top of her. The pain in her head vibrated down her spine. Her vision blurred and the noise of the world began to fade, until his ice-cold hands thrust into her sweatpants. This snapped her back to consciousness. As the weight of his body pinned her down, she punched and clawed until her knuckles broke and her nails became thick with skin and blood.

When she felt her underwear rip away, she screamed a piercing, shrill cry. But it lasted only a few seconds, until his hands found her throat and crushed her voice into raspy gasps. He was vicious and possessed as he silenced her, his hands clamping with a powerful rage around her neck. She sucked for air, but it would not come, and soon her arms fell like deflated balloons to her sides. And though her body could no longer respond to the panicked calls from her mind, she still resisted by never breaking eye contact with him. Until her vision faded like her voice.

Broken and bleeding, she lay there, her chest barely rising with shallow breaths. She drifted in and out, waking each time he brutalized her in angry, violent waves. It went on for an eternity before he left her. Before he fled through the sliding glass door of the family room, leaving it wide open and allowing the cold night air to fill the room and creep over her naked body. Becca's eyelids fell to slivers. All that was left now was white halogen glowing in the doorframe, bright against the dark night. Becca lay motionless, unable to blink or look away had the desire come to her. It did not. She was strangely content in her paralysis. Tears slid down her cheeks and climbed the curve of her earlobes before dripping silently to the floor. The worst was over. The pain was gone. His fists no longer pummeled her, and her throat was finally free from his crushing grip. His hot breath gone from her face, he was no longer on top of her, and his absence was all the freedom she wanted.

On the floor with her legs splayed and arms like two broken tree limbs attached to her sides, she faced the wide-open patio door. The lighthouse in the distance—with its bright beacon calling out to lost boats in the night—was all she knew and all she needed. It was life and she clung to its swaying image.

Far away a siren bounced through the night, low at first, then gathering strength. Help was coming, although she knew it was too late. Still, she welcomed the siren and the aid it would bring. It was not herself she was hoping to save.

Chapter 2

Kelsey Castle
Events *Magazine*
March 1, 2012
Two weeks after Becca's death

Kelsey Castle's return to work was quiet and without ceremony, just the way she wanted it. She parked in the rear lot so no one would notice her car, and rather than risk the elevator she snuck in the backdoor and climbed the stairs. Early still, most of the staff was battling rush hour or snoozing the alarm clock. She couldn't stay invisible forever. She would have to talk to *someone*. But Kelsey hoped to keep her office door closed and play catch-up for a few hours, uninterrupted by sad smiles and how-are-you stares.

The cubicles were empty when she poked her head out of the stairway. In a smooth stroll she walked the hallway, keeping her eyes set on her office door—a racehorse with blinders. The door to her editor's office was open with lights blazing. Kelsey knew she wouldn't beat him to the office, never did. After a few more steps she reached her office, slithered through the door, and quickly shut it behind her.

"What are you doing here?" Penn Courtney asked with a

look of disapproval. "You're not supposed to be back for two more weeks." He was sitting on her couch, feet on the coffee table, paging through drafts of articles that would run in this week's edition.

Kelsey took a deep breath as she turned from her closed door. "Why are you in my office? Whenever you need something, you wait in my office."

"Good to see you, too."

Kelsey walked to her desk and dropped her purse in the bottom drawer. "Sorry." She took another deep breath and smiled. "Good to see you, too, Penn. And thanks for everything you've done for me. You're a good friend."

"You're welcome." He paused a moment before continuing. "How you doing?"

"Good God, right through the gates and I get it. We talked about this already. I don't want everyone running around here asking me how I am every minute of the day."

"Hence the stealth return before the troops arrive? Let me guess, you took the stairs."

"I need the exercise."

"And parked in the back lot?"

She just stared at him.

"You can't hide from everyone. People are concerned about you."

"I get that. I just don't want all the mushy stuff, you know?"

Penn waved his hand. "Won't ask again." He organized the papers in front of him in neat stacks to keep his hands busy. "But really, what are you doing here?"

"I'm stir-crazy at home, so six weeks isn't going to work. I made it a month, that's all I can take. So back to my original question, why are you in my office?"

Penn stood from the couch, a stack of papers in his hands, and walked to the front of her desk. "I was going to do this in two weeks, but I guess I can ask you now."

Kelsey sat behind her desk. The computer screen already captured her attention as she scrolled through e-mails. "Look at all these e-mails. Hundreds. See? This is why I wanted to do some work from home."

"Forget the e-mails," Penn said. "They're all junk." He let her read for a minute before he continued. "Have you ever heard of Summit Lake?"

"No, what is it?"

"A little town in the Blue Ridge Mountains. Quaint. Cozy. Lots of out-of-towners who spend time at their weekend homes. Water sports when it's warm, ski trails and snow-mobiling when it's cold."

Kelsey glanced at him, then back to her computer. "You need any Propecia? There are about fifty e-mails here that hock it."

Penn ran a hand over his smooth scalp. "I think it's too late for that."

"Viagra? Do these idiots know I'm a woman? Yeah, most of these are junk."

"I want you to go there," Penn said, dropping the pages on her desk.

Kelsey stopped scrolling. Her eyes moved from her computer screen to the dropped pages and then up to her editor's eyes. "Go where?"

"Summit Lake."

"For what?"

"A story."

"Don't start this, Penn. I just told you."

"I'm not starting anything. There's a story there and I want you on it."

"What story could possibly be in a tiny tourist town?"

"An important one."

"Terrible answer," she said. "You're getting rid of me because you don't think I'm ready to come back."

"That's not true." He paused. "I'm getting rid of you because I think you need it."

"Dammit, Penn!" Kelsey stood up also. "Is this how it's going to be from now on? Tiptoeing around me like I'm a porcelain doll, giving me fluff pieces and sending me on vacations because you don't think I can handle my job?"

"To be honest, no, I don't think you can handle your job right now. No, I don't think you should come back so soon. And, no, this is not how it's going to be from now on." Penn lowered his voice, put his palms on her desk, and leaned closer, looking straight into her eyes. Twice her age, with two sons and a successful vasectomy, Kelsey Castle was the closest thing he'd ever have to a daughter. "But this is how it's going to be right now. There's a story in Summit Lake. I want you to track it down. Is it an accident the town has a gorgeous view of the mountains and a beautiful blue lake? No. Would the magazine normally set you up in a five-star hotel with all expenses paid? *Hell* no. But I own the damn magazine, you helped build the magazine, and I want this story done right. I'm sending you to Summit Lake for as long as it takes to figure it out." Penn sat in a chair in front of Kelsey's desk and exhaled a long, calming breath.

Kelsey closed her eyes and fell into her own chair. "Figure what out? What's the story?"

"A dead girl."

She raised her eyebrows, stared at him with her big, brown eyes. "Go on."

"It's the only recorded homicide in the history of Summit Lake, and currently a big deal up there. Happened a couple of weeks ago, and it's starting to make national headlines. The girl's dad is a prominent attorney. Family is wealthy. Police have no leads yet. No suspects. No persons of interest. Just a girl who was alive one day and dead the next. Something's not adding up. I want you to rattle some cages and poke around. Find what everyone else is missing. Then give me an article that people want to read. I want to plaster this poor girl's face on the cover of *Events*, not just with a story *about* her death, but with the truth. And I want to do it before the other vultures pick up the scent and descend on Summit Lake. Once that small town fills with reporters and tabloids, no one's going to talk."

Kelsey pulled the pages Penn dropped on her desk and skimmed through them. "Not as fluffy as I thought."

Penn made an ugly face. "Do you think I'd send my best crime reporter to write about cute shops and galleries?" He stood up. "Take a couple days here to do your research, then off you go. Find out if there's a story up there, and if there is, write the hell out of it. And I don't expect you back anytime soon. I want this for the May edition. That means even if you get this story straight the day you arrive, you've got the hotel for a month."

Kelsey smiled. "Thanks, Penn."

Chapter 3

Becca Eckersley
George Washington University
November 30, 2010
Fourteen months before her death

In the recesses of the George Washington University library, Becca Eckersley sat with her three friends. Desk lamps illuminated their table, brightening textbooks and papers, and highlighting their faces in the otherwise darkened space. Three years earlier, she arrived on campus with no high school friends, but Becca found no problems adjusting to college. Freshman year she roomed with Gail Moss, and the two quickly became friends. Becca and Gail, together with their two guy friends—Jack and Brad—were all headed for law school. They studied together regularly and made an unusual foursome.

"People say it all the time," Gail said.

"What people?" Brad asked. "Who talks about us so much?"

"I don't know," Gail said. "Just other kids. I've heard girls talk."

"And what's their problem?"

"They just think we're weird."

"Who cares what they think?" Brad said. "Seriously, this is all in your head."

"It's not in my head," Gail said. "Okay, I'll just put it out there and ask the question. Why are we friends?"

"What do you mean?" Becca asked. "Because we like each other. We all get along, have things in common. That's why anyone becomes friends."

"She means the sex, or lack of it, between us," Brad said. "She's just too shy to phrase it that way." He looked at Gail. "You better figure out a way to express yourself more clearly if you want to be a litigator."

"Fine," Gail said, closing her eyes momentarily to avoid eye contact. "Does anyone think it's odd that we've been friends since freshman year and there's been no hookups, no sleeping around, no drama?"

"You had a boyfriend for the first year we knew you," Jack said. "What was his name?"

"Gene."

Jack laughed and pointed at Gail. "That's right. Euge. I loved that guy. Sort of a tool, but in a geeky, cool kind of way."

Brad laughed also. "I forgot about that guy. He hated when we called him Euge. 'It's just Gene' he kept saying. Remember that weekend?"

Becca laughed now, too. "The 'Just Gene' weekend. Oh my God, that seems like more than three years ago."

Gail tried not to smile. "Yeah, very amusing. He never came back to DC after that weekend, anyone notice that?"

"He broke up with you a few weeks later, didn't he?" Jack asked.

"Yes, because of that weekend."

"Come on," Jack said. "Because we called him Euge?"

"Forget it," Gail said. "My point is that our little foursome here is unique. Two girls, two guys—all best friends, in college, without any of the crazy stuff to mess it up."

Jack closed his Business Law textbook. He patted Brad on the back. "Brad here will be the most powerful senator in Congress, you two will be schmuck lawyers working for him, I'll be a lobbyist getting him all his money, and we'll all still be best friends. Who cares why, and who cares if other people don't understand?" He threw his books into his backpack. "I've had enough for tonight. Let's get a beer at the 19th."

"Amen," Brad said.

They packed their things and stood to leave. Becca stared at Jack. "No one's worried about Professor Morton's final?" she asked.

"I'm worried," Jack said. "But I'm on the slow infusion process, which allows my brain to absorb his terribly boring and abstract lectures in small spoonfuls. If I cram it all in, most of it ends up seeping out."

"Yeah," Becca said. "That's a great plan for someone who's kept up with the readings all semester. But for the rest of us, we'll need to cram. You guys go without us, Gail and I are staying."

"Come on," Jack said. "Don't be lame."

"Finals are in two weeks," Becca said.

"Call it quits for tonight and we'll put in extra time tomorrow," Jack said.

Brad stood up and lifted his hands. "Boys and girls, Bradley Jefferson Reynolds has you covered. This was supposed to be a surprise, but I can see you all need to know now. I will have for us, by next week, a copy of Professor Morton's Business Law final exam. To be used and abused as you all see fit."

Becca pursed her lips. "Bullshit."

"No bullshit," Brad said. "I have a source, and that's all I can say for now. So let's all have a beer to celebrate."

Becca looked at Jack, who shrugged his shoulders. "Who are we to doubt this guy?" he said.

She reluctantly packed her things and looked at Gail. "This'll be like the time he promised everyone full-length essays for the Asian History exam freshman year and we were up until 5:00 a.m. finishing things for him when he 'hit a wall.'" She flexed her fingers to make quotation marks while looking at Brad. "Remember that?"

"This is different," Brad said.

"Sure it is." Becca threw her bag over her shoulder and grabbed Brad by the inside of the bicep, resting her head on his shoulder as they walked out of the library. "But I'll still love you when you don't come through. Even though I'll have a C to tarnish my transcripts."

Brad patted her head as they walked. "No Ivy League law school will accept you with a C on your transcript. Looks like I'll have to come through for you."

The 19th Bar in Washington's Foggy Bottom neighborhood held the normal crowd for a Tuesday night, overflowing with college students in the peak of their existence. Most came from wealthy East Coast families and had plans for political careers or law. Some wanted other things, but they were outnumbered.

They found an empty table near the front window, a floor-to-ceiling pane of glass that allowed passersby to look in with envy and see the lives of college kids on the way to stardom. They ordered draught beers and fell into their common routine of debating politics. After a few beers, Brad began his well-practiced, curse-riddled speech about there never having been a U.S. president who truly ran on his principles and then governed the same way.

"They always fall prey to the politics of Washington, always give in to special interests. Can anyone name a president who really had the citizens in mind during the majority of his decisions in office? None of them did, and the current one doesn't either. It's all about power, keeping power, and dishing out power to those who throw the most money at them."

"You tell 'em, Bradley," Becca said. "And you're going to put an end to it all, right?"

"Or die trying. And I'll start with the crooked son of a bitch who calls himself my father." He took a sip of beer. "As soon as I have the credentials."

"I'd build some contacts and support before you go after your own father. Or tort law in general."

"Good idea," Brad said, pointing at Becca and then sloshing another sip of beer like he was in an Irish pub about to arm wrestle. He ran his forearm across his mouth dramatically and stared off at the ceiling. The others were laughing now at the show. "It's gotta come out of right field, totally unsuspected. Yeah, I'll build a coalition and when the old man thinks he's got things covered, I'll take him down like Giuliani tackling the Teflon Don."

"Not even accepted to an accredited law school yet and this guy's comparing himself to Giuliani." Jack laughed. "Love your confidence."

Becca and her friends loved Brad's tirades. Jack and Gail listened for entertainment value, but Becca had a keener ear. She knew Brad best. She knew his secrets and his desires and his struggles. She understood his opinions were born out of rebellion. An oppressive father, who amassed a fortune running one of the biggest tort law offices on the East Coast, had tried too hard to steer his son's life in a direction Brad did not want to go. In a mixture of feigned surrender and secret revenge, Brad agreed to an education at George Washington University and would soon endure an Ivy League law degree. But instead of joining his father in thievery, as Brad put it, he would use the degree and education his father paid for to go after tort law, and one day shut his father down. So the plan went, anyway.

In the three years they knew each other, Becca had met Brad's father on a number of occasions. Becca's father knew him, too. Their dads had a professional relationship, with Brad's father hosting an annual weekend at the Reynoldses' hunting cabin where a dozen rich lawyers shot elk, smoked cigars, and talked business. Becca's father was invited the year before, and came home with stories about Mr. Reynolds being a true ballbuster. A cold, hard man who pushed his children in unhealthy ways, Becca never had difficulty understanding Brad's resentment. As punishment for his father's absenteeism from little league tournaments and soccer practices and Orioles games and anything in high school besides brief appearances at debates to let his son know his deficiencies, Brad decided to use his father's will against him. It was an insidious plan that would take years to accomplish, and if it ever came to fruition—if Brad's resentment didn't fade with maturity, and if his interests didn't change with time—Becca figured there was no worse slap in the face to a parent than for their child to use the education they paid for to set out on a career that would hinder their own. So Becca did more than listen when Brad went on his rants. She knew there was a point beyond Brad's words—it was therapeutic for him to plot a years-long rebellion against his father. It was his way of releasing his frustration without doing it to his father's face and without ruining a relationship that in adulthood might stand a chance at restoration.

They ordered more beer when Brad calmed down.

"Is everyone going home for Christmas this year?" Gail asked. "Because we're going to our place in Florida. My mom said you guys could come down."

"My parents would kill me if I didn't go home," Becca said.

"Yeah," Jack said. "My mother would not go for that. Christmas is too big of a deal."

"Maybe," Brad said.

"Really?" Gail asked.

Brad shrugged. "Yeah, maybe for a few days. My old man gets exhausting after about forty-eight hours. Christmas Eve and Christmas are about all I can handle with him. Maybe I'll head down for a few days after Christmas. Otherwise, I'll be back here and this place is dead until everyone gets back."

"We'll hang out on the beach and think of poor Jack freezing in Wisconsin."

"Rub it in," Jack said.

"It would be a lot of fun," Gail said. "You guys should think about it."

Jack took a sip of beer and looked at Becca, then back at Gail. "Maybe spring break, but I can't do it for Christmas."

Gail widened her eyes. "Spring break! My parents will be in Europe. We'd have the place to ourselves."

"Unless you boys would rather head to South Beach for hookups with University of Miami girls," Becca said.

Brad and Jack looked at each other and touched beers. "Yeah, we'll let you know about spring break. We might have to make a quick stop down South," Jack said.

"Asses," Gail said.

They laughed and ordered more beers. It was two weeks before finals. They were immortal.

Chapter 4

Kelsey Castle
Summit Lake
March 5, 2012
Day 1

High on a bluff in the mountains of Summit Lake, Kelsey Castle watched as the rising sun burned the horizon red and turned the wispy clouds into cherry cotton candy torn across the sky. Farther off the horizon, over the center of the lake, dark thunderclouds formed. A storm was coming and it reminded Kelsey of her youth. Of the sunny rainstorms that always came on her birthday, and of her grandfather's deep belly laugh when they saw the clouds roll in. The downpour happened quickly from newly developed clouds, and her grandfather would whisper in her ear as beads of water ran down their faces and wrinkled their clothes against their bodies—*happy birthday to the rainmaker.* Everyone else ran for cover, newspapers or jackets overhead. Kelsey and her grandfather danced and kicked puddles as the rain came down, all the while a bright blue sky, just beyond the storm clouds, threw slashes of sunlight across the ground and high-lighted the raindrops like diamonds pouring from the sky.

And just as quickly as the storm developed, it would pass, leaving dripping trees and street puddles that reflected the blue sky. It was an odd phenomenon Kelsey grew to love. That they happened each year on her birthday was a special tag on her life that said someone, somewhere, was watching over her on her special day. At least that's what her grandfather always told her.

She walked to the edge of the bluff now and took deep breaths to bring her breathing under control. Arriving in Summit Lake the night before, Kelsey jogged through town early this morning. Quiet and still in the dawn hours, she took twenty minutes to survey the center of town, jogging past storefronts and galleries and exploring side streets to get a feel for the place. After two laps around the town square, the waterfall was her next stop. It was, besides the lake itself, the most famous landmark this tiny town had to offer. And now, standing on the bluff where the falls originated and looking out over the sunrise and the town, Kelsey wanted to call Penn Courtney and thank him for getting her out of the city and away from her house. Thank him for giving her some time away she didn't want to admit she needed. There were books and experts that might help her, but Kelsey was not the type to confide in those structured aids. She always relied on an inner strength to get her through difficult spots in life, and this rough patch would be no different.

The waterfall fell for a hundred feet, passing just in front of the mountain face to eventually crash into the lagoon below. Spruce trees flanked the falls and bearded the mountainside, merging with a dense forest that isolated the lagoon. On the far side of the trees the town of Summit Lake took shape. From Kelsey's vantage point high on the bluff, the town belonged on a postcard. One main drag—Maple Street—ran through the center of town with five roads slicing across, each heaped with shops and boutiques and restaurants and galleries Kelsey had inspected earlier during her run. On the north end was the Winchester Hotel, an old Victorian building that had been hosting guests of Summit Lake for decades and where Penn Courtney arranged for her to stay. Five blocks from the Winchester, on the south end of Maple Street, St. Patrick's Church was a majestic structure built from white stone and decorated with gothic wooden entry doors and a tall steeple that looked like a needle ready to puncture the sky. To the east was the vast expanse of the lake after which the town was named, and together with the western mountains where Kelsey stood, it sandwiched the town of Summit Lake into a cozy setting known for summer houses and weekend getaways.

Homes trickled down from the foothills and circled the lake. A few tiptoed on stilts into the water. The stilt houses, with tiled roofs and large bay windows, were arranged in two long, arching rows to give each a beautiful view of the lake. This morning, the cresting sun threw starbursts off the windows. Kelsey stared over it all. Somewhere in this quaint tourist town, a girl had been murdered. It seemed too nice a place for such a thing to happen.

As she stared down from the bluff, Kelsey felt connected to the town. It had a story to tell her. And even though Penn Courtney sent her here to slowly get her swagger back, to ease her gently back into the occupation she once ruled, Kelsey had no intention of taking it easy. She had interviews to conduct, facts to gather, and evidence to discover. Still, Penn knew what he was doing. Kelsey spent the weekend in Miami researching the Eckersley case and picking through the scarce details about how the girl had died. Now in Summit Lake, she was scouting the town, scoping angles, plotting her path to discovery. Immersing herself in a different world and an unfamiliar setting. She was on the beat again, and it was the first time in five weeks she felt alive.

Kelsey knew, however, the distraction wouldn't last forever. She came to Summit Lake to write the story of a girl's murder, but she also came to put her own demons to rest. That would require self-reflection, something she was not good at. Sitting on the edge of a boulder, she took a deep breath. The creek gurgled as it flowed past, its steady current pulling the clear water around rocks and over submerged logs and to the edge of the cliff where the water began its roar as it fell. As Kelsey watched the water spill over the edge, a single raindrop tapped her nose. Then another, and another. After a minute a solid drizzle fell across the bluff, slowly increasing to a heavy rain that pelted the creek and rippled its surface. She smiled as the rain drenched her, soaked her clothes and matted her hair. She looked out at Summit Lake. The stilt houses were still bright with the dawning sunlight.

A sunny rainstorm, and it wasn't even her birthday.

Chapter 5

Becca Eckersley
George Washington University
December 2, 2010
Fourteen months before her death

Brad's arm supported her head as Becca lay in his bed. It was past three in the morning and not unusual for the pair to fill the empty hours of night with conversation. They talked about their dreams of being lawyers, of litigating cases in front of the Supreme Court, and changing the way Washington worked. They talked about the law schools they would pick if such a thing were possible—to pick a school rather than the other way around. They talked about love, and what they each looked for in the perfect mate. These all-night discussions, which bordered on intimate but never crossed into that territory, were not purposely kept a secret from Gail and Jack. It just happened that way. Without discussing why, they never shared their nights. They existed only between Becca and Brad.

"Okay," Brad said. "Give me one thing that's an absolute deal breaker for dating someone."

Becca took no time to answer. "Back hair."

"Back hair?" Brad said. "Come on. How's a guy supposed to avoid back hair?"

"Wax it or shave it, but don't display it. Complete turnoff."

"What if you dated a guy for two months, really liked him, and then learned he had a back like a sweater?"

"Over," Becca said.

"Just like that?"

"Well, that's your scenario. I don't accept the premise of the situation, since I'd never get as far as really liking a guy who had that much back hair."

"But how would you know? It's the middle of winter and you've never seen him with his shirt off. Shouldn't you work through it before you dump the poor guy? It's a minor problem."

"Eating with your mouth open is a minor problem. Back hair is something worse."

"Okay," Brad said, rolling onto his side and supporting his head with his bent elbow so they were face-to-face. "What does my back look like?"

"What is this, a test?"

"Just want to see how aware you are of something that bothers you so much."

"Okay," Becca said. "A few non-threatening follicles on your shoulder blades and a benign tuft at the small of your back. All in all, a perfectly acceptable back."

"You've got some kind of nasty fetish, huh? That was pretty accurate."

"We've spent about a hundred nights lying next to each other, talking until sunrise. I think I know what your back looks like. Plus, I watched you and Jack play volleyball at the beginning of the school year. Both of your backs are acceptable."

Becca rolled over and sunk her hands under her head. She

wore a pink T-shirt that was tight around her chest, and when she raised her arms it crept up her stomach to reveal dual pelvic bones that sat just above the band of her sweats. Brad always thought she was beautiful, with her blond hair and olive skin and perfect teeth. She was a stunner in every room she entered, and Becca drew the eye of most guys she encountered. But the moments Brad loved most were these. When she was all his, no one else around to steal her attention. She was most exquisite in this intimate setting, lying in his bed, relaxed and content, and not trying to be gorgeous. He knew these short clips of time would last only until the morning light, which was why he savored them so much. There would come a time when he would tell her how he felt, but he wanted things to happen naturally, without forcing them. He knew it was the best way for a long relationship to start. And somehow, for a testosterone-riddled twenty-one year-old, lying next to Becca all night never produced an anxiousness for sex. He was always content simply talking and exploring her mind, and when she fell asleep, listening to her breathe.

There was, of course, the time freshman year when they came home from a late-night party, buzzed from vodka punch, and ended up kissing in his dorm room before they both passed out. They never talked about that night, never discussed whether feelings had developed. Instead, it was hidden away under the easy cover of drunkenness, and both pretended not to remember the incident. Now, three years later, they had never been intimate since, although this did nothing but cause Brad to fall more in love with her. He waited nearly four years for something to happen between them, and he knew it would. Maybe after graduation, when they were out of the environment of college and away from Jack and Gail. Maybe then it would be less awkward. And that was fine, he could wait.

He heard Becca's breathing take on a slow, deep rhythm as she fell asleep. He put his head onto the pillow, resting his forehead against her temple and laying his arm over the twin peaks of her pelvic bone. Brad closed his eyes.

On these nights, the sun always came too soon.

She never stayed long in the mornings, and the bed was always empty when he woke. An avid runner and study junkie, Brad knew Becca was either snaking through campus with headphones dangling from her ears or already at the library with her hair in a ponytail, glasses in lieu of contact lenses, and a tall cup of coffee sitting next to whatever she was studying. Business Law, probably. Final exams were in two weeks, and Brad knew she was struggling.

He found her note on the pillow, where she always left them. They were not much. A sticky note or a torn piece of loose-leaf paper. Sometimes a napkin. They held her words, though, and it was something he loved. Notes like these were meant to be read and tossed. Discarded without thought. But Brad could never bring himself to throw them away. He read this one:

B— *Had fun last night. Thanks for sharing your pillow. No worries, your back looks good to me! —B*

Brad folded the sticky note and dropped it in the shoebox under his bed that held all the other BB notes she'd left him over the years. Then he hit the shower and worked all day on his plan. Becca told him she was in bad shape for finals, and it was all the motivation he needed. He had to come through for her.

It would take most of the day and some conniving, but when he showed up at the library that night he carried a look of satisfaction on his face. It was late. Gail and Becca had already gone home. Only Jack remained, sitting at a desk and poring over an open textbook, notes strewn around him.

"I got it," Brad said as he walked into the dimly lit alcove that marked their study spot.

A single, recessed bulb contrasted stiffly with the dark surroundings of the library and illuminated Jack's cubicle desk. They studied here often—a second-floor area where old periodicals were stored on brown metal shelves and covered in age. Four desks had been abandoned, but during their freshman year they spaced them out head-to-head, cleaned them off, and screwed in new lightbulbs. When serious study was necessary they used the desks, which offered privacy. When group study was easier, they sat at the large table with built-in, green awning lamps. There was no traffic in this abandoned part of the library, and they never had to worry about how loud they were. They cracked open cold cans of Newcastle beer after particularly good study sessions or at the end of finals week when they knew they wouldn't be back in the library for weeks. Brad managed to disarm the alarm on an infrequently used emergency door, and it became their escape route when the library closed and they stayed for an extra hour of cramming.

"Got what?" Jack asked, leaning back in his chair and stretching away the stiffness in his shoulders.

Brad smiled and dangled a key between his thumb and index finger. "Access to Milford Morton's office, and the Business Law final."

"Whatever," Jack said in a dismissive tone.

"Not whatever. I got the key to Morton's office."

"How?"

Brad walked closer. "Mike Swagger. Said he got it from someone last year but old Professor Morton was out on sabbatical, so he never used it. I had to beg him for it. Told me if it ever got back to anyone important that he gave me this key, he'd chop my nuts off—and that's a direct quote."

Jack took the key and studied it. Throughout the year it was a mythical thing, a drudged-up story that went around the fraternity and around campus and especially around the hundred or so kids of Professor Milford Morton's Business Law course that somewhere, someone had a key to the professor's office. And in years past, stealth operations had been conducted during finals week to perpetrate a heist of the final exam. The stories were large and embellished and mostly bullshit, Jack thought. Until now. Until he held what was supposed to be the key to the professor's office.

Jack studied it for a while longer. "No," he finally said. "It's all part of the myth."

"What do you mean?"

"Brad, you're not going to be this naïve when your opposite tries to paint you into a corner in the courtroom, are you? Think about it. The key shows up the year after Morton's sabbatical, so no one's around to confirm if it really works. The two of us take all the steps to use it—including breaking into the building—and then we look like idiots when we're standing in front of ProMo's office in the middle of the night jabbing at a lock with a key that doesn't work."

"Swagger said he got it from a senior last year who broke into Morton's office the year before and had a copy of the exam. The exact test—word for word."

"Right. All once removed and three years ago. It's like the guy who has a cousin who knows a guy who had his kidney stolen."

"What the hell are you talking about?"

"He meets a girl and goes back to her hotel. Next thing he knows, he wakes up in a bathtub filled with ice and a note that tells him to call 911 immediately because his kidney has been stolen for the black market."

"Shut up, Jack. This key is the real deal."

"So's the story about the guy's cousin's friend. Woke up, no kidney."

Brad grabbed the key from Jack's hand. "Trust me. It's legit."

"Says Mike Swagger. Isn't he in his seventh year of college?"

"Are you scared, Jackie Boy?"

"Do you even need a copy of the test?" Jack asked. "I thought you were acing this course."

"I'm doing fine. But ProMo is notoriously boring and vague, so who couldn't use a little help?" There was a gap of silence. "I know Becca could use some. She's struggling big time."

"Struggling for our dear little friend means she might not eke out an A, and the perfect student will have a B for the first time in her life."

"She's saying a C if things go badly. Maybe worse."

"Becca's always on her way to a C until her scores come in and she keeps the 4.0 GPA she's had since first grade. It's Becca's little thing she does. It gets her attention and then everyone congratulates her for rising to the challenge and pulling out an A. Don't fall for it."

"You're not getting out of this, Jack."

"Out of what?"

"We're friggin' breaking and entering."

Jack smiled. "We'll get the boot if we get caught."

Brad raised his eyebrows. "Let's not get caught."

Chapter 6

Kelsey Castle
Summit Lake
March 6, 2012
Day 2

On her second morning in Summit Lake, Kelsey woke under a down comforter in the Winchester Hotel, wrapped in thread counted sheets higher than anything she would purchase on her own. Pulling herself from the warmth of the bed was not an easy task, but she came to Summit Lake to chase a story and today the race began. She also came to heal, and in the last many weeks exercise had not been part of her routine. Typically a morning jogger, the four-mile path along the beach in Miami was a common route she took a few times each week. The doctors restricted her activity during her first two weeks of recovery; lack of motivation and fear had prevented her after that. But today she woke with an eagerness to move and sweat and burn her lungs.

It was a cool morning in Summit Lake as Kelsey took off along the canopied path that wound through the forest and led to the waterfall. There was a moment of hesitation just before entering the forest. Leaving the open area of the town center—where other people walked and shopped and gave off a general vibe of presence—to enter the dark, empty forest put a flutter in her heart. Being alone in her house for the past month was one thing. There, she could lock her door and close her windows. It was where she felt most comfortable. But running alone in the forest brought back the fear she was trying to rid herself of. The fear she was growing to hate.

Nope. Won't let you do it to yourself, Castle.

With a deep breath she took off into the forest in a slow jog. She wore shorts and a long sleeved running shirt, her auburn hair held back in a headband. After a quarter of a mile, she'd worked up a decent burn and her long, muscular legs glistened with perspiration. She found it was a popular trail, offering waves and "good mornings" to other joggers. The more people she passed, the more she calmed down. After half a mile, she stopped peering into the dark brush on each side of her. She was safe.

It was dark along the running path with only glimpses of sunlight poking through the foliage, but a cloudless spring morning welcomed her when she emerged at the falls a mile later. Several other joggers gathered around the lagoon and stared up at the falling water and the morning sunlight that caught the mist. Others sat on rocks and hung bare feet into the blue water. Kelsey took a quick count and settled on thirty people milling around the waterfall. Yesterday, the place was empty.

With her hands on her head, Kelsey made her way over to the water. Her lungs ached, something a mile run would not normally do to her. When she reached the lagoon she took deep breaths and stared at the water like everyone else.

"What's the attraction this morning?" Kelsey asked a woman who stood with her head cocked upward.

The girl smiled. "The morning falls."

"Yeah? Everyone comes just to look at the waterfall?"

"Yes. Well, no. Not just the waterfall. On clear mornings with no clouds, when the sun gets to a certain point over the horizon it hits the water just right and ricochets off the granite behind the falls. For a few minutes it's really pretty." The girl pointed. "There!"

Kelsey watched as the sun penetrated the falls and highlighted the rock face behind the water. The streaming water became backlit, and for two minutes the mountain bled orange-glowing liquid from its side. It was a magical sight Kelsey had never seen in the flatlands of Florida.

"Ta-dah," the girl said. "The morning falls." A few seconds later, the sun hit the water at a different angle and the orange glow faded. "That's it." The girl shrugged.

"Pretty amazing."

The girl paused when she looked away from the waterfall and made eye contact with Kelsey. Her sentences were slow and calculated.

"The sky has to be just right. No clouds, or not many. And the sun has to be at just the right angle. Some of us are fanatical about it. That's why it's so crowded on clear mornings like this. I assume it's your first time here?"

"Yes, first time."

"Sorry to put you on the spot," the girl said. "Aren't you Kelsey Castle?"

Kelsey smiled. "Yeah."

"I read your stuff. I mean, I read *Events*. And I read your novel."

"It's actually a true crime book. Nonfiction."

The girl laughed, a little nervous. "That's what I meant. It was crazy good. I recognize you from your author photo. Can't miss those pretty, brown eyes."

"Thanks," Kelsey said.

"Welcome to Summit Lake. I'm Rae."

"Nice to meet you, Rae."

Rae tapped her chin with her index finger, building up the confidence to ask her next question. Finally, she tapped one more time and then pointed at Kelsey. "Are you here to look into the Eckersley murder?"

Kelsey cocked her head. "I'm here to ask a few questions about it, yes."

"This thing's getting pretty big. Are you writing a piece about Becca in *Events*?"

"Depends what I find."

"And?"

"And what?"

"Figured anything out yet?"

Kelsey smiled. "Haven't interviewed anyone yet, or written one word. I just got here a couple nights ago."

"The town is in quite a tizzy over this, you know?"

"I've heard."

"Mostly because the police won't say anything about the case. It's always 'no comment' on this and 'no comment' on that. No one knows what's going on and people are really frustrated. Scared, too. We just want some answers, and the way the police are being so quiet about the details is weird. But that's a small town, I guess. Lots of weird stuff goes on."

Kelsey shrugged. "I'm from Miami, so I don't know small towns. But one thing I'm sure of. Someone always knows *something*. So either that person hasn't been found yet or hasn't decided to talk."

The crowd began to thin. Many took to the trail back through the woods, others followed paths on each side of the lagoon and disappeared around switchbacks.

"I hope you have some luck while you're here," Rae said. "Just remember, Summit Lake is not the same as Miami. People do things differently up here, especially the locals. They're very protective, so be careful in your approach."

Kelsey raised her eyebrows. "Good advice."

"I work at the coffee shop in town. Come by sometime and we'll have a latte."

Kelsey smiled. "I will."

"You a runner?"

"I'm getting back into it."

"Yeah? Me too. But not usually in the mornings. I'm always at the coffeehouse. Are you heading back to town?"

"Yeah."

"Mind if I join you?"

"Of course not."

They jogged into the cover of the forest. Kelsey ran next to the girl without talking, working hard to keep pace and happy for the company. Her lungs ached and her legs burned—a good ache and a good burn. She was on her way back, emerging from a crumbling building in life many others get trapped in, but one from which Kelsey Castle was determined to escape.

Showered and dressed an hour later, Kelsey found the Summit Lake Police Department. Located next to the firehouse on Minnehaha Avenue, one block west of the town center, the redbrick building was aged and tired. Gaps of missing grout sat between many bricks, and the concrete steps were chipped on the edges. Rust residue spilled from exposed rebar throughout the façade and stained the brick like bleeding wounds. An optimistic person would describe the building as having character, others would say it needed a massive renovation. It wouldn't fit on Maple Street, next to the impeccably manicured shops and galleries, but tucked away on a side street it was inconspicuous and invisible. Kelsey walked up three steps and pulled open the door. Inside a pleasant man with a security badge asked how he could help her.

"I'm here to speak with Commander Ferguson," she said. "My name's Kelsey Castle. I'm from *Events* magazine, running a piece on the Becca Eckersley case."

The man smiled. "A few other reporters have been asking around."

Not a good sign. "The case is drawing some attention, I know," Kelsey said.

"Wait just a minute, I'll see if the commander is in."

Kelsey strolled around the reception area of the small headquarters building and read headlines from framed articles that hung on the wall. This was truly a small town, Kelsey thought. The headlines were of store openings, an elderly couple's fiftieth wedding anniversary, and of the Winter Days Festival. A murder was something not only foreign to this quaint town, but unwanted. She wondered how well equipped the police force was to handle it.

"Kelsey Castle? Is that correct?"

She turned to see Stan Ferguson, a man she knew from her research and with whom she'd spoken last week as she planned her trip. He was well into his sixties, and the unlit cigarette that hung from his lips was surely the source of the wrinkles that road-mapped his face. The same habit contributed to his coarse voice, which was reminiscent of a man recovering from laryngitis.

"Yes," Kelsey said.

They shook hands and Commander Ferguson pointed to the front door, pinching the unlit cigarette between his fingers. "You mind if we talk outside?"

"Sure."

They stood on the sidewalk in front of the old building. The commander lit his cigarette like he'd done a million times before. When he spoke, diluted smoke dripped from his nostrils.

"What can I do for you, Miss Castle?"

"I'm here to write a piece about Becca Eckersley, and I was wondering if there was anything you could tell me about the case."

The commander smiled. "I could tell you a lot, depends on what you want to know."

"This is your police force, right? You're in charge here?"

"Never had another job. Been here forty-plus years."

Kelsey pulled a notepad from her purse. "Can you tell me a little about the night Becca was killed?"

The commander took a pull from the cigarette and looked down the street, toward the lake. "Becca Eckersley was killed on a Friday night—February 17th. What's that, two weeks ago? Just over? She was alone in the family's stilt house the night she died. You familiar with stilt row?" He pointed toward the lake.

Kelsey nodded. She remembered the row of stilt houses she saw during her trip to the top of the falls.

"Came up here from George Washington University, where she was a first-year law student, to study for an exam. Get away from all the distractions, I suppose. She spoke to her parents earlier in the day—a call placed from her cell phone in the morning hours when she was on the way down, and a second call placed from the Eckersleys' home phone just after seven in the evening. It was around 10 p.m. when the next-door neighbor noticed the Eckersleys' patio door wide open. With temperatures in the twenties, he knew something wasn't right. He poked around and found Becca unconscious on the living room floor." Another puff from the cigarette. "She died at Summit Lake Hospital the next morning."

"Did you see the house that night?" Kelsey asked.

The commander nodded.

"Can you describe the scene?"

"Evidence of a struggle. A helluva one, too. Overturned furniture, stools and such. Becca's study materials strewn across the floor. Dishes were broken, all in the kitchen, so we know most of the struggle happened there. But no evidence of forced entry—no broken windows, no jimmied locks. Doors were all in good working order and all the windows were locked."

"So she opened the door for him?" Kelsey asked.

"Or he had a key. Or he was already in the house when she got there. A few different possibilities."

"What's your take?"

The commander shrugged. "Doubt he had a key. The family could account for all of them—both parents and both kids. No duplicates. None were hidden, and no neighbors had any. I also doubt he was in the house before Becca got home. There was a security system that was always set when the Eckersleys were out of town. We checked with the security company and they pulled a log of each time the security code was entered. On the day Becca was killed, the code was registered at three in the afternoon—presumably when Becca got into town. She disengaged it when she entered the house. Then a half hour later—when she left the house, it was reengaged. A third and fourth time right about seven o'clock, when she got home. So it looks like she turned it off when she got home, then reset it immediately knowing she wasn't going out again. This coincided with the phone call she made to her parents at about that time. Then once again the code was entered, about eight o'clock."

"When she opened the door for her killer," Kelsey said.

"That's the thought."

"So it was someone she knew."

"That's one theory, yes. Mine, maybe. But not the most popular."

"No? What's the most popular theory?"

"The vic's purse was missing, so some around here are running with a burglary-gone-bad presumption."

"But no leads?"

"Not yet."

"Do you have any suspects?"

"Had a bunch at first. Always do. But click by click we checked 'em all off the list."

"Family members?"

"All cleared. Solid alibis and no motive. Good family, close. Wealthy and clean-cut. Parents aren't even on my radar, and Becca only had one brother, who was in New York the night she was killed."

"Boyfriends?"

"Working on it."

Kelsey paused. "I'm trying to get hold of the autopsy," she said. "And maybe the notes from the EMTs who were first on the scene. Can I access any of that from you or your department?"

The commander finished his cigarette. "What are you after here, Miss Castle?"

"The truth."

The commander let out a horsey laugh. "And you're going to find it before I do?"

"Before or after, sir. I'm just here to write an article for my magazine, not get in your way. But I want to write an *accurate* article. I want to write about what *actually* happened, not what some people *think* might have happened. I feel for this girl who senselessly died, and for her family. And for this town and this police department. So when I write about all that, I want to make sure I've got things straight."

The commander closed his eyes for a second. "Sorry to come at you. We've never had so much press around, asking questions and second-guessing everything we do."

"Let's make a deal," Kelsey said. "Besides maybe a newspaper or two that's got wide circulation, *Events* will be the biggest medium to cover this story. If you help me out—and I mean *only* me—give me exclusive access to what you know,

I'll make sure anything that gets printed has your approval first."

"And what if I don't like what you write?"

"It goes in the shredder and I start over," Kelsey said, knowing Penn Courtney would disapprove of such a promise. This shredder policy was usually reserved for him.

The commander raised his chin slightly as he considered this. "There's been some unflattering things written about us so far. Like we don't know what we're doing, and we're screwing this case up from here to Hell."

"You've got forty-plus years of experience to draw from, yes?"

"Sure. Not forty years of homicide cases, but I've been trained in such things and have been on the periphery of other homicides in neighboring counties."

Kelsey shrugged. "The way I see it, this is your town and nobody knows it better. If anyone's going to figure this out, it's you and your force. So help me out. And along the way, if I come across anything useful, you'll be the first to hear about it."

"Hold on," the commander said, disappearing up the steps and into the building. He came back fifteen minutes later with a heavy folder two inches thick. He did the stare down to the lake again, then handed her the folder. "This is everything I have so far."

"On the Eckersley case?"

He nodded.

"You're giving this to me?" Kelsey said, taking the folder.

"I know who you are, Miss Castle. I've read your stuff, and I know you're fair. There are some hacks up here, and they're gonna print anything that sells. The more sensational, the better. But the truth?" He shook his head. "That's on the back burner for them. I hold you and all your accolades to a different standard."

Kelsey quickly slipped the folder into her bag. "Thanks for your trust."

"On top of all that, a fresh set of eyes never hurts. And I didn't give you any of that information if anyone asks."

"You run this place, so who's going to ask?"

"I used to run it. The state guys are here now."

"Who?"

"The state detectives, assigned from the District Attorney's office. They've essentially put the cuffs on me and my department. Not only us here in Summit Lake, but the county sheriff, too. They've taken this case from us, end of story. I was involved for the first few days, then they took over under the pretense that they're better suited at handling a homicide than my little department here."

"How does that happen?"

"Politics. Becca was killed in my town. But because we're so small, her father put pressure on the governor—whom he's close with—and the governor put pressure on the DA, and the next thing you know we've got state police poking around up here, making sure we know what we're doing. Then state detectives showed up and reminded me that no one around here has ever handled a homicide before. I don't argue that point. But if I had a little room, and free flow of information, I'd do just fine."

"Isn't Becca's family from Greensboro?"

The commander nodded.

"How can her father—an attorney from Greensboro—control information the police receive here in Summit Lake?"

The commander held up his thumb and index finger. "Money and connections."

"But why? Wouldn't her father want this solved more than anyone?"

"I'm sure he does. But he wants it solved *his* way, and he wants all the messy details controlled. Becca's father, word has it, is getting ready to leave his private law practice for a judgeship. And if it comes out that your family, your daughter in particular, was out of control . . . well, it looks bad for him. How can he take the bench and control the public if he can't control his own daughter?"

Kelsey made some notes. "This robbery-gone-wrong theory. That comes from the state guys?"

The commander nodded.

"But you're not on board with it?"

"Not even close."

Kelsey thought for a moment. "You said you needed a free flow of information. Like what?"

"You asked me about the medical records and autopsy? I haven't seen either yet." There was a long pause as the commander fished a fresh cigarette from his pocket and stuck it between his lips. He cupped his hands around his face and flashed his lighter, bringing the cigarette to life. "So this town that's been mine for decades? I guess I don't run it as much as I thought." He blew smoke out of the corner of his mouth. "But not a minute goes by that I don't think of that girl who died in my town."

Kelsey nodded her head as she stared at Stan Ferguson, a troubled man plagued by a murder he'd never have the chance to solve.

"Anything else you can tell me before I dive into all this?" Kelsey asked.

He did the stare again, toward the lake and then back. Ran his tongue around the inside of his cheek, flicked an ash from his cigarette. "She was hiding something," he finally said.

"Who?"

"Becca."

"Hiding what?"

"I don't know. And trust me, I've spent many hours working on it."

"Why do you say that? That she was hiding something?"

"When a politically connected father works this hard to control the flow of information, it usually means there's something being covered up. Something they don't want the public to know, and certainly not an investigative reporter from Miami."

A familiar wave of anticipation coursed through her, a feeling Kelsey always experienced when she knew there was something to a story. She took some quick notes.

"Are you starting to see why I'm willing to help a reporter help me?" the commander asked.

"I am. But I'm not sure I'll be able to get any further than you. Not with these roadblocks in my way."

"Just stay in the shadows. Don't let the state guys know you're poking around. If you come across anything interesting, let me know about it."

"For sure. But to figure this out, I'll have to know everything about this girl. Who she dated, who she hung out with. I'll need her e-mails and Facebook postings. I'll need to talk to her family and friends and her professors."

"You're going to have to do without all that stuff, Miss Castle. Her family is not going to talk to any reporters, and there's no way for you to get to her e-mails. Her Facebook account was scrubbed the day after she was killed. And the state detectives will be on you in a heartbeat if you start tracking down Becca's friends, which is exactly what they're doing right now."

"Her e-mail and Facebook accounts didn't simply disappear."

Commander Ferguson cocked his head. "Worse. They were subpoenaed by the District Attorney's office, and from my current position—with staties all over me and this case—that means they've more than disappeared. They never existed."

"So where do I start?"

"Right here. Summit Lake is a small town, Miss Castle. But it's a special town, too. People around here love this place, and they don't like what happened here. Summit Lake has a way of talking to you, through those people who love it so much." He took a drag from his cigarette. "I know Becca spent some time at the coffeehouse the day she died. She was studying for a law school exam. She was there for a couple hours. Got eyewitnesses who placed her there, and the owner knows her parents real well and said she talked to Becca briefly that day. I've talked to everyone in this town, and no one saw Becca after she left that café."

Commander Ferguson pulled on the cigarette again until the red glow shrunk to the filter. He stubbed it out on the bottom of his shoe and stuck the filter in his pocket. He looked up and down the street, as if he were about to give up a secret. "If you want to heat up a cold case," he said with smoke billowing from his nostrils, "start by looking in the last place the victim was seen alive."

Chapter 7

Becca Eckersley
George Washington University
December 10, 2010
Fourteen months before her death

Thom Jorgensen was a GWU professor of logic and critical thinking, and Becca knew what she was doing was wrong. Technically. In reality, she reasoned it was harmless since she was no longer his student. There were no rules against students befriending professors, but the university had strict canons against professors engaging in inappropriate relations with students. The technicality, in Becca's mind, came from how one defined "inappropriate." Many would argue that she and Thom could not date one another, as this would breach the trust all students place in professors. The counter-argument that they *could* date since she was no longer his student was what lawyers called a "difference without distinction," a thought that made Becca cringe, since her mind was already working like her father's and she hadn't even been accepted to law school yet.

However she argued it, this rendezvous was just breakfast with an old professor who was leaving the university. And breakfast was better than getting drunk with him on rum and Cokes, like she did earlier in the semester when they ran into each other at a bar in Foggy Bottom. There was the occasional text message sent back and forth and a once-in-a-while coffee grab. If pressed, Becca would never deny that Thom Jorgensen was a good-looking man and that she liked his attention. But she always paid her own way and there was nothing illicit about the friendship. He was a thirtysomething-year-old, single, soon-to-be-former GWU professor who was on his way to New York. When friends leave, they say good-bye.

"So what's so great about New York?" Becca asked as the waitress poured coffee.

Thom shrugged. "Cornell? It's beautiful and it pays better. Plus . . . you know, the status."

"Oh, come on. It's Ivy League. Since when have you been into status?"

"It's prestigious, that's all. I can't turn it down."

She took a sip of coffee. "Well, I'll be sad to see you go. I always liked spending time with you."

"You're one of my more unique students. And whether I left GWU or not, you're done after this year so our paths were bound to diverge at some point."

"Maybe. I applied to GW Law. Haven't heard yet. But if I get accepted, I might be sticking around."

Thom shrugged. "What if Cornell accepts you?"

Becca turned her head sideways. "How did you know I applied to Cornell?"

"You told me. A couple months ago when we met for coffee. Plus Harvard and Penn. So don't get so disgusted about me heading to an Ivy League school when you've applied to three."

Becca smiled. She didn't remember this conversation, and she was certain only her parents and Gail knew all the law schools she applied to. "Fine, I'll cut you some slack about becoming an Ivy Leaguer. So what's the deal? When do you start?"

"Officially next year. But I'll be done here after this semester. I'll have an office at Cornell where I'll be preparing for my class, which starts fall semester next year. I'm required to publish, too, so I'll be working on that most of the spring semester."

"So you have a semester to do nothing?"

"No teaching and no students. Lots of paperwork and research."

The waitress walked over with their plates and refilled their coffee.

"So, listen," Thom said as he forked his sausage and eggs. "I was thinking, since I'll no longer be employed by the university in a week or so, maybe you and I could actually go have a meal without worrying about being seen together."

Becca stopped cutting her omelet and stared at her plate for a second. "What do you mean? We're having breakfast right now."

"Yeah, and we're both sitting here worried someone might see us. Worried we're doing something wrong. It would be nice if we could spend some time together without that fear hanging over our heads. No?"

Becca's eyes widened. "No. Yeah, I mean. That would be fun. I guess I'm always a little worried about getting in trouble when we hang out. Although I think, really, you'd get in more trouble than I would."

"Exactly. So what do you say?"

"I've got finals next week. Then I'm going home for Christmas. Won't you be gone by the time I get back?"

"I'll be moving, but not gone. I won't be leaving until the end of January, so I'll be in town for a while. We could get together when you get back from break."

"Okay," Becca said. "It'll be our farewell dinner."

"That sounds awful. Like we're never going to see each other again."

Becca smiled. Professor Jorgensen had a crush. "You're right. Our paths will cross again at some point," she lied. Because unless she was accepted to Cornell, which was unlikely, she would probably never see Thom Jorgensen once he left GWU.

They picked a Friday night, and much deliberation was applied to the strategy. Fridays saw less students on campus as most were out at bars and some traveled home, and there was very little chance a professor would be anywhere near Samson Hall. But most importantly, no one—professors, students, cleaning crews—would be back in the building until Monday morning, which granted time to fix any problems should something go wrong.

It was midnight and cold when Brad inserted the mysterious key into the lock on the side entrance to the building—an entrance meant only for faculty. He smiled when the door clicked open.

"Son of a bitch," Jack said. His breath floated from his mouth in a white whisper that rode on the Potomac breeze and swirled around them.

"You didn't expect it to work?" Brad asked.

"I don't know what I expected."

"No turning back now, Jackie Boy."

"This is truly crazy." Jack grabbed Brad's shoulder before they walked through the door. "Are you sure you want to do this? Becca's going to be fine for the final. She doesn't need the friggin' test."

"Let's go, Jack. Stop stalling."

The hallways were dark, lighted only by auxiliary bulbs in the corners and an odd fluorescent light that remained permanently glowing. The floors shined, reflecting the subtle lights and smelling from fresh lemon wax. An hour earlier, Jack and Brad watched the last of the cleaning crew leave. They walked the hallways of the building now, looking in each lecture hall and behind any unlocked doors, making sure the building was empty. To be caught in the building after hours on a Friday night was no crime—there was a bulletin board that attracted students at all hours, and offered the latest news on updates and schedule changes and essay questions from the previous week. That was their cover should they be caught—they were in the building to get info from the mob board. The excuse was thin for a Friday night, but irrefutable should they need to present it to anyone in authority.

After twenty minutes of searching, they agreed the building was empty. They entered the wing of professors' offices, a straight hallway with opposing doors, each littered with the instructor's signature beliefs or favorite quotes. Some were entirely empty but for the placard that gave their name, others looked like the refrigerator of a household with five grade-schoolers. As they approached the door of interest, its placard stated, PROF. MILFORD MORTON. Underneath was a cartoon of the president on all fours in a pigpen. The caption read, *Once you step in it, you may as well roll around a while.*

Brad looked at Jack. "I hope that's not metaphorical."

Jack shrugged as he looked at the cartoon. "We haven't stepped in anything yet."

"We're about to. Step, roll, and dunk our heads. But it's us. We don't get dirty."

They lifted surgical gloves from the medical school's anatomy lab earlier in the week and slipped their hands into them. Neither had ever been arrested, and fingerprinting was not part of the enrollment process at GWU, but such precautions felt like the right thing to do. At the very least it filled them with a needed boost of adrenaline.

The key worked a second time and Prof. Morton's door opened without problem.

"Holy shit, Jack. We're really doing this."

"Let's kiss and hug later. Find the damn test."

With a small flashlight they scoured the file cabinet in the corner and found in the third drawer a series of folders titled "Final Exam—Hard Copy." There was a copy for each of the last six years. With shaking hands they each took three packets and skimmed them, quickly deducing there was very little difference between them aside from the essay questions at the end. They laid them all on the desk. Brad worked the camera on his cell phone while Jack turned the pages. They took photos of each of the eight pages of the latest test, and all the essay questions from the past six years. Brad checked to make sure the quality was acceptable and the questions legible. Seventeen minutes after they entered the office, they closed and locked the door behind them, threw the surgical gloves in a garbage can, and walked in the shadows along the side of the building and eventually out into the campus. Their hearts were racing and theirs hands trembled.

It was cold and dark, two weeks before Christmas break. They never spotted a soul until they were three blocks away from Samson Hall when they saw a freshman couple, holding hands and heading back to the dorms.

They were invisible.

"So what was the big mystery last night?" Becca asked.

They sat in a booth at Founding Farmers and drank coffee while they waited for their breakfast.

"You had your little sorority thing," Brad said. "We had our little thing."

"Oh," Becca said. She looked at Gail. "They're jealous."

Brad laughed. "Jealous? Of what?"

"Our hookups last night," Gail said.

Out late, and now up early, Becca had her blond hair pulled back in a ponytail. She wore no makeup besides the gloss that coated her full lips, which curled into a smile at Gail's tease. She looked, in her heavy GWU sweatshirt, both cute and stunning in the same glance.

"You guys hooked up?" Brad said with a smile. "With Sig Eps?"

Jack sat back in his chair and smiled while he sipped coffee. He looked at Becca over the edge of his cup. When she met his gaze, he slitted his eyes.

"Are you listening to this?" Brad asked.

"Listening, processing, storing," Jack said, sipping more coffee.

"Time out," Gail said. "What's the problem if I hook up with someone? I'm not dating either of you."

"And he was kind of cute," Becca said, finally looking away from Jack. "For a Sig Ep."

"Shut up," Gail said.

"No, I'm serious. He just sort of had the man-boob thing going. But if he hit the gym he could take care of that."

This got Jack laughing, but Brad was still serious.

"So you guys really did hook up?" Brad asked. Now he was staring at Becca.

Becca pointed to Gail. "I went to bed after the social. Cinderella here strolled in at about three this morning."

Gail tried to hide behind her coffee mug.

Jack was still leaning back in his chair. "I heard that's the hardest place to lose weight. For a guy. In the chest."

Gail put her cup down. "Stop it."

"I'm not kidding. It's called gynecomastia—large breasts on a man. And you can't get rid of it through exercise because of metabolism or something. Read it in a fitness magazine. *Men's Life,* I think. Because of the way blood flows to the pectoral region, when you exercise you'll lose cellulite from the stomach, hips, butt—just about everywhere before you lose it from the breast."

Gail rolled her eyes.

Jack held up his hand. "Wait a minute, Gail. I'm making a serious point here."

"Which is?"

Jack's face was stoic. "If this guy's about twenty now, with significant gynecomastia, I'm thinking if this works out between you two, by the time he's thirty he'll be wearing your bras."

This got the whole table laughing, and Gail put her hand over her eyes. "His face was cute."

"Sure it was," Jack said. "I'm just telling you what to expect in a few years."

"Okay," Becca said. "So now you guys know how we spent our evening. I'll assume no one really wants the specifics on what happened with Gail from midnight till three. So what did you guys do?"

"Not much," Brad said. Then he stopped and raised his finger. "Oh, we did break into ProMo's office and steal a copy of the final exam for next week."

No one talked for a minute. The waitress came and set plates in front of each of them, refilled their coffees, and walked away. Jack and Brad let the silence linger as they stabbed their food. Becca leaned forward and quieted her voice. "You guys broke into Professor Morton's office?"

Jack winked at her.

"I don't know what that means," she said. "Yes? No?"

Jack wiped his mouth and leaned back again with his coffee. "Yes."

Becca widened her eyes. "No!"

Jack shrugged his shoulders and looked at Brad. "Told you they wouldn't believe us."

Gail shook her head. "I don't believe you."

Brad looked at Jack with wide eyes. "No faith in us, Jackie Boy."

"You're messing with us."

"No," Jack said. "While you were messing with a Sig Ep, we were securing As for the four of us." He took a sip of coffee. "You can thank us later."

"Prove it," Gail said.

Brad handed over his cell phone and went back to his eggs.

"Holy crap," Gail said as she scrolled through the photos with Becca over her shoulder. "How did you get this?"

Jack let Brad tell the story, he seemed more proud of it.

Gail shook her head when Brad was done. "How do we know it's the same test he'll give us?"

Jack took a bite of eggs. "We don't."

"But we looked back at the last several years of tests," Brad said. "They were all on hard copy in his file cabinet, and none was much different. Except for the essay questions, so we took pictures of all those. So even if it's not exact, it should be pretty damn close." Brad looked at Becca. "I told you I'd come through for you."

Ten days later, the night before Milford Morton's final exam, Becca sat with Jack in the quiet reference section of the library where they often studied. Brad and Gail skipped out early. With a copy of the final exam, there was little for them to study.

Becca and Jack sat at opposite desks, which were isolated by wooden cubicles and offered privacy. Becca stood and peeked over the top of the desk to look at what Jack was reading. An open textbook sat illuminated by the desk lamp, several handwritten notebook pages next to him.

"You're not using the exam, are you?" Becca asked.

Jack looked up. "Hi, nosey, how are you?"

"Come on, Jack. I'm not as dumb as you think. How long does it take to memorize a stolen test?"

Jack leaned back and embarrassingly spread his hands to reveal his study material. "You caught me."

"I don't get it. I mean, I get it, you don't want to cheat. I'm the same way but don't have the will power not to peek. Plus, the whole slow infusion process, or whatever you call it, is a lost art on me. But why take the risk? Why break into Morton's office if you're not going to use the test?"

Jack shrugged. "Brad got the key. He was excited, it got me excited. I don't know, I guess I wanted the adventure." He laughed. "I don't really know why I did it, I guess so when we're fifty we can tell good stories."

"You don't even want to take a peek at the questions?"

"I don't need to."

"Oh," Becca said, placing her hand over her heart. "That hurts. Right in my ego."

Jack smiled. "I don't think you really need it either, but that's another story." He waved his hand. "So what was the deal with you yesterday? Gail said you were upset about something."

"Oh, just girl stuff."

"You don't get girl-stuff problems. Fess up."

"Richard stopped by."

"Again? That guy's an idiot."

Becca didn't say anything.

"Have you asked him to leave you alone?"

"We're friends, Jack. And our parents are friends. I can't ask him to leave me alone."

"First of all, he's not your friend, he's your ex-boyfriend. Second, your parents should support you on this. Every time the shithead comes around, you're upset for two days. Plus, it's finals week, so what's the jackass doing here?"

"Harvard finished last week and he was driving home. Just stopped by."

"Knowing you'd be upset for the rest of the week when you need to study. I've had it with this guy."

"It's fine, Jack."

"What did he want this time?"

"Wants to get together over Christmas break."

"Great. I hope you said no."

"I told him I was busy. Hurry up and finish cramming, I'm getting tired."

Becca sat back down behind her desk, out of sight. She put her head on her folded hands and closed her eyes.

"I'm going to be another hour or so," Jack said.

"I'll wait."

Chapter 8

Millie's Coffee House sat on the corner of Maple Street and Tomahawk and was the only game in town for custom brews and homemade pastries. Set toward the south end of town, across from St. Patrick's Church, the corner location featured a cobblestone patio scattered with umbrellaed tables in front of a glass façade. Inside, the smell of coffee and sweets filled the air. Kelsey also noticed the subtle aroma of pinewood burning in the fireplace, holding off the final remnants of winter that refused to release their grip on the first part of March.

Large and welcoming, the cafe was decked in deep cherrywood—from the baseboards to the thick ceiling beams. A redbrick, dual-sided fireplace sat in the middle of the coffeehouse with four leather chairs around it. Tall pub tables hugged the windows, while traditional cafe-style tables took up the floor plan. A shiny mahogany bar ran along the back wall, behind which employees donned red aprons while they whipped up coffee orders and dropped pastries onto plates for waiting customers.

At the corner of the bar, a small group was in an animated discussion. When Kelsey heard Becca's name, she sat down two stools away and randomly scrolled through her phone while she listened. An older, orange-haired woman, who Kelsey quickly noticed spoke with her eyes closed, sounded like she was on the defensive.

"That's not what I heard," Red said, eyes closed and shaking her head. "I heard she dropped out of school and was up here in Summit Lake for two weeks *before* that night."

"No, no, no," a younger man, mid-forties, said. "Where do you hear this stuff? She never dropped out of school. She came here specifically to study for an exam. She came here the same day she was killed, so someone obviously followed her. The question is who?"

"Maybe some psycho spotted her on the road, you know?" This from a heavyset woman at the end of the bar. "Saw she was all alone and decided to follow her."

"Too random," the forty-year-old said. "Not impossible, but, I mean, how would the guy know where she was going or that she wasn't headed to meet someone else? Just too random."

"Well, that's what the police are saying. Some stranger broke in and robbed the house blind. Killed Becca by accident."

"In this whole town, a random stranger picked a random house that Becca was randomly in on a random night when she would normally have been at school?" The forty-year-old shook his head. "I'm sorry, but that's too . . . random."

"I still think it had to do with the girl dropping out of school," Red said.

The group let out a collective sigh. Listening for only a

minute, Kelsey realized how far she'd gotten in just a couple of days. As she put her phone away, Kelsey recognized the girl who walked from the kitchen behind the bar. She watched the morning falls with her yesterday. The girl delivered a breakfast sandwich to a waiting customer and greeted two others before she made her way back behind the mahogany bar. Pretty in that young way that took no effort, she had a bright smile that was perfect for a coffeehouse tucked into the mountains. With short, sandy hair, dimpled cheeks, and magnetism about her, it was easy for Kelsey to imagine this girl as the face of the establishment.

"Hi," Kelsey said.

The girl looked surprised to see her.

"Hey," she said. "How are you?"

"Good. Rae, right?"

"Right. Welcome. What can I make you?"

Kelsey glanced at the list of coffees on the wall behind Rae. "Caramel latte."

"Are you drinking this here or taking it to go?"

"Here."

Rae glanced over at the gossip group. "Take a seat by the fireplace," Rae said. "I'll bring it over."

Kelsey moved from the bar and sat in one of the overstuffed leather chairs, then pulled out her notes on the Eckersley case. She scanned them as she waited for her coffee. Her research so far told her Becca Eckersley was a good kid from North Carolina who'd attended George Washington University on a partial academic scholarship and who'd elbowed her way into the law school of the same university. Straight as an arrow, never in trouble, and a thriving first-year law school student when she was killed two weeks ago. Kelsey thought back to her conversation with Commander Ferguson and wondered what sort of trouble Becca was in before she was killed, and what, exactly, a young law student might be hiding. From Commander Ferguson's case file, Kelsey created a timeline of the day Becca was killed—from the time she left GWU in Washington, DC, to when she arrived in Summit Lake, to when she settled into her parents' house on stilt row. Sometime that day, Becca came here, to this cafe.

Rae delivered her latte and sat in the chair next to Kelsey. "I'm glad you came by," she said.

Kelsey took a sip. "I can't turn down a coffee invitation. I love this place. It's beautiful, feels perfect for this town."

Rae smiled. "It's a popular attraction, for sure."

"How long have you worked here?"

"A while. I run the place now, since Livvy wanted a break. She's the owner."

"Yeah? I was actually hoping to talk to the owner. For my article."

Rae made an I'm-sorry face. "That would be Livvy Houston. She's hardly ever around anymore. Comes in occasionally, but not much. And not at all since Becca was killed."

"Why?"

"It was too much for her. Police were asking her questions, then customers, too. Some detectives showed up from down South. It was too much."

"Are you here a lot?"

"Every day now."

"Were you here the day Becca Eckersley was killed?"

Rae nodded. "I was."

"Did you see her here?"

"Yeah."

"Talk to her?"

"No."

"Did Mrs. Houston?"

"Yeah, they talked for a while. Livvy is friends with Becca's parents."

"The police chief thinks Livvy Houston might have been the last person to talk to Becca before she was killed."

"From what I know," Rae said, "she was. But if you want to talk with Livvy, you won't find her here. She's fallen off the map since Becca was killed. She lives here in town, though. West side, in the foothills. You could try making a house call. Not sure she'll talk to you, though."

Kelsey pulled out her notepad and wrote down Livvy Houston's name.

"Anything you can tell me about that day? About Becca?"

"Not much," Rae said. "I was working in the kitchen and it was pretty slow, so I wasn't out here much."

"You know most of the customers?"

"Sure. Know their faces, anyway. Most of their names. Except on the weekends, we get a lot of out-of-towners."

"You remember anyone from the day Becca was killed who stands out to you?"

Rae thought a minute. "Not really. No one I can think of. It was just a normal Friday."

"How long was Becca here that day?"

"Couple hours at least. She was working on a bunch of stuff."

"Yeah, studying for a law school exam. You see anyone other than Livvy talk to her?"

"No, from what I remember, she came in alone and left the same way."

Kelsey paused, looking at her notes and taking a sip of coffee. "Okay. You mind if I come back to talk to you about that day if I need anything else?"

"Yeah, sure." Rae pointed to the gossip group at the bar. "Everyone who comes in here talks about it. The regulars sip lattes and splash gossip around every morning, and they all have their own theories about what happened to Becca. Some of it's pretty wild." Rae smiled. "You're welcome to join the conversation any morning."

"Thanks," Kelsey said. "And thanks for the coffee."

"Good luck."

It was four blocks to the Winchester Hotel and then another quarter mile until she reached the hospital grounds north of the town center. The hospital sat on the banks of Summit Lake, and the automatic doors slid open when Kelsey approached the front entrance. At the reception desk she made inquiries until she was directed to the third floor, where she found the nurses' station.

"Hi," Kelsey said. "I'm looking for Dr. Peter Ambrose."

"Sure," the nurse said. "He should be in his office. Last door on the right." The nurse pointed down the hallway.

Kelsey smiled and headed down the corridor. When she reached the office, the door was open and she knocked on the frame. Peter Ambrose was sitting behind the desk paging through charts and typing on his computer. He wore blue surgical scrubs and a long white coat that had his name stenciled on the breast pocket. A nice-looking man with short, cropped hair and sideburns that bled into a shadow of scruff across his face, he had an All-American look. Kelsey could imagine him as the valedictorian of his high school class or the bowman of the Yale crew team, where he studied. Kelsey had done a little research into Dr. Ambrose. She always did some picking before she asked someone for help.

He looked up. "Hi."

"Hi. Dr. Ambrose?"

"Yeah."

"My name's Kelsey Castle. They told me downstairs you might be able to help me."

He cleared a space on the desk by stacking charts to the side, then pulled the surgical cap from his head. "Come in." He pointed to the chair. "What can I do for you?"

"I'm in town writing a story on the Becca Eckersley case. I write for *Events* magazine." She handed Dr. Ambrose a card as she sat down. "Are you familiar with the case?"

He studied her card for a moment. "Only because the girl was treated here. I wasn't directly involved."

"I'm trying to get hold of Becca's autopsy and medical records from the night she was brought in. Is that something you can help me with?"

Dr. Ambrose swiveled in his chair and threw his surgical cap into the trash. "I don't think so. Medical records are protected, so you'd have to get permission from the family."

"That's not happening. The family is very private. They're not going to allow me to look at the records."

"Without their approval, I'm not sure there's much I can do for you."

She paused for a moment.

"You have full access, though. Right? To the medical records?"

"Sure. If I wanted to look."

"Do you want to look?"

Dr. Ambrose smiled. "I told you, I wasn't the treating physician, so I have no *reason* to look."

"What if I told you I thought things were missed. I just need help getting my hands on some of this information and I know I'd be able to piece a few things together."

"Isn't this an active investigation?"

"It is."

"Why don't you just let the police piece it together?"

"They're trying."

"And you're going to do a better job than the police?"

"Not better, just different. Homicides are solved all the time when new eyes look at old evidence."

"I bet that's accurate. But again, I'd have to get permission from the family before I could hand anything over to you."

Kelsey nodded. "Okay. I understand."

"Why don't you talk to the family? You might be surprised."

"Maybe," Kelsey said as she stood up. "Thanks for your time."

"What's the interest?" Dr. Ambrose asked as she was leaving.

Kelsey turned in the doorway. With a runner's body and big caramel eyes, Kelsey knew how to use her presence to get her point across. "First and only murder in Summit Lake. Prominent family. Young law student with everything going for her, squeaky clean and straight as an arrow. State authorities have taken the case from the local boys because this story stinks, and someone wants something buried and hidden. It's exactly what my magazine publishes, and the type of thing I'm really good at figuring out." She shrugged. "Thanks again for your time." Kelsey stepped into the corridor.

"Stinks of what?"

"A cover-up."

"You know her?" Dr. Ambrose asked.

"Who?"

"The victim?"

"No, but the little I've learned about her makes me think something's off with the whole story and the current police theory."

"Which is?"

"That a stranger broke into her house, assaulted her, and fled into the night without anyone seeing a thing."

"Sounds flimsy."

"And lazy," Kelsey said.

He ran a hand over his chin as he thought. "Who's covering things up?"

"I don't know."

"And why would someone hide details of a young law student's death?"

"Good question."

"You think my hospital is involved? My staff? That's ridiculous."

"I don't know who's involved, Dr. Ambrose. I'm not making accusations, I'm looking for answers. And I need some help finding them."

He rubbed his hands together, finally folding them on the desk as if in prayer, then checked his watch. "How about this. I have to round on some patients this afternoon, then I'll poke around and see what I come up with. I can't get you any records or documents, but I can quietly read through what's available and tell you what I find."

"You'd do that for me?"

"I'll do it for myself. Now I'm curious."

"Thank you."

"Give me a day to see what I can come up with. Let's get together tomorrow night."

Kelsey nodded. "Perfect."

"There's a place called Water's Edge, just off Tahoma Avenue."

"Seven?"

"That works."

Kelsey smiled. "Thanks for your help."

"I haven't done anything yet."

She waved good-bye and rode the elevator to the ground floor, mentally checking off items on her to-do list. This was what early fieldwork looked like. She talked to many people and started down several avenues of discovery, some she knew would run off to dead ends and others would lead to more information that required further investigation. But if enough trails were started, Kelsey knew one of them would lead somewhere important.

Chapter 9

Becca Eckersley
George Washington University
December 21, 2010
Fourteen months before her death

December in the District of Columbia was bitter, with winds off the Potomac that ran up your back and into your spine. Becca pulled her scarf to her eyes and jogged to Old Main for her last exam before Christmas break. Butterflies floated in her stomach. Not from fear of Prof. Morton's final exam and whether it would resemble the stolen test she had memorized, but instead from the anticipation of what waited after this semester. She harbored her feelings for three years, keeping them secretly stowed. Sharing them with no one, not even Gail. But now she finally decided to unlock those feelings and put them on display.

There would be some explaining to do, and perhaps some awkward days or weeks ahead. They would pass, though. And if they didn't, graduation was on the other side of winter, not six months away. The confines of the social circle she constructed around herself would no longer limit her, and if friendships faded, Becca would assume it was the way life after college worked. In the world that waited outside George Washington University, secrecy about the man she loved would play no role.

It took three years of friendship to lay the groundwork, and on such strong footing it was not hard to understand how she fell so far so fast. Now she was two hours from finishing her seventh semester. Only one left after this and Becca wondered where that semester would lead. She envisioned happiness and bliss and finally holding his hand during strolls through campus. Saturday morning breakfasts—which they currently could only enjoy when they snuck out of Foggy Bottom and found a deserted cafe—could be enjoyed openly, like any other couple. She was tired of lying to Gail, and it was definitely time to stop sneaking herself out of his bed early in the morning before the campus woke.

As she jogged to Professor Morton's exam, her stomach continued to stir. The butterflies grew more intense as she imagined the coming year.

The campus thinned during the ten days that constituted finals week as students scribbled their exams and left for home. Only the unluckiest of students had to wait until the last morning for their freedom. Most were done the day before and well into Christmas break by that night, which was something of an event around campus—a sayonara to the semester of hard work. And for Becca Eckersley and her three friends it was a final passage; the last time they would celebrate the end of a semester and the coming break. It was the end of an era. Next time this happened they would be at the end of their college careers. There would be no breaks in front of them, except for the summer before law school, which was likely to scatter them across the country.

They met at the 19th, which was filled with GWU students and a few young professors who wore turtlenecks under elbow-patched sport coats. Becca and her friends sat at a tall, round table for four, a pitcher of beer half-spent and their glasses filled.

"It was exact, am I right?" Brad asked.

Gail gave a little smile. "Exact, exact. Like, no differences at all."

Becca took a sip of beer. "I have to admit, Brad. You delivered in the clutch."

Brad mimicked a high-pitched, female voice. "I'll still love you when you don't come through."

"Okay, okay. You came through for once, and we all owe you everything we have in school and life and in our future careers."

"I wouldn't go that far," Brad said. He looked up in contemplation. "Actually, that's pretty right on. Do you have anything else to add?"

"I do," Jack said. "For a two-hour exam, it would've looked a little better had you not finished in thirty minutes."

Brad laughed. "I know, right? I was the first one out of there and then it was like an avalanche."

Gail laughed. "People bolted as soon as you stood up. It was like everyone was waiting for the first person to commit."

Becca laughed along with Gail but saw the concern in Jack's eyes.

"How many people had the damn thing?" Jack asked. He made a circular motion with his fingers. "I thought this was our little secret."

"I gave it to a couple buddies." Brad shrugged.

"I'd say half," Becca said. "Considering how many people left early."

Jack shook his head. "Bradley, that's just a good way to broadcast that something's up."

"Come on. Morton wasn't even proctoring. It was the old guy from the library and that lady." Brad snapped his fingers as he thought. "From the admissions office or something. They don't know how long the test was supposed to take. That geeky kid, what's his name . . . with the half mullet?"

"Andrew Price," Becca said.

"Right. He's out of every exam in thirty minutes."

Jack poked a toothpick between his teeth. "Not exams with essay questions at the end."

"Trust me, if good ol' ProMo had been in the room, I'd have stuck around for the full two hours. Which, by the way, was what you did. What's up with that? Were you that nervous about leaving early?"

Jack shrugged his shoulders and sipped his beer. "Wanted to make it look good."

"You're a good actor, and you have a hell of a lot more patience than I do. I would have gone nuts just sitting there."

Jack looked at Becca. "I just hope things stay contained, if you know what I mean. And I hope everyone you gave the test to had the sense to miss a few questions. A perfect score from fifty kids with C averages spells Shitcan City for us."

Brad knocked Jack's pint with his own, giving off a loud clink and splashing cheap beer onto the table. "Cheers, brother. Stop stressing. In the next few weeks we should all know where we're going to law school and then it's smooth sailing. As long as you don't fail a course, the schools don't even look at your final semester. Now drink your beer and relax. We're on Christmas break."

"He's really freaked out, isn't he?" Brad asked.

Becca raised her eyebrows and shrugged. "It didn't look good that everyone left so quickly. And in Jack's defense, I agree that maybe we should have just kept the test to the four of us."

"Maybe," Brad said. "But some guys knew I had the key to Morton's office, and I guess I didn't want it to look like I was too scared to do anything with it. Plus, the guys I gave it to really needed it. They were in bad shape going in. Kinda like you."

"Right, but like Jack said, if a bunch of kids with Cs suddenly ace the final exam, people are going to suspect something."

"I know one girl with a C who aced it, right?"

Becca shrugged. "Yes, it helped a lot. Took some pressure off."

Jack and Gail had gone home early from the bar. Brad and Becca stayed and finished the pitcher before walking back to Becca's apartment. Gail was sound asleep, and Becca quietly closed her bedroom door. She and Brad sat in the living room, Becca lying on the couch with her bare feet on Brad's lap.

"You know I did it for you," Brad said.

"Shush," Becca said. "I don't want Gail to know you're here."

"I don't care if Gail knows I'm here."

"I just don't want her to wake up and come out here."

"Okay," Brad said in an exaggeratedly hushed voice. "You know I did it for you?" he said again.

"Did what?"

"Got the test. You said you really needed help."

"Thank you," Becca said. "I probably would have survived without it, but like I said it took some pressure off."

"Look how freaked out you are. You guys are overthinking this. And I'm getting a headache worrying about it." Brad rubbed Becca's feet. "This reminds me of the good old days."

"What do you mean?"

Brad didn't know how to tell her, couldn't find the words to express how he felt about her. He knew she had similar feelings, and he was just about ready to ask her about them. Just about ready to let the words flow off his tongue. He'd thought many times of how that conversation would go. The "why did we wait so long to admit this" and "I'm so glad we don't have to hide this any longer" slogans passed through his head when he imagined finally discussing his feelings with her. And now, here they were and here it was, the moment when they would get it all out in the open.

But he choked. For some reason, the words wouldn't form.

"What do you mean?" Becca asked again. "About the good old days."

There were nights last year when he thought he was falling in love with her, but never found the courage to tell her, or even to kiss her again the way he had freshman year. His feelings brewed and simmered throughout junior year until summer break; then they said good-bye. Tentative plans to get together over summer fell through, and it wasn't until the beginning of senior year that he finally got to see her again. By then, having missed her so badly, Brad knew without question he loved her. But the unspoken attraction and pent-up feelings worked against them during this past semester. The late nights of talking until the sun rose and until they both drifted off to sleep happened infrequently at the beginning of the semester, and barely ever now. A week before when she slept over, and now tonight, were the only times all semester Brad could remember having Becca just to himself.

"Brad," Becca said again. "What's going on?"

Finally pressed on the subject, and perhaps wanting to be, Brad felt his cheeks warm. "I don't know, I guess I just miss this." He threw his finger back and forth. "You know, you and me talking all night. We used to do it all the time, but this year has been weird for us. You know?"

He saw Becca's eyes dart right and left as he spoke, recognizing that she felt the same way. She sat up and pulled her feet slowly from his lap.

Brad," Becca said. "You know you're one of my dearest friends, right?"

"Sure," Brad said. "And you're one of mine."

"So stop talking about the good old days, okay? What are we, old people? We're going to be friends forever."

"I like hearing you say that," Brad said. "Because I like being friends with you, and I like being close to you, and I like spending all night talking to you. And those stupid BB notes you leave for me in the mornings mean a lot to me."

"What notes?"

"The little sticky notes you write me when you stay over and leave before I'm awake. I don't know, I just like them." He pointed toward Gail's bedroom. "And I don't care who knows that we like spending time together."

They weren't the words he had practiced so many times. He wanted to say that he loved her. He wanted to tell her that he couldn't imagine *only* being her friend for the rest of his life, because that would mean every woman he met would be compared to her, and he knew none would stack up. But even though the correct words did not form tonight, what came out was a good start. It was further than they ever came before in dealing with their feelings for each other.

"Everyone knows you and I are close," Becca said. "It's no secret."

"I know we're close. But my comment about the good old days comes from . . . I don't know, I just feel like something happened over the summer. Last year we used to stay up all night and talk, and we haven't had many of those nights this year. I miss them, that's all."

Becca moved her feet back onto his lap. "My flight doesn't leave until tomorrow afternoon. We can stay up and talk tonight. I'd like that."

Brad grabbed her feet and massaged them as they rested on his lap. This was a perfect way to end the semester, but

Brad knew he couldn't go through another—their last—hiding his feelings. The conversation eventually drifted to Brad's father. Becca was the best listener on the subject. Becca's father had been invited again to the Reynoldses' hunting cabin for the annual weekend where stiff-suited lawyers acted like outdoorsmen. Brad pressed for information about what Becca's father thought of his dad. Becca kept the fact that her dad thought Mr. Reynolds was a jagoff to herself, but the topic took them late into the night. The whole time they talked Brad thought about kissing her, but the right moment never came.

Later, he listened to Becca's breath as she slept next to him. Brad closed his eyes and imagined them as a couple.

Next year would be different.

Chapter 10

Kelsey Castle
Summit Lake
March 8, 2012
Day 4

It took a few calls the next morning to find the address and phone number. It was late afternoon when the woman was able to meet. Kelsey walked from the Winchester Hotel and found Hiawatha Avenue. She sucked up the crisp spring air as she made her way west through town, toward the mountains. The houses here were older Colonials with wraparound porches and manicured lawns. She found 632 painted on the mailbox, headed up the front steps, and rang the bell. It was her fourth day in Summit Lake.

A moment later, an elderly woman came to the door with a pleasant smile. "Hello?" the woman said.

"Hi. Livvy?"

"No, no. Livvy's my daughter." She had a cute Southern twang covered by the gravel of age.

"My name is Kelsey Castle. We spoke earlier on the phone."

"Oh, yes. You're the writer."

"Correct. A journalist for *Events* magazine."

"You gonna figure out what happened to Becca?" the woman asked.

"I'm going to write a story about her, yes." Through the screen door, Kelsey guessed the woman was in her eighties, maybe older. Her gray hair was recently sculpted, and Kelsey suspected she kept a weekly appointment at the beauty shop in town. Her skin had deep creases, but her smile was bright and her eyes sharp.

"Is your daughter home?"

"Oh, no," the woman said. "She's gone now. Too many people asking her too many questions."

Kelsey paused a moment and slivered her eyes. "When I talked to you on the phone you said she was here."

"No, ma'am. You asked if she lived here, and I told you she did. Had you asked if she were home, I'd have told you she was sick and tired of talking to y'all."

Kelsey smiled at the old lady's backhanded charm. "My apologies," she said. "I misunderstood. Mind if I ask *you* a few questions?"

"Of course not. No one's asked me a thing."

"I didn't get your name."

"Mildred Mays. But you can call me Millie, everyone else does."

Kelsey smiled through the screen door. "Millie? Like Millie's Coffee House?"

"You got it. Started that little place many, many years ago."

"I was there yesterday. It's really pretty."

"Sure is. Livvy did a great job remodeling when she took over."

"I understand Becca Eckersley was at the cafe that day." Kelsey paused. "The day she died. I heard Livvy talked to her."

"It's such a shame," Millie said, opening the screen door and motioning Kelsey inside. "Livvy and her husband are close with William and Mary." She turned to Kelsey as they walked through the hallway. "That's Becca's parents." She pointed to a bar stool at the kitchen island. "Take a seat. I'll make some tea."

Kelsey sat down. Through the bay window was a spectacular panoramic view of the mountains. "This is a beautiful home," Kelsey said.

"Thank you." Millie set water on the stove to boil. She draped three Lausanne tea bags over the edge of the pot. "Some people enjoy the lake. Like the Eckersleys, with that beautiful house on the water and that wonderful view. We prefer the mountains."

"Both are nice options." Kelsey pulled her notepad from her purse.

"Oh, sure. Only problem out here are the hunters. Lots of hunting cabins deeper in the foothills, and they make a helluva racket some mornings. Shooting those guns. But I'm an early riser, so it doesn't bother me much."

Kelsey waited a moment. "So how was it that Livvy knew Becca?"

"Livvy lived in the same neighborhood as the Eckersleys, back in Greensboro. That was before she and Nicholas moved up here permanently. Nicholas is my son-in-law. Livvy and Nicholas are the ones who introduced William and Mary to Summit Lake when their kids were very young. My husband and I have been up here for years. When I was ready to move on from the coffeehouse, it was Livvy's turn to take over. Livvy and Nicholas have owned a house here for many years, and they used to invite the Eckersleys up for long weekends when the kids were young. William and Mary fell in love with this town and soon bought the stilt house. Livvy has children the same age as Becca and her brother. She used to watch the Eckersley clan a bunch when they were little kids."

"Watch them how?"

"William was always busy with his law practice, and Mary worked back then. Livvy stayed at home and her house back in Greensboro was where the kids gathered in the summer. Livvy just took on the role of watching Becca and her brother when William and Mary were at work."

"Have the Eckersleys been back up here since Becca died? To that stilt house?"

"Oh, no. They rushed up the night it all happened, but after Becca died the house was roped off. They stayed at the Winchester for a couple of nights to help the police any way they could; then they went home to Greensboro and haven't been back since. I heard they're going to sell the house. They couldn't possibly enjoy it knowing what happened there. I don't blame them one bit, but I doubt the house will sell easily. Which is unusual for those homes. Whenever they go on the market, they're usually snatched up real quick. Because of their location and so forth. But this is a small town, and everyone knows what happened to Becca."

Kelsey made some notes while Millie pulled two tea glasses from the cabinet. "Did Livvy tell you she talked to Becca that day? At the coffeehouse? A few hours before she died."

Millie smiled as she worked. "I'm her mother. Livvy told me everything about that day." In a softer voice, and with more twang, she added, "And plenty more."

The water came to a rolling boil and Millie turned the burner off and covered the pot to let the tea simmer. She pulled a glass pitcher from the fridge. It was empty but for a strange sludge at the bottom, which was barely visible through the frosted glass. "I've found if you chill this overnight it sticks to the tea better." Millie swirled the concoction in the pitcher.

"What is it?"

"My special recipe for sweet tea." Millie placed the pitcher next to the brewing tea. "You tell me what you think when it's ready."

"Can't wait," Kelsey said. "Can you tell me anything about Livvy's conversation with Becca that day at the cafe?"

"Oh, sure. I can tell you all about it. Becca came to Summit Lake to study for her exams. She was studying to be a lawyer, you know?"

"She was at George Washington Law, isn't that right?"

This caused Millie to laugh. "For her father, there was no other choice. It was his alma mater and he was intensely proud of his school. Becca's brother attended a few years before she did and then joined his father's firm. That was the plan for Becca, I suppose."

"How long was she at the cafe that day?"

"Couple of hours, from what Livvy said. She had papers and books all over the place—on the table, on the chairs. A real mess. Had her computer out and was tapping along. Livvy didn't want to bother her or take her focus off her studies. So mostly, she just let Becca work. Refilled her coffee when she asked for more."

"When they finally did talk, what did Livvy say they talked about?"

"After she packed up her things Livvy walked over to say hello. Becca was always a good girl. Real polite. Livvy asked her about school and Becca showed her what she was reading. Real boring stuff. Constitutional law that sounded awful to cram in your brain. And contracts, too." Millie shook her head. "But Becca said she liked it, so Livvy was excited for her. You've gotta remember, Livvy used to babysit this girl when she was still in diapers, so to see her studying to be a lawyer was a real treat. Livvy told me, though, she could tell something was wrong. Something about Becca was off."

"Like what?"

"She looked worried, I guess. Livvy never really explained it, she's just good at reading people. You know someone from the time they were a little girl, you can tell when something's bothering them."

"Livvy ask her about it?"

Millie paused before answering. "She did."

"And?"

"Well, you see, Miss Castle, Livvy never told William and Mary about this because Becca swore her to secrecy. So I'm not sure she'd want me to say anything to you."

A veteran at conducting interviews, Kelsey knew when to push hard for information and when to back off. When Millie offered nothing more, Kelsey scribbled on her notepad and changed the subject. "Has Livvy been in touch with the Eckersleys since Becca died?"

"Not that I know of. Livvy and Nicholas are up here most of the year running the coffeehouse, and since the kids have all gone off to college she hasn't been as close to William and Mary. She sent a card and saw them at the funeral but hasn't talked to them besides that. Plus, William and Mary have been busy with the investigation."

Millie stood and walked to the stove. She poured the hot tea into the frosted pitcher and stirred it thoroughly to dissolve the sweet sludge at the bottom. From an ice maker near the kitchen bar she scooped two shovelfuls of ice into the pitcher. After some more stirring, she made herself a sample and examined it as if she were in a Napa vineyard. Finally she tasted it, staring through the bay window while she let her palate examine her work. Then she nodded.

"Perfect." She filled two glasses and placed one in front of Kelsey. "See for yourself."

Kelsey took a sip. Raised in Florida, she was no stranger to sweet tea, and Kelsey had to admit that Millie's sludge put a taste on the tea that was different from anything she'd experienced before. "Very good."

"Isn't it? I'm quite proud of it."

Kelsey took another sip. "This might be the best tea I've ever tasted. You should sell this."

"I do. Over at the coffeehouse. It's on the menu: *Millie's Sweet Tea.*" Her Southern twang was more pronounced with some tea on her tongue.

"No kidding?"

"When I owned the place I had a few customers ask for it every now and then, but I never told many people about it. But when that young girl came to run the place for Livvy, she liked the tea so much she put it on the menu and named it after me."

"Who's that?"

"The young girl who's running the cafe while Livvy's gone."

"Rae?"

"Yes, nice girl. You know her?"

"I met her the other day," Kelsey said.

"Great girl. Sharp as a nail, too. Everybody really likes her around this town. After she put my name on the menu, she'll always have a place in my heart."

Millie walked over to the counter and gathered the ingredients to put them away. She shoved the laminated page containing her sweet tea recipe into a binder.

"Is your recipe available to the public?" Kelsey asked.

"Oh, no, sweetheart," Milled said, holding up her recipe binder—a felt-covered book that rested on her counter. "This book is strictly off-limits. If I let people know what was in here, all my secrets would be revealed. I'm eighty-six years old. My secrets are all I have left."

Kelsey nodded and drank her tea, staying quiet for a moment. She looked over her notes before deciding enough time had passed. "Any hint about what was on Becca's mind that day at the cafe? What might have been bothering her? You said she swore Livvy to secrecy about something."

Millie sighed. She shoved her recipe book into a row of cookbooks on the kitchen counter and then sat down with Kelsey. She took a sip of tea, looked at Kelsey with a little smile. "She was excited about a boy she was dating."

Kelsey scribbled again on her notepad. "Did she tell Livvy anything about this boy?"

"Quite a bit. When Livvy finally went over to talk to her, after Becca gathered up her study materials and textbooks, she was scribbling away in her journal. Livvy said she was gushing."

Kelsey's spine straightened and her eyes narrowed. "Becca was writing in a journal?"

"That's what Livvy told me."

"Did Livvy see the journal?"

"Just what Becca showed her about the boyfriend."

"Which was?"

"He was someone from law school, or maybe he was already a lawyer. I guess I'm not too sure about that. I just remember Livvy saying Becca was really glowing about him, and . . ." Millie trailed off.

"And what?" Kelsey asked.

"Well, you see . . . I feel strange telling you this because Becca's parents don't even know. Even now, I don't think they know. Becca never told them."

"Told them what? That she was dating this guy?"

"Oh, no, her parents knew she was dating him."

"Then what?"

Millie wrapped both hands around her tea and closed her eyes. "They didn't know Becca had gone off and married this fella."

Chapter 11

Becca Eckersley
George Washington University
December 22, 2010
Fourteen months before her death

Jack slammed the back hatch of the Ford Explorer and walked to the driver's side window. "See you, buddy. Have a good Christmas."

"Yeah," Brad said.

Brad stared straight through the windshield, and Jack recognized the familiar look in his roommate's eyes. He always noticed it when Brad headed home.

"It won't be that bad," Jack said. "Just don't get into it with him."

Brad feigned a smile. "He's such a pompous ass. I can't wait until I'm on my own."

"He already told you he's not paying for law school, so there you go. Get an apartment next year and borrow your way to freedom, that's what student loans are for. You can spend every holiday at my place." Jack leaned against the car, his breath a swirling white vapor as it came from his mouth.

"Where will your place be?" Brad asked.

"Next year? Depends where I get accepted."

"How about Becca? She hear from any schools yet?"

"I don't think so. I haven't really talked to her about it." Jack laughed. "Don't worry about Becca and where she's going next year. You get like this every time you head home."

"Like what?"

"Freaked out about everything. Listen, in ten years you and your old man might be best friends, so just grin and bear it for one more Christmas. Aren't you heading down to Florida, anyway? To hang with Gail?"

"Yeah, maybe. Let's get a beer before I leave."

"You're not drinking beer before you drive a hundred miles."

"Fine. Let's get a burger."

"What's up with you? Your old man is a pain in the ass, but I've never seen you so messed up. Is it about Morton's final?"

"I've gotta tell you something, and it's gonna screw everything up."

Jack stared into the car and checked his watch. "Okay, let's get lunch."

They drove to McFadden's and found a booth in the back. Boise State was playing Utah in a college bowl game, and several flat-screen televisions displayed the action. They ordered burgers and Cokes and stared at each other for a while, half watching the game until their food arrived.

"You're weirding me out, man," Jack finally said. "Spit it out, what's on your mind?"

Brad took a swallow of Coke and washed down his burger. "Okay, here's the deal. I think I'm in love with Becca."

Jack's forehead wrinkled and his eyebrows slowly elevated. "What?"

Brad nodded. "It's totally screwed up, I know. But I needed to tell you. I want your advice."

"On what?" Jack shook his head. "Say it again."

"I love her. I'm . . . in love with her."

"Okay, slow down, Brad. You're not in love with Becca."

"Don't say that to me, Jack. You don't know what's been going on between us. I'm telling you. I've had these feelings for a long time."

"How can you be in love with someone you've never dated or kissed or slept with? Maybe infatuated, but not in love."

"Whatever. It's complicated. We're really close. She stays over all the time, and we talk until the sun comes up. I never told you about it because it's a private thing between us. We went through a strange period where we stopped the sleepovers, whatever you want to call them. But lately, the last couple of weeks, we're back at it. You know, we just talk all night. Last night we had this thing, I don't know. Like a moment. Like we were about to tell each other how we felt. I know she feels the same way about me, but it'd be too complicated if we got together, you know? Neither of us knows where we'll be next year. We're friends, and she doesn't want to screw that up." Brad stirred his Coke with a straw. "I just wanted to give you a heads-up. My mind is spinning right now."

Jack shook his head. "Give me a heads-up on what?"

"You know, with the four of us all being friends I think we both feel like it would screw things up, Becca and me. If we got together. But I don't really care about that anymore. I hope it doesn't bother you if Becca and I become . . . you know, start dating."

"Slow down for a second." Jack looked at his friend. "Did Becca tell you she felt the same way? That she wants to get together with you? Or date you. Or that she loves you?"

"No, I mean, not exactly. She tells me she loves me all the time, but she says that to everyone. I think she's worried about the dynamics of our little group if she and I get together."

Jack thought for a second. "You've got a lot going on, okay? You're emotional about going home and dealing with your asshole father. You're waiting to find out about law school. Maybe a little freaked out about next year. You just got done with finals and the whole Professor Morton thing. It all piles up."

"None of that matters." Brad shook his head. "I can stay up until dawn talking to her, and she totally understands what I'm going through with my father. She just, I don't know, she just listens to me and understands me. She's perfect for me and I know we'd be perfect together."

"What if Becca doesn't feel the same way?"

"I don't know. It's hard to explain, but I know she does. I guess I'm going to find out, anyway."

"How?"

Brad shrugged. "I'm gonna tell her. Wait until we get back from break and then tell her how I feel."

They finished their burgers and pretended to watch the bowl game.

"Okay," Jack said. "Let things simmer for a couple weeks. We'll talk after Christmas."

"Yeah," Brad said. "What time's your flight?"

Jack checked his watch. "Soon. I've gotta run."

They drove back to their apartment and Brad stopped in the parking lot. "I better hit the road. Have a good flight, and say hi to your parents."

"I will," Jack said. "Be nice to your old man, maybe he's mellowed since Thanksgiving." Jack stepped out of the car and held the door open.

"See you in a couple weeks," Brad said.

"All right." Jack closed the door and Brad backed into the street. The driver's side window was open. "Hey, Brad," Jack yelled from parking lot. "Don't sweat it. This stuff has a way of working out."

Brad waved and rolled the window up as he drove away.

Jack watched his roommate cruise down H Street, past the Cathedral buildings the campus was famous for, and then onto the boulevard that would take him to I-95 and eventually Maryland. Jack looked at his watch and scrambled up the steps to his apartment. He grabbed his stuffed duffle bag off the bed, threw it over his shoulder, flicked off the lights, and locked the door in a panic. He took the stairs two at a time and tossed his duffle into the back of his hubcap-less Volvo, then raced to the airport. His unexpected lunch with Brad put him an hour behind schedule and very late for his flight. His cell phone had buzzed five times in the last hour. He didn't dare answer it, not with his mind running so fast.

He found a spot in the closest lot, which would cost him three times as much as the economy lot, but he had no time to catch the tram back to the terminal. A line of Christmas travelers zigzagged back and forth four times in front of the United desk. It was an easy thirty-minute wait to check in and Jack didn't have that much time. He walked straight for the front of the line. A gray-haired man waited for the next clerk with his identification in hand and his roller suitcase stacked next to him.

"Excuse me, sir," Jack said. His duffle bag was over his shoulder, his oxford shirt untucked and hanging below his jacket, and his finals week scruff trying to become a beard. An athlete his entire life, he had always managed to use his tall frame and broad shoulders as tools for comfort rather than intimidation. Today, he'd use his charm and good looks and physique in any way necessary to get on the plane. "My flight leaves in twenty minutes, can I please cut in front of you?"

The man looked annoyed, stared at the line behind him, and then motioned for Jack to head to the open counter.

"They're already boarding," the ticket agent said. "You might not make it through security and to the gate in time."

Jack rolled his finger in a loop to hurry things along. "I'll try."

"Are you checking bags?"

"Not anymore."

She tapped the keyboard with proficiency and printed the boarding pass. "B-6. Terminal two. I suggest you hurry."

Jack grabbed his boarding pass and snaked his way to the front of the security line, raising insults from those he passed. "My flight's boarding," he told the people who confronted him. He threw his duffle and shoes onto the conveyor belt, dropped his shaving kit—containing razors, fingernail clippers, and other essential toiletries that would prevent him from making it through security—into the garbage. He made it through the metal detector on the first try, strapped his duffle bag over his shoulder, and ran in his socks to gate B-6. The seats outside the gate were empty.

"Here he is," the gate agent said to her supervisor, who stood with a passenger list in her hand.

"Sorry," he said, raising his shoes as he jogged to the counter.

"Thirty more seconds and the doors were closing."

"Thank you for waiting."

They checked his ID and scanned the boarding pass. "15-E. It's a full flight."

"Thanks." Jack trotted down the skyway, hopping as he pulled on his shoes, and smiled at the flight attendants who waited for him. He pulled his duffle bag from his shoulder and carried it in front of him as he walked down the narrow center aisle of the 737. He ignored the faces of the hundred people who stared at him, concentrating only on the person seated in seat 15-D. He saw her and smiled, and finally sat down with his duffle bag on his lap.

"What the hell?" Becca said. "They were about to close the door."

"Sir, your bag will have to be stowed under the seat in front of you," the flight attendant told him.

"Sorry." He shoved the bag under the seat, taking deep breaths.

"And you'll need to fasten your seatbelt."

Jack smiled at the flight attendant and avoided eye contact with the surrounding passengers who stared at him. He buckled his belt.

"What happened?" Becca asked.

Jack pointed at his fastened seat belt and gave a thumbs-up to the flight attendant who was presiding over him. "Tell you later. But I'm gonna need to stop and get a toothbrush before we get to your house."

"Are you that nervous to meet my parents?"

"Ah, a little nervous. Yes. And I need to shave when we land."

Becca took his hand. "They're going to love you."

"They are?" Jack tried to catch his breath. "How do you know?"

She kissed his unresponsive lips. "Because I do. Now tell me why you're late."

PART II

SELF-HELP

Chapter 12

Kelsey Castle
Summit Lake
March 8, 2012
Day 4

Her conversation with Millie Mays was the first glimmer of light shed on the dark mystery of Becca Eckersley. Being married opened up a motive and created at least one suspect. That Becca eloped was another avenue she would need to pursue. But first, Kelsey wanted to figure out who this guy was, and if he had any reason to kill his new wife. With her mind racing around the fresh developments, Kelsey headed to the Water's Edge restaurant to meet Peter Ambrose and see if he came through with the medical records and autopsy report.

She turned down a side street off Maple and found the restaurant on the corner. Peter was already seated at a table by the window and waved when she entered.

"Hi," Kelsey said as she walked over.

"Hi," Peter said, pointing to the chair across from him. Out of his scrubs now, he wore a blue sport coat over a Ralph Lauren button-down.

Kelsey, too, had changed for this dinner meeting into slacks and high heels. She wore a white blouse under a gray blazer, and had swiped her eyelashes with mascara and pulled her hair back before leaving the Winchester.

"Thanks again for doing this for me, Dr. Ambrose," she said.

Peter waved as he sat down. "Call me Peter. And don't thank me yet."

Had they not been about to discuss a young girl's death, they looked very much like two young professionals on a dinner date. With a sharp angled jaw and crisp, hazel eyes, Peter Ambrose was attractive. And if Kelsey didn't want to admit that she noticed his good looks, she would have to find another reason to explain why she'd applied bronzer and lipstick for the first time in over a month.

"What's wrong? Couldn't find anything?"

"No, I found quite a bit. But it wasn't easy. Someone's trying to keep the details of the case quiet."

"Yeah? That's what the police chief told me." Kelsey draped her purse over the back of the chair. "The District Attorney's office thinks the Summit Lake police force is without the resources and know-how to handle a homicide, so the state detectives took over up here." She pulled her chair in. "What did you find with the medical records?"

"Getting my hands on this information was not easy, and I wasn't able to get everything you asked for."

"Why was it so hard?"

"The medical records should be easily accessible through our electronic medical records system, but I'll be damned if I didn't have to jump through hoops to find out about the night Becca Eckersley was brought to the ER. Her file was elevated, which means very few people have access to it. No nurses—or any paramedical staff—are able to pull up her file, and very few physicians. I had to dig for a password before I could get to her records."

"Sorry to put you out, I thought you'd just pull a file. I hope I'm not getting you in any trouble."

Peter shook his head. "Everything's electronic now. Pulling a file anymore means looking it up on a computer. And I have the clearance, I've just never had to use it before."

The waitress came over. "Can I start you with a drink?"

"Sure." Kelsey looked at the table and saw Peter had a glass of wine in front of him. "I'll have a glass of wine."

"Sauvignon blanc," Peter said.

The waitress smiled and left.

"You're a surgeon, right?" Kelsey asked. "I did a little background on you."

"Trained as a surgeon, yes. General surgery. But since taking this job, I feel like I do more administrative work than surgery."

"Are there many surgical cases up here in the mountains? I'd think with that specialty you'd want to be in an urban location."

"I was. For a few years I ran the surgery department at St. Luke's in New York."

"So why are you up here pushing papers?" Kelsey asked.

Peter smiled.

"Sorry," Kelsey said. "I'm used to interviewing people, so I sometimes have trouble conversing without drilling for information."

"No, it's a good question. But there are cases up here. People have a way of finding you. I was getting burned out in New York. Too many cases, too many hours, too much stress. We're a much smaller operation up here, but the cases we handle are still complicated and challenging. I can concentrate on each patient more closely, without delegating so much off to residents and fellows."

"You have a family?"

"No. Well, a wife."

"How is she adjusting to the move up here?"

Peter pursed his lips in a reluctant smile. "Sorry. Ex-wife." Peter broke eye contact and stared at his wine, grabbed the stem, and swirled it. He took a sip. "Still piecing things together."

The waitress delivered Kelsey's wine and took their dinner orders.

"I was offered this job and decided it would be good for me to get out of New York for a while. I know people say otherwise, but no marriage ends well."

"Sorry, Peter."

He smiled again. "I'm not the first divorced surgeon the world has ever seen. I'll be okay. Here, let me show you what I found." Peter pulled a thin manila folder from his leather bag. "These are the notes from the night the girl was brought to the ER. I printed them out." Peter handed the pages to Kelsey. "You can't keep these, but you're welcome to look at them here."

Kelsey took the packet and read through the emergency room physician's notes.

"Help me out here," Kelsey said. "Some of it's medical jargon I don't understand."

"I looked through the records this afternoon," Peter said. "The Eckersley girl was brought by ambulance to the ER and arrived at about 10:00 p.m. Really bad shape. Her biggest problem being a fractured trachea."

"Her neck was broken?"

"Windpipe was crushed. She was strangled."

Kelsey blinked several times as she processed this. Peter continued. "Most deaths from strangulation are caused from asphyxiation. The assailant clamps their hands around a victim's neck hard enough to stop airflow through the windpipe—the trachea—and if this is done long enough it causes a lack of oxygen to the brain and organs, and eventual death. In Becca Eckersley's case, the assailant did this in such a ruthless manner that her trachea collapsed."

Kelsey made an ugly face. "That's terrible."

"Terribly brutal, yes. And when she arrived at the hospital that night there was very little the doctors could do. The EMTs had started a tracheotomy, which was the correct measure to take, just too late."

"What's that?"

"A trach? They put a hole in her throat. When they realized her windpipe was fractured, and they weren't able to push air into her lungs through her mouth as they normally would do, the EMTs attempted to intubate—insert a tube into her throat to deliver oxygen to the lungs—but were unable to accomplish this because of the fracture. Instead, they made an incision in her throat below the fracture to gain access to the undamaged segment of the trachea. They administered oxygen through a pump bag. When they arrived at the hospital, she had only a faint pulse. The ER staff continued working on her. Had her stabilized for a while, but she was just too far gone. They managed to keep her alive until her parents arrived. She died the next morning."

The waitress delivered their salads and Kelsey pushed hers aside. "Sorry," she smiled at Peter. "I'm not hungry anymore."

"Probably a bad idea to do this over dinner."

Kelsey shook her head. "I didn't know it was this brutal."

"Let's take our drinks to the bar. Sound better?"

Kelsey crinkled her nose. "Much."

Peter talked to the waitress and paid for their uneaten dinners. At the bar they sat on corner stools so they could face each other. Kelsey pulled out her notes again and laid them on the bar.

"Were you able to talk to any of the medical staff? The ER docs?"

Peter shook his head. "No. This wasn't my case and there's no reason for me to get involved, so I don't feel comfortable asking questions . . . yet. I need to figure out how to approach my problem."

"What problem?"

Peter took a sip of wine. "The old days of fudging medical records are over," he said. "A physician can no longer simply open a patient's file and change a diagnosis or insert a pertinent finding or delete something that shouldn't be there the way he used to, sometimes weeks later, by jotting it down in ink or crossing it out. Now everything's electronic, and once the record is signed, it's final. In order to change the medical record after it's been officially signed, you need to *unsign* it, make your changes and then sign it again. And when this is done, it leaves a trail."

"Becca's chart was unsigned?"

"Twice," Peter said.

"What was changed?"

"That's impossible to tell. I can only see that it was signed the night she was brought to the ER, and then unsigned the day after and again two days later."

"But you can't see what was changed?"

"No," Peter said. "And I'm curious because of what I found with the autopsy."

"Okay," Kelsey said slowly, mulling over the idea that Becca's medical records could have been altered. She consulted her notes. "Becca was brought to the ER and pronounced dead the next morning. When was the autopsy done?"

"The autopsy was a little trickier," Peter said. "Since the girl's death was ruled a homicide, the hospital pathologist here in town didn't perform the autopsy. It was done by the Buchanan County medical examiner." Peter pulled more notes from his bag and placed them on the bar. "Autopsy was performed the next day by Dr. Michelle Maddox, but I couldn't manage to get a copy of the actual report. It hasn't been released yet. The best I could do was a synopsis of some of the findings."

"And?"

"Some general external findings," Peter said, running a finger down the page, "confirming strangulation, including petechia to the lids and subconjunctival hemorrhages."

Kelsey raised her eyebrows.

"Bleeding in the whites of the eyes," Peter said. "When blood flow is restricted during strangulation, the pressure inside the blood vessels increases. This causes small blood vessels—capillaries—to burst. This is visible in the eyes. And, internally, also the lungs." Peter looked back to his notes. "External exam also noted bruising to the neck, with dramatic soft tissue damage and fractures to the hyoid bone and cricoid cartilage. All common in strangulations. Internal examination of the laryngeal skeleton confirmed the tracheal fracture." Peter turned the page. "A tuft of missing hair on the back of her scalp and a large subdural hematoma at the base of her skull."

"The bastard hit her with something?"

"No, the missing tuft was pulled manually, based on follicle absence and random patterns of the hair loss. The bleeding is believed to be the result of a fall." Peter shrugged. "She stumbled backward, I guess, and hit her head when she landed." He went back to the page. "Also, two dislocated knuckles on the victim's right hand."

"So she went down swinging," Kelsey said.

"And scratching. There was skin under her fingernails." Peter looked to the notes again. "There were also contusions. . . ." He paused. "I don't know how much you know about this case."

"I've just started digging, so I know only what I've learned in the last couple of days."

"And you didn't know the victim?"

"No. Why?"

"There were contusions to the victim's vaginal area, indicating rape."

Kelsey slowly sat back on her stool and crossed her arms. "I didn't . . . I was unaware Becca had been raped."

"Sorry to be so blunt."

Kelsey shook her head. "It's fine. I was under the impression it was a simple homicide."

"I'm not surprised you didn't know about the rape. Not many people do. It's not mentioned in the medical records from the ER, and if it was, it's been removed. And this record here—the Report of Investigation, as it's called, created by the county medical examiner—is a partial synopsis of the autopsy and is supposed to be public record. So presumably any reporter should be able to talk to the medical examiner or pathologist to get a copy of this."

"But?"

"The county hasn't released it yet."

Kelsey made some notes. "Not unreasonable. They have six weeks, right?"

"They do, but I managed to get my hands on the official synopsis that's set for release and it doesn't include the assumption of rape."

Kelsey cocked her head. "The Report of Investigation that will be released is different from the one you found?"

"Exactly," Peter said.

"So how did you get this copy?"

"I've got a contact at the Buchanan County Government Center. He did me a favor."

"Why would they be hiding that Becca was raped?"

"Not sure. Probably just delaying the information until

they get a better handle on the investigation. But the Report of Investigation is always the first document released, then the ME is allowed to release an amended version some weeks later. Then the final—formal—autopsy report after that, which includes definitive cause of death and toxicology reports."

"I've been there before," Kelsey said. "*Later* means when no one's looking any longer."

"No reporters, anyway," Peter said.

"We never stop looking, but the public loses interest and that's what they want." She remembered her conversation with Commander Ferguson, about Becca's father running for a spot on the bench. That his only daughter had secretly married and was then raped is something he might want to keep from his constituents. Kelsey went back to her notes and scribbled for a minute. "According to the synopsis you have there, did they find anything on the body?"

"Yes," Peter said. "Semen, hair, skin cells. Dr. Maddox believes some of the hair was from a beard."

"How can she determine that?"

"Some of the hair specimens contained the bulb, or root, suggesting they were pulled out during the struggle. Some were long, and they were determined to be from the perpetrator's scalp. Others were short. Based on their length, and the fact that they had full shafts connected to the root, they were determined to come from facial hair."

Kelsey made notes about long hair and beards while Peter talked.

"Also fibers," Peter said. "Presumably from a wool coat."

"So the attack happened shortly after he entered the stilt house."

"Yeah," Peter said. "Never took off his coat."

"So found on the body was everything they need for a conviction?"

"From the fluid and hair recovery, it would be an easy DNA match, yes."

"If they had anyone to match it to," Kelsey said. She went back to her notes and studied them for a minute. "Ever heard of a protective father suppressing information?"

"You mean about this being a rape?"

"Yeah."

"You'd have to be quite powerful to do that. And very connected on top of it."

"William Eckersley is both. A big-time lawyer who's gearing up to be a judge. He has both money and political clout."

"I don't doubt it. Clearance on the electronic medical records has been elevated, and the records themselves have been changed or at least reopened. Filing of the autopsy synopsis report will be abbreviated, and the full autopsy report is out there somewhere and sure to be very delayed."

"Out there where?"

"Don't know. But Dr. Maddox would know, and probably the state detectives also."

"What are the chances I could get my hands on that full report?"

Peter smiled. "Not very good."

Kelsey shook her head. "I'd love to see it."

"So would I, now that I know something's up."

Kelsey felt an adrenaline rush. She always did when she knew a story had some bite. "Your friend who helped you get the Report of Investigation synopsis, you think he could help with the actual autopsy?"

Peter thought a moment. "I doubt he'd want to get involved with stealing an autopsy report." He shrugged. "I'll ask around and see what I can do."

"Thanks for all your help." Kelsey packed up her things and stuffed them in her purse. "It's been eye opening."

"Keep me posted on what you find. Now I'm curious."

"You too," Kelsey said.

It was close to 10:00 p.m. when she made it back to the Winchester. She called Penn Courtney and left a message. His plan of sequestering her up in the mountains to chase a story that didn't exist had been foiled, she explained to his voice mail. She'd stumbled onto something here in Summit Lake, and her investigational radar told her it was something interesting. She hung up the phone and spent the rest of the night poring through her notes and rereading the new information she gathered about Becca Eckersley. A story was forming in her mind. It was too early to see the entire arc, but she'd been through the process before. From nothing, a small narrative was taking form about Becca Eckersley's life and death. There were many gaps in the story and hundreds of unanswered questions. But the process was working and Kelsey knew, like a train moving downhill, there was no stopping this story from making it to the page.

She took her computer and notes to the balcony. The night air was cool and it helped clear her mind. The Winchester Hotel stood at the north end of Maple Street, and from her third-story balcony Kelsey's view spanned through town to St. Patrick's Church on the south end, whose façade was lighted by upward-shooting spotlights that broke through the dark night and illuminated the bleached white stone in V-shaped cascades. Lampposts stood on all four corners of intersections and brightened the streets. The maple trees running down the middle island were budding with early spring, and the street was littered with old leaves from fall. A lake breeze swept across town and stirred them in funnels.

To the east Kelsey saw the lighthouse sitting on a point somewhere on the other side of the water, its powerful light cutting through the darkness. Her gaze moved to the stilt houses running into the shallow water of Summit Lake. She stared at the Eckersley home for a while, thinking of Becca and all she went through in that house. A sanctuary, warm and safe, turned into Hell. Kelsey pulled out Commander Ferguson's file and riffled through the pages. She found the inventory list itemizing the evidence collected at the Eckersleys' home the night Becca was killed. The list was long and tortuous to read. It included such items as:

E-1   *Constitutional Law textbook, open on kitchen floor*
E-2   *Apple MacBook, open, facedown on kitchen floor, screen cracked*
E-3   *(5)Notebook pages, scattered on kitchen floor, handwritten study notes*
E-4   *iPod and speakers*
E-5   *(1)Heavy sock/slipper in living room, size small*

The list went on for two pages—a tedium of items written in a man's ugly chicken scratch. Kelsey was so interested she read the list twice to make sure. Nowhere on the pages was there mention of a journal.

Without being aware of the passing hours, Kelsey noticed it was approaching midnight. She was suddenly cold and tired. She packed up her research and carried her laptop inside where she climbed under the covers. As she drifted off, she was restless, tossing and turning as her mind worked. When she finally made it to sleep, a vivid dream placed her inside Becca Eckersley's home. She walked through the kitchen— floated really, it took no effort at all. On the kitchen island was a textbook and notes and an open computer. But something else, too. A hard-covered binder, small and compact. Becca's journal? Yes, of course. Kelsey reached for it, hoping to page through it and find the answers to all her questions. But her movements were congested, and the harder she tried the farther away she floated. Finally there were three loud knocks on the mudroom door. She floated to the door, pulling it open to reveal Becca's killer. But she found only darkness outside. Then something. A flash of light from the lakeside of the house. Kelsey ran to the patio deck and saw the lighthouse across the lake. Then she heard the pounding of feet as someone ran along the dock. When she turned, she saw Peter Ambrose jogging up the dock and into the night. When she looked back to the house, a faceless man was standing in the shadows. She tried to scream but could only manage to exhale heavily. Then she ran. The slow gallop of running through knee-high water. She was back in Miami now, attempting to run along her jogging path. The path by the water she took each morning. The path through the woods, where her life had gone to Hell. She felt his presence and tried to move faster. In a flash, he came at her from the woods, crunching over twigs and leaves. Her breathing became erratic, hyperventilating just as the man grabbed her. It was enough to startle her awake.

She sat up in bed, her lungs frantic as if she'd actually been running. Her thumping heart so palpable she heard it in her ears. An every-night occurrence at first, the dreams had subsided of late, absent from her entire time in Summit Lake. Until tonight. Until she discovered Becca was raped. Now, her nightmare stomped on the muddy bottom and clouded Kelsey's mind with all the fears from that morning in the woods she'd been working so hard to settle.

Kelsey spent that first month inside her home. She hadn't been beyond her locked door but for a few times before she forced herself back to the office, knowing if she stayed in her house any longer, she might never leave. Healing might come with time, as the doctors told her, but the longer she waited the more far off recovery felt. Closure would only come, Kelsey knew, when she decided to chase it. And learning about Becca's rape brought her own ordeal back, dangled it in front of her nose and dared her to go after it. Hearing the details from Peter—the first man other than Penn whom she'd spoken to in weeks—added to her angst.

She lay back down, the pillow absorbing her head, and closed her eyes. Sleep never came.

Chapter 13

Becca Eckersley
Summit Lake
December 22, 2010
Fourteen months before her death

The flight from DC to Charlotte was smooth and quiet. Becca slept with her head on Jack's shoulder while Jack's mind worked on the idea that his best friend was in love with his girlfriend. They may have been able to conquer the secrecy of their relationship, had they come clean last summer when everyone returned for senior year. But now, Jack knew, months later and with this new revelation about Brad, their relationship would be much harder to explain.

Becca's parents met them at arrivals, and they threw their bags in the back of the Escalade. Jack stood in the background while Becca hugged her parents.

"Mom and Dad," Becca said, giddy with excitement. "This is Jack."

"Hi, Jack," Becca's mom said as she hugged him.

Jack shook Mr. Eckersley's hand and they all climbed into the Escalade.

"Thanks for having me for Christmas," Jack said as they pulled away.

"You're very welcome," Mrs. Eckersley said.

"So, Jack," Mr. Eckersley said. "Becca tells us you're looking at some very impressive law schools."

"Same ones as Becca. Mostly."

"He's already heard from Stanford," Becca said, looking at Jack and smiling with those perfect teeth.

"Is that right?"

Jack nodded in the backseat while he gave Becca a dirty look. His acceptance to Stanford was something he told only Becca, but no one else. He hadn't even told his own parents yet, and he definitely didn't want to discuss law school during this trip. He knew William Eckersley was a mega-lawyer with his own power firm and was rumored to be heading for the bench. Having no real interest in the profession, Jack wanted to avoid law talk altogether. He had no intention of slogging to work every day in a stiff suit, trying to outperform the other stiff suits who were trying to outperform him. "Yeah, I just heard last week."

"Early," Mr. Eckersley said.

"They offer a few early admissions to some of their top prospects," Becca said.

"That's not exactly true," Jack said. "You have to have . . . I just had a good recommendation."

"From Senator Ward—of Maryland—who Jack worked for over the summer. He's a Stanford alum."

"Well, congratulations," Mrs. Eckersley said. "Are you taking the offer?"

"I'm not sure about California."

"He doesn't get excited about it because he doesn't even want to be a lawyer. He wants to write," Becca said.

"Write what?" Mr. Eckersley asked.

Jack widened his eyes at Becca. They agreed not to talk about any of this with her parents. His counselor already told him his career choice was suicide and that if he got into a top-notch law school he should work hard and take a big-firm job after graduation. His counselor pulled out graphs of the salary projections for Ivy League law graduates and told Jack exactly how much he should be earning in five years. Trying to be a speechwriter was wildly risky, his counselor told him. He went on for fifteen minutes about other kids who missed opportunities and where they were now in life. Jack wanted to ask which opportunity his counselor missed along the way that stuck him now in a ten-by-ten office pushing papers and steering persuadable kids away from their dreams.

"Political speeches, maybe," Jack said. "Becca and the rest of our friends are going to law school also, so I'm sure one of them will end up in Congress. Maybe they'll hire me." He smiled at Becca.

"Brad's the only one who wants to run for office. Gail and I will open our own practice and be millionaires before thirty."

"Keep talking like that and you'll give me a heart attack," Mr. Eckersley said.

"Don't worry, Daddy, I'll add the third *Eckersley* to the firm's name."

"So where does this aspiration for political speechwriting come from?" Mr. Eckersley asked Jack.

"I interned for a couple of summers back in Wisconsin for the governor's campaign and had the opportunity to write a bit here and there. And then the last three summers at a program on Capitol Hill."

"He wrote the draft for Senator Ward when he addressed Congress about military spending," Becca said.

"Really?" Mrs. Eckersley said. "Milt Ward?"

Jack nodded.

"You wrote his speech?"

"Me and the rest of the interns," Jack clarified. "And most of my stuff got cut out."

"You always do that," Becca said. "I hate when you put yourself down."

Jack laughed. "That's not a putdown, it's a fact. My part was on defense spending and most of it got cut."

"Only because of time restraints." Becca leaned forward between the seats so her parents could hear clearly. "The senator called Jack later to tell him he had more promise than any of the other interns."

Becca's mom turned in the passenger seat. "Really?"

"I think it was a courtesy call," Jack said. "He sponsored the program, so I imagine he called all the interns and said something similar."

Becca shook her head as she leaned back. "He did not call the other interns. Sammi Ahern was in the same program and she never got a call from Ward. That's just you being modest. Senator Ward wrote one recommendation letter this year, even though a hundred students probably asked him. It went to Jack."

"So why law school if you want to write speeches?" Mr. Eckersley asked.

"I'll intern during the summers and get some more experience, and law school will be a good résumé booster. I guess it'll make me more legit if I write about policy stuff."

"Well, the law is a fascinating occupation and maybe you'll change your mind when you start school. Either way, it sounds like you've got your head screwed on straight." William Eckersley turned his head to look back at Becca while he drove. "So I'm finally piecing together why you were so adamant about staying in DC last summer instead of clerking for me. Is this official now? You two are dating?"

"No one at school knows," Becca said. "But we're telling everyone when we get back."

An acidic gas bubble burst somewhere in Jack's esophagus, causing instant heartburn. He stifled the belch and faked a smile to Becca.

Mr. Eckersley changed his focus to the rearview mirror, where he could see his daughter's face. "And why the secrecy about you guys dating?"

"I already told you, Daddy. We're all friends and we just want to wait to tell everyone."

"Wait for what, honey?"

"We're waiting for the right time, Dad. It's just one of those situations you're not going to understand."

"Ah, of course. But remember, you were three years old before your mother and I told anyone about you, so I might understand more than you think."

"You're such a dork, Dad."

They drove in silence for ten minutes before Mr. Eckersley spoke. "Jack, are you familiar with the Blue Ridge Mountains?"

"Not so much," Jack said. "I'm from Wisconsin, so mountains are a new phenomenon to me."

"They're part of the Great Smoky Mountain Range. They're sort of the interior of the Appalachians and formed a barrier to the original settlers. Not until late in the 1700s—"

"Dad! We just finished finals, we don't need a history lesson."

"It's not a lesson, it's interesting background on where we're headed. Anyway, we have a home up in the mountains where we like to spend Christmas each year. It's a lake home and we also spend quite a bit of time up there in the summer. I used to like to run my Catalina around the lake, until Becca decided she was the new captain. I only take orders now. The town is called Summit Lake," Mr. Eckersley said.

"Becca told me about your house. It sits on the water, right? On stilts or something?"

"If you fell off the porch you'd land in the lake," Becca said.

"A stilt house," Jack said. "I'm really excited to see it."

Becca's brother was engaged to a girl whose parents lived in Manhattan, so he was spending his Christmas in New York. And being a newly minted member of his father's law office, he was flying back to Greensboro on Christmas night to be in the office on the 26th. That made Jack, Becca, and her parents the only participants in the Eckersleys' holiday trek to Summit Lake. The same pressures of making her mark were coming for Becca when she joined her father's firm. But she'd have to tackle law school first before she joined the other gunners who thought ninety hours a week was the only way to prove their worth.

It was approaching 6:00 p.m. when they pulled into Summit Lake. Even without daylight Becca and Jack could sense the mountains staring down on them.

"See, look," Becca said as they came into town. She pointed to the lake where two rows of ten houses ran into the water, supported by long pillars. Decorated in Christmas lights, the houses were ablaze and reflected off the lake below. A narrow road ran behind the houses and Mr. Eckersley steered the Escalade along the path. He parked in a small spot next to the last house in the line. They all piled out. It was chillier here than at sea level. Becca took Jack by the hand and led him to the deck that ran 360 degrees around the house. They walked to the back of the house where they looked out at the lake.

"What do you think?"

"This is amazing. Now I know why you love it so much. What's out there?" Jack asked as he stared at a light on the other side of the lake.

"The Summit Lake lighthouse. On Christmas night, it alternates red and green. It sits on the point right where the mountains end. On the other side, the lake opens up for many miles." She excitedly turned him in the other direction and pointed at the town. "See the tree?"

Over the two-story buildings Jack saw the top of a pine tree glowing with colored lights and a bright star. Becca squeezed his hand, reading his mind the way she always did.

"Don't get sad. We're going to Green Bay next year for Christmas."

"I know. I can just see my mom crying Christmas morning when I'm not there."

"Next year my mom will be doing the same thing. When I'm thirty years old she'll still cry if I'm not around on Christmas morning."

They unpacked the car and then headed into town. Becca carried a wrapped box containing the latest rage doll, while Jack carried a Tonka truck. They walked along the dock that ran behind the stilt houses and then onto Maple Street, which was five blocks long and concluded with a three-story hotel at the end. Shops and restaurants lined the road and in the middle of town they came to the giant pine that would not have been misplaced in Rockefeller Center. They each put their donation underneath it.

"Come on," Becca said. "I want to show you the town."

They headed to the end of Maple Street, turned around, and walked back on the other side. Foot traffic was sporadic as people strolled in and out of shops grabbing gifts a few days before Christmas. Without the intrusion of city lights, the night sky was decorated with stars. It reminded Jack of home. He stared off at the houses that ran up the mountain. They were alive with Christmas decorations and he imagined a life where a second home waited in the mountains, where family and friends gathered for long weekends and holidays. He got to know wealthy kids since he started at George

Washington, some so rich they made his life back in Green Bay look like a page out of *National Geographic*. Becca and her family, he knew, approached this type of wealth. His own family never had much money, and could never afford a vacation house up in Door County where some of his friends went during the summer, but none of that ever mattered to him. His parents gave him and his sisters everything they had, and from that Jack was able to attend GWU. Maybe from that opportunity a life like the one Becca had lived for twenty years might be possible. Maybe.

For the first time, doubt crept into his mind and stained the way he thought about his future. As he stood in this town, he was nervous about what he would have to offer the girl he loved. Was his counselor correct in his guidance? Jack thought of ninety-hour workweeks digging through research in the basement of a New York firm. No, he decided. He'd crash and burn and live off food stamps before he gave up on his dreams, or fell into the rut of a nine-to-five life. Or a five-to-nine life as many first-year graduates in New York live.

"That's our church," Becca said, pointing to the large structure at the end of Maple Street. "They have a really pretty service for Midnight Mass."

Jack smiled. "I can't wait."

"Are you glad you came?"

"I am."

Becca wrapped her arm around his waist as they walked through town. He lifted his arm around her shoulder and pulled her close.

Chapter 14

Kelsey Castle
Summit Lake
March 9, 2012
Day 5

She woke early and took to the streets in a slow jog. Despite her dream, or perhaps because of it, she was determined to run this morning. The town was asleep at 5:30 a.m. as Kelsey snaked her way along the sidewalks and through the avenues until she reached the lake. A dirt path took her past the hospital and around the water to the Summit Lake Lighthouse two miles away. A paved path led through the courtyard to the entryway of the lighthouse tower. She climbed the stairs—spiral, metal planks that clinked under her shoes. Forty-watt bulbs offered dim resistance to the darkness outside. She was breathing heavy when she made it to the top and exited from the small doorway that felt like it belonged on a submarine. The breeze was stronger at the top of the tower and Kelsey grabbed the railing to steady herself.

She looked across the lake. The town was just starting to rise now, with lights visible in scattered homes and chimneys twisting smoke into the morning. She walked around to the other side of the tower, where the lake opened up to a vast expanse of water that covered many miles. From her perspective, she could see the horizon burning with predawn. The metal grating was cold as she sat down and slipped her legs between the railings, dangling her feet over the side. Hugging the two railing bars, Kelsey stuck her face between them and watched the sunrise.

When the sun peeked over the horizon and painted a highway along the surface of Summit Lake, Kelsey's mind settled on Becca Eckersley. If Kelsey's information was correct, and Becca had married in secret—why? The list of possibilities was long. Becca's parents did not approve of the guy. Their relationship was new and they were young and no one would understand getting married so soon. He was older—a professor perhaps, or maybe an attorney—and their affair had to be kept quiet.

Despite the reason, the result was the same—Becca's parents knew nothing about the marriage. Or at least they didn't the night she was killed. Kelsey shifted her gaze across the lake. The arc of the stilt houses was visible. At the end, the Eckersley home caught the morning light. Kelsey pursed her lips and exhaled a long, slow breath that was scantly visible in the cool air. She needed Becca's journal. If it existed, it surely held the identity of the man she married. And if Becca did write in it at the coffeehouse the night she was killed, someone knew about this journal. Kelsey spent thirty minutes on top of the lighthouse, mulling over the facts of Becca's murder and piecing together her information. Finally, with the sun over the horizon, she headed down the stairs and jogged back around the lake.

He offered to meet her at 7:00 a.m. and it was just a few minutes past when Kelsey finished her jog and slowed her pace. She walked onto the dock next to the stilt houses and spotted him at the far end of the pier. She cooled down as she walked the length of the dock and stopped in front of the Eckersleys' home. Commander Ferguson approached her, stuck a cigarette between his lips, and lit the end of it, pulling for a few seconds before talking.

"Good morning, young lady." Smoke leaked from his mouth and rode away on the lake breeze. "Looks like you've had a hell of a day already."

"Early jog. I didn't sleep well." Kelsey pointed to the Eckersleys' house. "Thanks for doing this."

"Not sure what you're going to learn from going inside, but let's do it before anyone in this town wakes up and sees me letting a reporter into a crime scene."

They bypassed the yellow tape that encircled the deck and flapped in the breeze. Commander Ferguson rattled some keys and fidgeted with the patio doors. He pulled the sliding glass door to the side and Kelsey followed him inside. She walked through the living room and into the large kitchen where, she knew, Becca was assaulted. Kelsey had been here in her dreams the night before. She looked around now and saw a long island with four stools. Pinewood cabinets reached the ceiling. Stainless-steel appliances and granite countertops gave the place a polished look. She noticed the doorway off the kitchen that led into a mudroom—the door the attacker entered the night Becca was killed.

She imagined that night. Becca's law school materials spread across the island as she sat on the stool. Somehow the man entered the house, either walked straight in through an unlocked door or was allowed in by Becca. Then, a struggle. Becca's knuckles were bruised, and two of them on her right hand broken. Skin beneath her fingernails and facial hair stuck in her palms. Papers and textbooks strewn across the kitchen, and dishes shattered on the ground. As she ran the scene through her mind, Kelsey found herself tensing and rooting for Becca to fight harder, to somehow change the outcome.

The fight happened right here, where Kelsey stood. The remnants of that night—the broken dishes and upended furniture—were still present. An eerie feeling came over her as Kelsey considered she was standing in the same place another woman had been assaulted—something Kelsey went through just weeks before.

Pulled from her jogging trail that morning, Kelsey fought for her life the same as Becca. And the questions Kelsey was asking of Becca and her life were the same ones that lurked in the dark corners of her own mind. Questions about why she was attacked, and if there was something she did to cause it. If she could have done anything different that morning to prevent it. Questions about why the bastard picked her and not someone else. About how long he had waited for her and watched her, and whether she knew the man behind the mask or if he was just a random stranger choosing a random woman.

Walking through the Eckersleys' home caused these dark corners of her mind to shine brightly, and all the questions she was avoiding came sharply into focus. And she wondered now if Penn Courtney—her surrogate father—knew more than he was letting on about Becca's case. If he knew the only way for Kelsey to conquer her fears was to do so through work and with a case that forced her to look long and hard at herself and what had happened.

But whether she was giving Penn more credit than he deserved, one thing was certain. There was a reason Kelsey took so quickly to this story, and as she stood in the very spot where Becca Eckersley had been raped and murdered, she realized it. Kelsey felt connected to Becca. There was a sense of knowing exactly what she went through. Knowing how she felt that night. As she stood amidst the crime scene, Kelsey knew she wasn't simply writing an article to fill the quota of pages for her monthly grind. She was searching for answers to return some dignity to an innocent girl who never had a chance at closure. Becca Eckersley deserved a conclusion to this ordeal, and if Kelsey could find those answers and provide that conclusion, maybe *she* would benefit as much as Becca. Perhaps she could go back to her life and set a course on doing the same thing for herself.

Commander Ferguson took ten minutes to describe the scene from that night. Small details Kelsey scribbled on her notepad, information that alone would never solve anything, but, pieced together with what she already knew, added to the narrative.

"Mind if I look around?" she asked.

"Place has been cleared out. What are you hoping to find?"

"Insight." Kelsey smiled.

"You've got five minutes, and don't touch anything." Commander Ferguson sat on a kitchen stool and drummed his fingers on the granite.

Knowing the kitchen was the main crime scene, and all evidence would have been carefully gathered from there, she walked down a hallway and into the den. A desk and chair and a wall of bookshelves made up the room. Unlike the kitchen and family room, this room was immaculate and untouched. Against orders, she quietly pulled open drawers and fingered the contents of the shelves. Upstairs next, Kelsey entered each of the three bedrooms. She spent the most time in Becca's room. She checked the nightstand first, then under the mattress. The closet was mostly empty and the armoire filled with nothing of value. After five minutes, she brushed a stray hair from her face while she looked around Becca's bedroom. The quiet room of a dead girl who would never again use any of the things that sat on her dresser or in her drawers or on her shelves. Finally, Kelsey headed downstairs.

"Find what you were looking for?" Commander Ferguson asked as she entered the kitchen.

"Nope."

"Did you make a mess while you were slamming drawers and opening closets I told you not to touch?"

"Nope again."

"Let's get outta here before I lose my job."

They headed back outside and Commander Ferguson locked up the house. They walked down the pier.

"Okay, young lady, what's this news you have to tell me?"

"I know Becca's secret," Kelsey said as they walked.

Commander Ferguson sucked again on his cigarette as his eyebrows rose. With his index and middle fingers he pulled the cigarette from his lips and turned his palm faceup. "Let's hear it."

"She eloped. Ran off and got married without her parents knowing about it."

Another pull while the commander considered this. He looked off to the mountains and Kelsey could tell his mind was working. This was a detective who had an unsolved case that spoke daily to him, begging him to solve it. When he pulled the cigarette from his mouth, smoke rose over his upper lip and into his nostrils. Kelsey thought this might be a new definition for secondhand smoke, and she wanted to mention to the great detective that if the initial puff didn't kill him, taking it in a second time just might. Instead she waved the odor away from her face.

This brought the commander back from his thoughts. "Sorry about that." He quickly snuffed the cigarette on the bottom of his shoe and shoved it in his pocket. He waved away the residual smoke, but his mind was clearly elsewhere. "That doesn't make any sense," he finally said.

"What's that?"

"Becca being married. I looked into her past pretty deep. Never came across any record that suggested such a thing. To get married, you need a marriage license. After the wedding ceremony, a marriage certificate is issued and must be filed with the county to make the marriage legal. It's part of our great bureaucracy, which is to say it's nothing more than a moneymaker for the counties, but still required by law. I never found any such record."

Kelsey thought about that. They walked down Maple Street until they reached Minnehaha Avenue, then stopped in front of the Summit Lake police headquarters. Could Millie Mays have been mistaken? Did the old lady misunderstand her daughter's description of her conversation with Becca? Had a touch of dementia and embellishment grown the story in Millie's mind? Possibly, Kelsey thought. But unlikely. Kelsey had interviewed thousands of sources in the same fashion she did Millie—casually, without pressure to get detailed information—and Kelsey had a feel for when people were stretching what they knew. Sometimes people embellished their knowledge to feel more important and maybe get their name in a magazine. Other times people had no real clue about what Kelsey was asking and couldn't bring themselves to admit it, so they created a story out of nothing. Millie fell into neither of these categories. She was reluctant to divulge the secret she kept, and surely wouldn't have given up any information had Kelsey not manipulated her.

"What if they ran off to Vegas and got married on a whim?" she asked.

Commander Ferguson shook his head. "Doesn't matter if it's Vegas or Jamaica. You have to file a marriage certificate, and it would have shown up when we ran her through our national database. If this supposed marriage happened outside the U.S., the certificate would have to route through the U.S. Embassy in the foreign country before arriving back here in the States, but it would still get here. Maybe a few weeks later, so the argument could be that it's still out there being processed. Problem with that theory is that there's no record of Becca leaving the country. So if she got married, it was right here in the U.S. of A., and there's no record of it. So she either bucked the system or you're wrong, Miss Castle." Commander Ferguson brushed his hand over his goatee. "Where'd you get this idea about Becca being married anyway?"

Kelsey gave him a smile, as if he should know better than to ask such a question.

"Fine," he said. "How credible is this person?"

"If the marriage angle is true, she's very credible. I guess we'll have to dig a little for the answer."

The commander pulled his stubbed cigarette from his pocket and brought it back to life. He took extra care to keep the smoke to himself. "Only way that scenario is possible would be if they got married on the sly, real quick, without anybody knowing, then never filed the marriage certificate, which they'd have to do together."

"So maybe Becca was killed before they filed?"

Commander Ferguson pointed his cigarette at her. "Exactly. That's the only way."

They both stood in silence for a while.

"I've looked very carefully through the information you gave me," Kelsey finally said.

"So have I."

"Do you know anything about Becca keeping a journal?"

"What sort of journal?"

"You know, a diary."

The commander shook his head. "Never heard she did. Why? She kept one?"

"So I've heard."

"Where is it? Her parents?"

"Doubt it," Kelsey said. "Supposedly she was writing in it just hours before she was killed. It should have been in the evidence collected that night from the stilt house."

"There was no journal found that night."

"I know."

"And you're saying there should have been?"

"I'm saying that if Becca was writing in a journal while she was here in Summit Lake, it has to be somewhere."

"And I assume it wasn't in any of the drawers or cabinets you were just banging around back at the Eckersleys'?"

Kelsey shook her head. "Who collected the evidence that night? Created that evidence list?"

"My guys," Commander Ferguson said. "Under my supervision."

"Not your state friends?"

"They didn't arrive until late that night, after most of the evidence was documented. If a diary was in that house, we'd have found it."

"And documented it?"

"Of course."

Kelsey closed her eyes and rubbed her temples.

"Still doesn't help us much," the commander said. "Even if it's true about Becca being married."

Kelsey cocked her head to the side. "No? You told me to find Becca's secret."

"I did," Commander Ferguson said as he sucked the life from the cigarette. "But finding a secret is never the key. Figuring out why a secret is a secret"—he lifted his cigarette into the air—"that will lead you somewhere."

Chapter 15

Becca Eckersley
Summit Lake
December 28, 2010
Fourteen months before her death

They spent three days after Christmas in Summit Lake. Becca and Jack walked the town, drank coffee at Millie's Coffee House, ate dinners with Becca's parents, and spent quiet nights at the stilt house watching movies and playing cards. Mr. Eckersley tried to impress on Jack the wonders of practicing law, instead of simply possessing a law degree. Jack promised not to make any decisions until he finished school.

On their last night, Jack and Becca went to dinner alone.

"This summer," Becca said. "You'll have to come to Greensboro so I can show you where I live. We'll drive to the coast and watch the waves roll in from the Caribbean. Maybe after law school we'll take a vacation there."

"Where?"

"The Caribbean. St. Lucia or St. Thomas. Or maybe we'll charter a sailboat and cruise around the British Virgin Islands."

"I don't know how to sail."

"I'll teach you this summer. I'll take you to Mumford Cove where we keep our Catalina. It's right on the coast."

"Great idea," Jack said. "So a Catalina is a sailboat?"

Becca smiled. "Yes."

"I don't speak the same language as you. We never had a boat in my family."

"So what. It doesn't take long to learn to sail."

"What are you going to do after law school?" Jack asked.

"What do you mean?"

"I mean, look at your life here. You go to a very expensive college—and so do I, but I have a full ride. I assume your parents write a check each semester. You've got a vacation home in the mountains, a huge house in Greensboro, and a Catalina. Two of them, right? One back home and one up here?"

"So? We also have a house in Vail. What does it matter?"

"If you saw my life in Wisconsin—and I don't mean this in a bad way, because I'm not ashamed of it—but if you saw where I lived, the house I grew up in, the car we drive, I think you'd see a very different life than all this."

"What does that have to do with what I'm going to do after law school?"

"First-year lawyers don't exactly kill it, unless you go to New York and sell yourself as a slave to a big firm. But I know that's not what you want to do. And your dad is smart enough not to bring his little girl into the firm a few years after he brought in his son and throw a huge salary at her before she proves herself."

"So I get an apartment and drive a used car and eat cheap meals. You don't think I can do that?"

"I think you can do it, it's just that for me, I'm used to it."

"But we'll be together, so it doesn't matter where we live or what we have." Becca smiled. "You're enough for me. But

I have news for you, Jack. You're going to be quite successful in whatever you do."

He shrugged. "I guess we both have to get through one more semester of college and then law school before we worry about any of that."

"It's so weird, isn't it?" Becca said. "Thinking about life after college? No more running around, no more hiding things. We can get our own place and actually sleep together, all night. No more sneaking home in the middle of the night. It's going to be weird telling Gail and Brad, but I think Gail suspects something anyway."

"Yeah," Jack said as he stared out the window of the restaurant. "Gonna be real weird."

"Becca Eckersley!"

The voice was deep and practiced, and when Jack looked up he was surprised to see someone his age attached to it. The guy wore a trying-way-too-hard beard that was meticulously maintained, and of which he was obviously very proud.

"Hi," Becca said, shooting a quick glance at Jack. Her eyes widened briefly—a little thing she did to let Jack know something awkward was happening. Becca stood up and offered the guy an obligatory hug. "What are you doing up here?" she asked.

"Home from school and here with my parents. How's GW?"

"Good," Becca said. "Really, really good. How about Harvard?"

"It is what it's supposed to be. A stepping stone, right? Everything's kosher."

Jack saw her wipe her hands on her skirt. Another one of her tells. "This is Jack," Becca said.

Jack stood. He was a few inches taller and significantly wider than the guy in front of him. He offered his hand.

The guy grabbed it and shook hard. The alpha male. "Richard Walker. Becca and I are old friends," he said, like they were forty years old and on a two-decade sabbatical.

"Richard and I went to high school together," Becca said.

"Yeah," the guy said. "We dated." He looked at Jack. "We were what they call *high school sweethearts*."

Jack kept his gaze on Richard and offered an expressionless face. "I'm familiar with the term." Jack was also now familiar with Richard Walker. This was the idiot who stopped by school every so often to upset Becca and make her cry. When Jack and Becca first met, she was untying the dating knot that snared these two throughout high school. Four years later, she was still working at it. Jack remembered Becca's red-rimmed eyes during finals week when this jackass stopped by to again pledge his love for her and explain how brokenhearted he was without her. Jack also recalled from his discussions with Becca that this guy's family owned a house here in Summit Lake, where the two spent every summer during high school.

"You been in town for a while?" Richard asked.

"About a week. We came up for Christmas. Leaving tomorrow."

"You both came up?"

Becca nodded.

"How do you guys know each other?" Richard asked.

"We go to school together," Becca said.

"We're what they call *college sweethearts*," Jack said.

Richard's face froze for a second, then a forced smile appeared and Jack could tell instantly this guy was full of himself, and shit.

"Gotcha. Good for you guys. Where you from, chief?"

Chief? "Green Bay."

"Wisconsin?" Richard made a strange face. "The sticks, huh? Welcome to civilization."

Jack stared at him but said nothing.

Richard broke away and looked at Becca again. "Can I talk to you a minute?"

Becca's eyebrows rose. "Sure."

"In private?"

Becca smiled awkwardly, looked quickly at Jack and then back to Richard. "I'm out to dinner, Richard. So I'm not going to run in the corner with you like we're in high school."

Jack laughed under his breath. He loved this girl for a reason.

"Gotcha," Richard said again. "Didn't mean to intrude. It was really nice seeing you."

"You too," Becca said as she gave a reluctant hug.

"Take it easy, chief."

"See ya, Dick," Jack said.

"What's that?"

"Dick. It's short for Richard."

"I just go by Richard."

Jack sat down and pulled his napkin over his lap. "See ya, Richard."

The forced smile came back to Richard's face. "Really classy, Becca. I'm sure your dad's happy you're running around with this guy."

"Bye, Richard," Becca said. "Have a good New Year's."

Richard stared at Becca. Finally, he took a step backward. "Yeah."

Jack watched him leave. "What's Paul Bunyan's problem?"

"I don't know," Becca said. "God, that was awkward."

"Has he always talked like that, with that fake broadcaster's voice?"

Becca shrugged. "He wants to litigate. I guess he thinks it will help."

"It'll help the jury think he's an idiot." Jack looked at Becca. "And you used to date that guy? That's the guy?"

She smiled. "Stop."

"He seems a little off, no?" Jack asked.

"Yeah, he did look a little strange. He's still . . . you know, he's never really gotten over us."

"You think?" Jack said.

"Did you call him Dick?"

"By accident."

Becca shook her head. "What am I going to do with you?"

They finished dinner and walked down Maple Street on the way back to the stilt house.

"My parents love you, by the way. Don't worry about Richard, he was trying to get under your skin."

"I may not become the lawyer your dad wants you to marry, but compared to Dick Walker I'm certain your parents think I'm a real catch. Unless your parents fell for that fake smile I almost wiped off his face."

"My dad always liked him in high school, but only because I was dating him. Richard's dad is a big trial lawyer, so my dad knows him. Richard used to play that angle. But that's enough about high school. We'll see who we run into next year when we visit your parents."

Jack laughed. "I have no Dick Walkers in my closet, trust me."

"Well, Richard was our coming-out party. He's the first person we've told about us dating, besides our parents. What's our plan for when we get back to school? We're telling everyone, right? Gail and Brad?"

Jack shrugged. "Yeah."

"You don't seem so sure," Becca said as they walked.

"I think we need to talk about it."

"About what?"

He looked at her. "I think we're going to have some issues when we get back to school."

"What kind of issues? You're starting to get me worried."

"Not issues between you and me. Issues with our friends. We've been keeping this whole thing a secret for so long, it's sort of become scandalous. I'm starting to think we should've just come clean from the beginning, last summer when everything happened between us. It would have saved us from a bunch of trouble we're about to run into."

They turned onto a side street and headed east toward the lake.

"I know what you're saying," Becca said. "But I think everything will be okay. Maybe a little weird at first, but that's about it."

"Gail is one thing," Jack said as they started along the dock in front of the Eckersleys' house. "Brad is another."

"What do you mean?"

Jack didn't have time to answer. As he and Becca made their way along the dock they saw Brad sitting on the bench on Becca's patio. Confusion shaped his face as Brad saw Becca approach with Jack.

"Brad?" Becca said as a slow smile formed on her face, not understanding what was happening. "Oh my God. What do you guys have going on?" she smiled at Jack. "Did you know about this?"

"Shit," Jack said, letting go of Becca's hand.

Becca walked closer to Brad and tried to give him a hug.

Brad held away her advance with a straight arm, staring only at Jack. "Did you tell her?" he asked.

"No." Jack said. "I haven't said a word about anything."

"Brad," Becca said. "What's going on?" Her smile faded. "What's wrong?"

Brad stared at Jack, unable to look at Becca. Finally he pulled his gaze to hers. "I came to tell you I had feelings for you. I thought you felt the same way. That's what you said the other night." Brad shook his head and let out a forced laugh. "I came to tell you I'm in love with you. But what? You're running around behind my back with Jack?" He looked back to Jack. "I thought your mom would *kill* you if you weren't home for Christmas."

"We just planned this a few weeks ago, Brad," Becca said.

Brad's eyes were squinted as he pieced things together. "Are you guys together or something?" Brad asked.

Becca nodded with no expression on her face. "Since summer," she said. "But it wasn't all of a sudden, Brad. We had feelings for each other for a while."

Brad shook his head. "So all the talks we had, about my father and all his shit; all the times we stayed up until sunrise, during all that you were with Jack? Thinking about Jack?"

"Thinking about . . . no," Becca said. "I was thinking about you and your situation. Because we're friends, Brad. You and I have always stayed up late talking about things. That's what you and I have always done. You're a great listener and one of my best friends."

"I'm going to head inside, let you guys talk," Jack said.

"Why didn't you tell me the other day at lunch?" Brad asked.

Jack let out a long breath. "I don't know, Brad. I was shocked to hear what you were telling me. The same way you would have been shocked had I told you."

"So you let me go on like a fool, telling you how I thought Becca and I were going to get together. And you were fine letting me spend all Christmas break thinking I had a chance with her. Trying to figure out a way to tell her how I feel. The whole time you knew you were going to be with her over break, laughing at me?"

"No one's laughing at you, Brad. I'd never do that. And the other day wasn't the right time to tell you. I had to get my thoughts straight."

"And you came here behind my back to get your thoughts straight?"

"No," Jack said with some force behind his voice. "I came here to spend Christmas with Becca, because she and her family invited me. None of it was done behind your back because before the other day I didn't know my relationship with Becca had anything to do with you."

"Okay, guys. Let's take a break for a minute," Becca said.

"Does Gail know?"

"No one knows," Becca said. "We didn't know how to tell you guys."

Brad slowly walked past them to the front of the house where his rental was parked. He climbed in and started the engine.

"Where are you going?" Becca asked as she followed him.

"Not here."

"Come inside, Brad. Meet my parents. Spend the night so we can talk."

"I already met your parents, and they probably think I'm an idiot."

He backed the rental from the driveway. Becca and Jack watched their friend drive away without saying good-bye. They were left with each other, standing in front of stilt houses decorated with Christmas lights.

Chapter 16

Kelsey Castle
Summit Lake
March 10, 2012
Day 6

The red numbers on her digital alarm clock flashed again. 4:45 a.m. Tossing for an hour now, she finally sat up in bed and slid her legs from under the covers until her bare feet touched the carpet. Her hands shook as she stared into the dark room. She sat still for several minutes, trying to control her breathing and her emotions and her mind. Finally, she buried her face in her palms and began to cry. Her mind struggled all night to find answers to why she endured a savage attack and survived, while Becca Eckersley had not.

Forcing herself back to work and then coming to Summit Lake to take on Becca's story felt like cheating—using Becca as a way to repair her own spirit. But Kelsey didn't know a better way. Her immediate reaction in the wake of her survival had been to complain about Penn Courtney giving her a paid month off from work, and to stand ready to strike like a rattlesnake at anyone who offered her sympathy or dared to ask how she was doing. But now, having walked through the

Eckersleys' home and in Becca's footsteps, Kelsey's perspective changed. She had her life. She was alive. She was healthy and healing.

As she sat in her dark hotel room in a small town in the Blue Ridge Mountains, Kelsey Castle knew she was being called—if not by Becca herself, then by some higher entity—to find the answers that had eluded this town. With a deep breath, she climbed out of bed and put on jeans and a sweater. She locked her hotel room and took the empty stairwell to the lobby. Outside, a brisk lake breeze greeted her. The wind ran up the mountains to the west and cascaded back in a circular jaunt that brought with it the smoky scent of wood-burning fireplaces. Darkness filled the sky without a hint of sunrise. Only streetlamps offered a soft yellow glow at intersections. Summit Lake was peacefully quiet.

Kelsey sucked in the clean mountain air as she headed down the main drag on her way to the shore. As she walked toward the corner of Maple and Tomahawk, Kelsey noticed lights above the coffeehouse—a startling contrast to the darkness the rest of the town hid under. She saw the drapes were open and as she got closer she heard a knock on the second-story window, which shot open. Rae stuck her head into the cold morning air.

"What are you doing out there?"

"Couldn't sleep," Kelsey said.

"Get in here. I'll open the front door."

A few seconds later Rae unlocked the café and held the door open. Kelsey noticed she was already dressed and showered. Her eyes were young and bright, without sleep or puffiness. Her sandy hair was newly blown dry and carried a soft glow of fresh conditioner.

Kelsey ran a hand over her puffy hair and licked her chapped lips as she walked into the cafe. "You look perfect, all fresh and perky. What time do you get up?"

"Just before four. The oven goes on at four-thirty."

"That's insane."

"Maybe for some, but I love it," Rae said. "Come back to the kitchen, I've gotta pull the scones. Coffee's on."

Kelsey followed Rae past the long mahogany bar and through the opening next to the register. She walked into the kitchen where Rae motioned for her to help herself to the stainless steel coffeepot on the counter. As she poured two mugs, she saw Rae don a red apron and pull a tray of scones from the oven. It was just before 5:00 a.m., and Kelsey watched Rae move around the kitchen as if it were noon.

"I take a little cream," Rae said. "And lots of sugar."

Kelsey prepared the coffee, then placed the cup on the island where Rae was running icing over the scones.

"Smells good." Kelsey said.

"Doesn't it?" Rae said. Her eyes jetted to Kelsey, then back to the scones. "I see you looking at me like I'm nuts."

"Me? No, I wasn't."

"Don't worry. I give most people that impression when they find out I get up so early, and sometimes stay so late. You'd think I'd get used to it or bored with it, but I don't. Not with the smells or the work or the crowd that comes through. Lots of regulars whom I've gotten to know well, and I love talking to them." Rae pointed the icer at Kelsey. "That's how you know you're doing what you were meant to do. When you never get bored with it, and you never want to do anything else."

"Ever thought of opening your own cafe?"

"Oh, yeah. All the time. Even told Livvy Houston I was thinking of becoming her competition. But the thing is, Livvy doesn't want this place. She's decided to move on, so Millie— Livvy's mom—offered the place to me. This year is my test run—to see if I can handle the place by myself. Make sure I'm sure."

"And?"

"So far, so good. Livvy never stops by anymore and Millie's too old to do much around here, so I already feel like the place is mine."

Rae finished the scones and put them to the side to cool. She threw a second batch in the oven and started dropping bagels into an automatic slicer. "How about you? You love your job?"

Kelsey thought for a minute. "Yeah, I do. Can't imagine doing anything else."

"Don't you feel sad for people who hate their jobs? I mean, to wake up each day and do something you don't like is no way to live. It's poor parenting, I think. When you're a kid, you don't know what you want. No ten-year-old kid dreams of being an accountant. No little girl wants to grow up to be a sales rep. Right? And those are fine jobs and lots of people are happy doing them all their life. But if no one tells you when you're a kid to dream, then you just go through life and do the things everyone else does, sometimes the things your parents do." Rae grabbed her coffee and took a sip. "I don't know, I'm too philosophical in the morning, but you know what I'm saying? Do what you love to do. And if you end up not loving it, do something else."

Kelsey smiled at the girl's enthusiasm. "I know exactly what you're saying, and it's good advice. I don't think you're too anything this morning except happy with your life. Maybe a little too amped up on caffeine at 5:00 a.m., but there's nothing wrong with that."

Rae laughed. "I think you and I are gonna get along. So why can't you sleep?"

Kelsey looked at the ceiling. "Why can't I sleep?" she said to herself, mulling the question. "You have a few hours?"

"Oh," Rae said. Nodding her head. "Sounds like boy issues."

Kelsey raised her eyebrows. "Hardly."

"I heard there was a doctor at the hospital who was helping you with research or something."

"Really? Where did you hear this?"

Rae shrugged her shoulders. "I also heard he's nice looking."

"What are you talking about?" Kelsey was laughing now. "He's twice my age."

"That's not true. I heard he's, like, forty. Maybe forty-five. How old are you?"

"Thirty."

"Twice your age is sixty, so stop exaggerating and avoiding the question. Is he good looking?"

"Where are you getting your information?"

Rae smiled. "I run the only coffee shop in a very small town where everyone is talking about Becca Eckersley's death. And everyone knows there's a journalist from *Events* magazine poking around. People talk, and in this town those people usually talk to me. So if you're trying to keep a secret while you're here, you won't be able to."

"Unless you murder a young law student, then you can disappear into the night."

Rae puckered her lower lip. "Touché. But my point is that if you don't want me to know you're hanging out with a good-looking doctor, don't have dinner with him a block away from here."

"He helped me with some medical records I was looking for."

"Really," Rae said. "And that's it? Nothing more to the story?"

"What do you mean?"

"When I find you wandering the streets before sunrise, I assume a boy is the reason."

Kelsey smiled. "I assure you, Peter Ambrose is not keeping me up at night. We just met."

"Ooh," Rae said with wide eyes. "Then that's called 'pre-romantic' boy issues, and they can be more complicated than full-on, in-the-trenches *romantic* boy problems." She dropped the last bagel into the slicer and pointed to the oven where another batch of scones was baking. "Those will take about forty minutes. Let's head up front."

Still before sunrise, the corner lamppost spilled through the windows and cast quiet shadows across the café. Rae clicked on a standing lamp next to the fireplace, washing the leather chairs in warm auburn light. She put logs into the fireplace and placed a match below them. As she and Kelsey settled into the chairs the logs resisted the flames with loud cracking noises.

"So if it's not a boy, then what's the reason you can't sleep?" Rae asked.

"I guess you could say Becca Eckersley is keeping me up at night."

"Really? That's creepy."

"It's the way I am. Once I get hooked on a case, it's all I can think about. And the things I'm learning about this case have my mind going a hundred miles an hour." Kelsey paused. "And I can't stop . . ."

"Stop what?"

"I don't know. Thinking about life and death and how it can all be taken from us so quickly."

"Yeah?" Rae stared at her, reading the expression on Kelsey's face. "This case got you thinking of all that?"

"It did."

"Dish."

"What's that?"

"Dish. Tell me what's going on with you."

Kelsey made a funny face.

"Stop it," Rae said. "I've read everything you've ever written. Your book—twice—and all your articles, which include many homicides. You wrote about a missing six-year-old last year, which ended very badly. And you wrote about the nut job down there in Florida who made her kid sniff chloroform and accidentally OD'd her, then buried her a mile from her home. So don't tell me you can't handle coming to a small town and writing about the death of a law student. I don't buy it. So what's up? Why are you so bothered by this?"

Kelsey sipped her coffee. It was strange how people knew her so well through her writings. "Ever thought about being a shrink?"

"Never. Now dish."

Kelsey wasn't sure why she wanted to tell this girl about the things that were bothering her. Or why, after barely knowing her, she felt she could confide in Rae. She couldn't explain the reason she was about to tell this girl something she had refused to talk to the psychologist about. But there was something about Rae. A charisma that broke through to Kelsey, made her feel comfortable. She took a deep breath.

"I walked through the stilt house yesterday."

Rae pointed out the window toward the lake. "The Ecker-sleys'?"

"Yeah."

"I thought it was off-limits."

"It is. But the police chief let me take a look. Pulled the tape for a few minutes."

"How'd you manage that?"

Kelsey shrugged. "He's frustrated with the state guys taking over. He doesn't like the direction they're moving the investigation in. So I'm sort of his private way to get things done correctly."

"Yeah? What did you find?"

"I don't know. Nothing, I guess. But I stood where Becca stood. Walked in the footsteps of a girl who was raped and then murdered, and it got me thinking that the same thing damn near happened to me."

Rae slowly lifted her chin. She didn't need to ask another question or push any harder.

Kelsey exhaled a long, shaky breath. "This assignment was meant to get me out of the office and back on my feet after some time off. Time off I was forced to take after I was . . . you know, assaulted—same as Becca."

"Jesus, Kelsey. When?"

"Few weeks ago."

"What happened?"

Kelsey's eyes were glassy with tears, but she refused to let them spill down her cheeks. "I was jogging one morning. On the same path I've taken a thousand times before. Had my headphones in and was in my own little endorphin world. He came from the woods. A straight grab-and-drag, the kind I've written about before, but I was suddenly living it myself. I was startled at first, didn't know what was happening. When I finally figured it all out, it was too late. I fought for my life. Woke up in the hospital a day later."

Rae just stared at her for a minute. "I don't know what to say. I'm usually blunt and direct, but I didn't mean to—you don't have to tell me any more."

"No, no. You didn't pull it out of me. The truth is, I need to talk about it. Haven't actually talked with anyone about it, including the shrink they set me up with." Kelsey forced a smile. "You should feel honored, Rae. This is a coffeehouse confession of epic proportions for me."

Rae smiled. "I'm glad you've got a good attitude."

"The other choice is to let it control me, and I'm determined not to."

"They catch the guy?"

Kelsey shook her head. "He wore a mask. Couldn't ID him."

There was silence for a minute.

"How are you?" Rae finally asked.

"I'm moving on. Putting myself back together. And I was doing a helluva job at it, I really was. Until I walked into that house yesterday and it made it all so real and close." Kelsey looked into the fire. "The same thing could have happened to me, and someone else might be writing about my death."

"Yeah, but it didn't."

"No, it didn't. But why not? Why Becca and not me? *That* question is why I can't sleep. And I realized in the middle of the night that I've got to find a way to help this girl. I've got to get some closure for her."

"Sounds like a good way to help yourself, too."

Kelsey shrugged and took a sip of coffee. "Probably."

There was a knock on the front door and Kelsey saw a couple standing on the sidewalk.

"Damn," Rae said, looking at the wall clock. "Six o'clock comes early. Gotta open this place and get those scones out of the oven."

"Sorry to keep you."

"You didn't keep me from anything. Thanks for the company this morning, and for trusting me with your story. Keep fighting, Kelsey. You're a tough girl, I can tell."

Kelsey smiled and headed for the door. "I'll unlock the front. Don't let those scones burn."

"Thanks," Rae said. "And, Kelsey, come back and visit sometime. I want to hear more, or anything you feel like telling me."

"I will."

"I might even be able to help you with the Eckersley case."

"Oh yeah? How's that?"

"You know the gossip group? The busybodies who sit at the bar? From the other morning?"

Kelsey nodded, remembering the coffeehouse debate that took place at the bar.

"Rumor has it she kept a journal."

Kelsey stopped walking and turned.

Rae smiled. "I'll do some snooping and see what I come up with. Give me a day or so."

She disappeared into the kitchen. Kelsey unlocked the front door and let the couple into the cafe, then walked down Tomahawk Drive toward the lake to watch the sunrise.

Chapter 17

Becca Eckersley
George Washington University
March 14, 2011
Eleven months before her death

The semester crawled by with long days spent figuring out their schedules and the best way to avoid each other. Awkward encounters, however, were impossible to avoid. The last time they talked was on the deck of the stilt house, and after a month of failure, Becca and Jack stopped trying to get through to Brad. Nothing could be said to change his opinion of them. So Becca and Jack avoided him as much as they could. When forced to go home, Jack did so late at night. Brad's bedroom door was usually closed, and on the rare occasion Jack entered the apartment to find Brad in the living room, a common scene followed of Brad standing from the couch, clicking off the television, and closing his bedroom door behind him.

Becca talked to Jack about moving out, but he was tied to the apartment for the rest of the semester and his free ride included just about everything but room and board. What his parents sent each month was barely half his rent, and he covered the rest with his job on campus. He turned down Becca's offer to help him with her own money. He would hunker down for two more months and finish his senior year in the apartment. It wasn't hard to find an alternate place to stay. Gail was genuinely happy for them, and didn't care that Jack spent almost every night in Becca's room.

In March, Becca received her acceptance letter to George Washington Law and she and Jack celebrated with a nice dinner. Two weeks later, Gail got into the law program at Stanford, and she and Becca celebrated with beers at Bucky's, then cried when they realized they would be so far away from each other. Jack's letter from Harvard came a day later and the three of them toasted in Becca's apartment, where they laid the three acceptance letters next to each other and raised their glasses to what lay ahead.

Jack had his doubts during these celebrations. He camouflaged them with fake smiles and imitation bravado. He knew as spring dawned on the east coast, so, too, did something Jack thought might wake someday. He was surprised it took so long. He expected it when they returned from Christmas break, and not even the dissolution of the strongest friendship he had ever been part of could entirely distract his internal radar from what was coming.

No one knew how it leaked, or who leaked it, or in what fashion it trickled down to those who shouldn't have discovered it. But Jack didn't need an article in the paper or a campus blogger detailing the events that brought on Milford Morton's suspicion. What was meant for the four of them had spread to at least a few people who Brad hoped to impress, and those few slipped it to a few more, and a few more after that, until eventually 74 of the 122 seniors who sat for the final in Milford Morton's Business Law course had a copy of the stolen exam.

Once out of the bag, the proverbial cat ran wild around

campus. The investigation and the details it uncovered spread like spilled ink on a thirsty cloth—so thick and dark that only some serious work, and probably penalties, could erase the sort of graffiti a scandal like this would leave on the walls of the university. Someone needed to take the fall, shoulder the blame, and jeopardize their future—as an example for other kids who made such poor decisions, but mostly to show the world of academia that GWU was an outstanding university that did not tolerate such betrayal of standards.

The faculty knew the right questions to ask and the proper buttons to push to make students talk, especially those with law degrees and political futures on the line. Not to mention prominent parents hoping to avoid public embarrassment. Jack understood now why it took until March for this to break. As law school acceptance letters trickled in, they would be used to make the right kids talk. By the time tulips readied to bud and the grass began the nourishing process that would bring it back to green, a poisonous trail very opposite to spring's transformation ran its way to Brad and Jack's doorstep. The president of the university called and asked to see each of them at three o'clock that afternoon.

They had not spoken since Christmas, but their current predicament got them both quickly over the awkwardness.

"My father'll kill me when this comes out," Brad said.

He and Jack sat on the hood of Jack's beaten Volvo, which was parked at the bank of the Potomac. They watched a big tugboat hauling sand from Maine crawl past. It was still too cold for recreational boats, and the water was mostly an empty canvas glistening with the midmorning sun of early March.

Brad put his face in his palms. "We just screwed up our lives."

Jack heard the despair in his friend's voice, saw it in his eyes when Brad finally looked up with welled tears hanging on his eyelids. "Here's the deal," Jack said, staring straight ahead at the Potomac and the tugboat that moved over its surface. "I broke into Morton's office by myself. I took the exam alone and distributed it. Over seventy other kids saw the exam, you're just one of them. Nothing more. They're not going to kick seventy seniors out of school; they want one person to pin this on."

Brad slowly raised his hands. "What are you talking about?"

"I'm taking the fall for this."

"No, that's not happening."

Jack laughed. "It's gotta happen. It's either me or you. Trust me on this, Brad. The kids they talked to have pinned this on us with nail guns. The dean sat them down, laid out their acceptance letters or their financial firm offers, and then made an offer himself. What do you think they did? Stayed quiet? Please. They threw us under the bus to save their own asses. There's no reason for both of us to go down."

The tug let out a long, low whistle, and a mile downriver a drawbridge began to separate.

"Listen," Jack said. "This has nothing to do with Becca or what happened over break, okay? The truth is I've got nothing going on. I'm a poor kid from Wisconsin who really doesn't give a shit if Harvard retracts its offer. That was for my résumé, not because of any great love I have to be an attorney. There are dozens of other schools that would gladly take a Harvard reject, and I've got no psychotic father to answer to. I want to write speeches someday and a blemish on my transcript isn't going to prevent that. Running for senator, maybe. But not writing for one."

"Jack, I came to you with the key. I solicited you to come with me to get the test."

"And I'm a big boy. I said yes. I wanted the adrenaline rush of breaking in. And I'm taking the fall, Brad."

"You didn't even use the test. I mean, that's what Becca said. You didn't even use it and you want to take the heat for stealing it?"

"It wasn't about the test, Brad. It was about the adventure. And I stole the damn thing just as much as you did."

"I don't know, Jack."

But Jack did know. His friend would take the offer. Brad knew, too. The rest was just a game, a way of accepting through the backdoor—not really wanting such a thing but only taking it because it was offered so sternly.

"I don't know what to say," Brad said.

"Say yes when Penn asks you into their law program. Or Harvard, but I know Penn is your first choice." Jack jumped off the hood of his car. "And say yes again when ol' Jackie Boy comes begging for a job in a few years." Jack pulled open the driver's side door. "Come on. Let's get our stories straight before we see the dean." As they climbed in the car, Jack grabbed the steering wheel and looked over at Brad. "You know they say the crime is not what brings people down."

Brad smiled. "Yeah, it's the cover-up."

"What's that?" Jack asked, pointing at a torn envelope on the kitchen table and a letter next to it. They were in Becca's apartment.

"Cornell," Becca said.

"Yes? No?"

Becca nodded.

"What the hell?" Jack said in an excited voice. "Why didn't you tell me?"

She shrugged. "I don't know. I'm too worried. It came a couple days ago, but we have all this pressure on us with the

Morton thing and I haven't felt like celebrating. And now you're about to see the dean to confess to something that wasn't your idea. It's not a good idea, Jack."

"First, it's already been decided. Second, holy shit! You got into an Ivy League school!"

She took a deep breath. "Still think I'm staying at GW. I'm here, I'm familiar with the area, I'm comfortable. And to be honest, if I'm serious about joining my father's firm, there's no difference between GW Law and Cornell. Maybe some snooty client will only want an Ivy League grad working for them, but unlikely."

"Really? Well, it's good to have options."

"Plus, who knows, Jack? We don't know what's about to happen with all this. I cheated on a final exam and if that gets out . . . I guess I don't have to say it. Which is why I don't think you should do this, Jack. Yes, you stole it. But you didn't even use it. Why are you taking all the blame?"

"There's no other way for it to work, Becca. Brad's not taking the blame by himself, okay? That's just not how he operates. And if neither of us owns up to this, you know what happens? The blame starts to spread. Guess where the first stop will be after Brad and me?"

Becca looked away.

"Guess."

"Me," Becca said.

"Correct. You, and then Gail. Wanna know why? Because every kid who cheated knows Brad and I stole the test. Brad couldn't keep his mouth shut. And they know you and Gail had the first look. And if the university puts pressure on those kids, they'll tell the dean and the president and anyone else who asks exactly what they know. So it's either me or all of us."

"Why not Brad?"

Jack laughed. "Come on, Becca, that's not going to happen." Jack stood up. "Supposed to talk to the dean at three, so I've gotta go. Congrats on Cornell."

Becca stood up and wrapped her arms around his waist, placing her head on his shoulder. "Good luck."

He kissed her forehead. "Tell me when good things happen to you from now on, okay?"

Becca nodded her head as she silently cried on his chest.

Chapter 18

During the past week in Summit Lake, intrigued by the story she was chasing and captivated by the girl who was killed, Kelsey found an oasis from her own trouble. But back now, since walking through the Eckersleys' home, was a repeating loop of vague memories and foggy images of the morning she was attacked. Of the man she could not place, a masked face she could not identify. Kelsey spent many hours over the last month pulling those memories into sharper focus, arranging them in chronological order and working to piece together the events of that day. It was as if her mind wore an electric collar, though, and could go only so far without hurting itself. Kelsey could get to a particular point in her memory and then go no further. Part of it, she knew, was that she didn't *want* to go further. Didn't want to see the details of that morning, or to relive the horror. Some part of her believed she could bury those memories and let them decompose. Another part knew it couldn't be so easy.

Placed on the other side of the crime—victim instead of investigator—she hated the process and the procedure and the fact-gathering. She despised the detectives' questions and connotations about what she wore that morning and whom she was seeing outside of work and how she conducted herself at the office. Never coming straight out and announcing their suspicions, Kelsey knew damn well the detectives were asking if she was a promiscuous woman who flirted with colleagues and wore inappropriate clothing. They didn't have the courage to ask her if she might have brought the whole situation on herself, but after a couple days of questioning Kelsey knew what they were suggesting. She was relieved when they left her alone and went out to futilely look for the man with no face and no name and no chance of being caught.

Then, Kelsey turned off her phone and locked her front door and didn't leave for a month. In the weeks off from work and while disconnected from the world, Kelsey succumbed one afternoon to researching what she'd been through. Poring through reference material and making sense out of volumes of information was how she figured things out in her career, and so she tried the same thing in her personal life. She bought a bag of self-help books from the bookstore that dealt with the healing process women go through after assault. She read them all in a three-day span made of little sleep, loads of coffee, and leftover Chinese.

After her reading binge, she took comfort knowing that all the emotions swirling through her mind and her body were not unique. Others shared her pain. The books suggested she would feel loneliness and isolation—and she did. Some of it was because Penn Courtney had not allowed her into the office for a month, but it was also from refusing to walk out her door for fear of what waited. Anger and resentment toward men, too, she read, would be part of the process. And though there was no bitterness in her heart or mind, Peter Ambrose was the first man she'd been around and her bizarre dream the other night of Peter running down the dock in front of the Eckersleys' house made Kelsey question herself about trusting a man. She allowed herself this emotion.

Nighttime would be especially difficult, the books told her. Her nightmares proved this. But she took pride in the fact that when she wasn't sleeping, the dark hours of night were her favorite time. It was when she watched old movies and finished the novels she was reading. It was a time when she knew the rest of the world was asleep and only then was she comfortable relaxing, knowing she wasn't missing anything.

She would be scared, the books told her, and it might take months or longer to walk down the sidewalk or to her car, or to jog the streets. Sometimes, these things would never again be possible. And this much was true—she *was* scared, there was no denying this. But running was her *thing*. Her passion. A private time when she reviewed cases and articles in her mind. When she was stuck on an article, the isolation of running allowed Kelsey to sort her thoughts. And if she ever felt overwhelmed or too close to a story, the miles were spent simply getting away from all those thoughts that ran through her head. Erase it all for an hour or two and come back refreshed. In the weeks just after the rape, though, the thought of running anywhere—let alone through the woods where the attack happened—was too much. But here in Summit Lake, Kelsey made a decision. She refused to allow her fear to take away what she loved so much. She forced herself to walk the town and jog through the canopied forest to the waterfall. The horror of that morning still coursed through her, but each mile took her a little farther from it.

Most of all, the books told her, she would feel a sense of loss. Almost, although not quite, the experts wrote, like someone had died. And this was essential to the rebirth she would need to experience to fully heal. Perhaps this was the sensation that overwhelmed her in the stilt house the other morning.

What she took from the self-help books was that everyone heals in their own way and at their own pace. Some reflect more than others on the things they encounter in life, and weigh those happenings differently. Kelsey finally decided *she* would pick which events shaped her life and defined her personality. This single, awful day would not be one of them. Simple as that.

She wasn't able to throw the books away, so she tossed them into the return bin at the local library and headed back to work the next day. A week later, she was in Summit Lake, on the trail of young Becca Eckersley, who had gone through the same thing as Kelsey but who was not so fortunate to wake up in a hospital bed the next day. Always a believer in fate, and a student of the persistent voice in her head that guided her and helped her find her way, Kelsey knew she was in Summit Lake for a reason greater than herself. For something more than the three-piece article she was sent to write.

Night fell and by 8:00 p.m. the sky was alive with stars. Kelsey pulled the collar of her jacket against the lake breeze. She stood in front of the Winchester Hotel and watched a black SUV roll up. The passenger side window came down and Peter Ambrose was behind the wheel.

She walked over and rested her elbows on the window frame. "You sure about this?" she asked.

"It's your story, so it's up to you. But I'm a willing participant."

"Will you get in trouble?"

"If we get caught, we'll both get in trouble."

Kelsey looked down Maple Street at nothing in particular, then pulled open the door and climbed in. They were on a winding mountain road out of Summit Lake a few minutes later.

"So tell me again where you got this information," Kelsey said as they drove.

"I put in a call to a pathologist friend of mine who works for the county. He knows about the Eckersley case—no specifics, only that it's all very hush-hush. He and the other pathologists and technicians were told to stay out of the way of this investigation while the state authorities take over. Only the Buchanan County medical examiner has any privileges."

"That's who wrote the partial autopsy report you got for me a few days ago?"

"Correct. My friend tells me there's something else going on with this case, rumors are wild and speculation is high."

"What are the rumors?"

"Something's being covered up. The ME is ready to resign over the secrecy and it's causing major trouble down at the county building. It's got everyone talking, and so when I put a call in to my buddy he was very happy to know someone was looking into this story."

"And how is he going to help us?"

"He's not—just in case anyone asks you. But I ended up with an access card to the county building and a password for the Eckersley file. I'm hoping if we have a look, we'll find the full autopsy report. See what the fuss is about."

They took the winding roads out of the mountains for half an hour until they entered the town of Eastgate, where the Buchanan County Government Center was located. It was close to 9:00 p.m. when they pulled into the parking lot of a pizza joint. They found a booth by the window and ordered beers and a pepperoni pizza.

Kelsey took a sip of her draft. "Why are you doing this for me? You could get in a lot of trouble."

"You've got me interested in this case. If something's being covered up, I want to help you find it. Plus," Peter said as he took a sip of beer, "if you can't tell, I like you. You seem like a good person with the right intentions."

"Thanks. I just hope this doesn't cause you any problems."

Peter smiled. "We're not stealing classified government documents, we're looking at an autopsy report that should be public record anyways. Tell me what you've found since we talked last."

"Where do I start? How about that Becca got married just before she was killed."

"To whom?"

"I'm working on that."

"You don't know?"

"Not yet."

"Aren't there records?"

"Not that I can find. It doesn't make sense, but I'm sure about my source, so I have to figure that one out."

The waitress came over with a deep-dish pizza and placed a slice in front of each of them.

"My working theory is that Becca eloped and was killed before a marriage certificate was filed, therefore leaving no record."

"No record, but a suspect."

"Exactly, if I can figure out who she married." Kelsey took a bite of pizza. "Also, Becca kept a journal. One she wrote in—or at least read from—the day she was killed."

"Like a diary?"

"Yeah."

"Doesn't it mention the name of the guy she married?"

"Probably does, but no one seems to know where it is." Kelsey put her pizza down. "Becca had her journal two hours before she was killed, when she was studying at the coffeehouse in town. But there's no record of a journal listed on the evidence report, and when I had the opportunity to poke around the Eckersleys' house, I saw no sign of it."

"So where is it?"

Kelsey shrugged. "Someone has it. Either the state authorities found it and kept it off the evidence list, or . . ."

"Or what?"

"Or whoever killed her took the journal because he knew how damning it would be."

"If the police found this journal, why would they hide it?"

"Don't know. Maybe for the same reason we're about to snoop around the county building looking for an autopsy report they won't publish."

"What's your boss say about all this?"

"He's interested, just not excited about my approach."

"I thought you said this is exactly what your magazine publishes. Shouldn't he be salivating over a homicide with potential cover-ups?"

"Oh, he is. Trust me. He's just mad about the timing. He sent me here to get me out of the way for a while. Tie me up with a fluff piece for a couple of weeks. At least, I thought he did. He's mixed on the fact that I've actually stumbled onto something."

"Yeah?" Peter said. "Why does your editor want his star reporter out of the way?"

Kelsey took a sip of beer and unknowingly crossed her arms, shaking her head. "That's a story for another time."

"I'd like to hear it sometime, because I did some investigating on my own and understand you're a pretty big deal. You've got a best-selling true crime book, and you've got quite a following for your *Events* pieces. So why would your boss waste your talents on a fluff piece?"

"It's a long story. Let's just say he wanted me out of the office for a while."

"You get along with him?"

"Yeah," Kelsey said. "I love him."

Peter took a bite of pizza and raised an eyebrow.

"Not like that," Kelsey said. "He's seventy years old. I love him like a father. Hate him the same way sometimes."

Kelsey was still sitting with her arms crossed. Peter pointed at her half-eaten pizza slice. "You don't like it?"

"Too nervous."

Peter looked out the window at the Government Center across the street. The building was mostly dark besides a few stray lights on the third floor. He dropped his pizza on the plate and wiped his mouth. "Ready, then?"

Kelsey nodded. "As ready as I'll be tonight."

"Let's go."

Peter paid the bill and together they walked across the street, leaving the car in the restaurant parking lot. The Government Center campus was lighted by yellow halogen as they walked along the sidewalk to the front of the building. He pulled the card key from his pocket and inserted it into the slot. The red light changed to green and Peter swung the door open. Kelsey took a deep breath and followed him inside.

They walked past the elevators and entered the stairwell. The three flights caused Kelsey's pulse to elevate more than it already was. Peter pulled the stairwell door open, the handle making a loud clinking noise. Everything, from their footsteps to the door handle, was intensified when set against the stillness of the empty building.

"Okay," Peter said. "He told me 3C."

They walked down the hallway. A glass wall stood to their left, through which they could see the dark workspace of a government office. A large reception area with chairs behind a chest-high counter. Beyond that, cubicles with a few computer monitors still glowing. When they came to suite 3C, Peter again inserted the access card and listened for the lock to disengage. Kelsey looked down the hallway one last time before entering. 3C was a private office with a single desk and computer. Peter sat behind it and Kelsey crouched down next to him. He touched the mouse and the computer came to life. He entered the password his friend had supplied to access the system, then entered: ECKERSLEY, BECCA.

A low tone sounded and then a message: INVALID ENTRY.

Peter looked at Kelsey.

"Here," Kelsey said. "Try this."

She pulled the keyboard toward her and typed: ECKERSLEY, REBECCA ALICE.

A higher, more pleasant ring sounded. Then a box appeared, asking for a password. Peter typed it from memory and a second later Becca's full autopsy and toxicology report blinked onto the screen.

"Don't print it," Kelsey said. "That will definitely leave a footprint. Probably entering the file has lit up a red light somewhere. You read, I'll take notes. Go."

Kelsey pulled out her notepad. Peter read from the screen.

"Official cause of death: suffocation. The trachea and larynx were collapsed by trauma, and this prevented oxygen from getting to the lungs. Said trauma determined to be caused by manual pressure to the neck. Most likely from someone's hands. No lacerations to the neck, or other indications of tightening objects such as belts, ropes, or ligature."

Peter waited a second while Kelsey scribbled.

"Go."

Peter read through some incidentals they had previously covered in the partial autopsy report while Kelsey took shorthand.

"Okay," Peter said. "It speaks here more extensively about the vaginal damage that confirms rape." Peter scrolled down the screen. "Here. Page four. We haven't seen this. Evidence sequestered from the body and turned over to police: semen, hair (head, facial, and pubic), fibers (wool—coat or gloves), skin shaving from seven fingernails."

Peter scrolled further. "DNA sequestered from all samples match each other, indicating one attacker. See toxicology. Hold on." Peter clicked on another screen and the toxicology report popped up. "Okay, it looks like they took DNA samples from Becca's father and brother and three cousins. No match on them." He mumbled a minute as he read quickly and flipped between screens. "Okay. It looks like a construction crew who had worked in the house was also sampled—five men, no matches."

"So no DNA matches at all?"

"Not on the toxo report."

"No other DNA taken—like a husband?"

"Not listed on this report, no."

From down the hallway, the elevator chimed and they both froze. They left the door to suite 3C cracked, and Kelsey grabbed Peter's arm when she heard the elevator doors slide open. Quickly, Peter stood and went to the office door. He twisted the handle and silently pulled the door fully closed. He stood still and placed his ear to the wood. Kelsey was next to him with her ear, too, against the door. Their faces were inches apart and their breathing heavy. They tried to control their lungs and listen. They finally heard a muffled conversation and then whistling, which after a minute faded away.

Peter placed his finger across his lips: "Shh."

He grabbed the handle and pushed the door open, sticking his head into the hallway. Kelsey did the same, just below him. They saw a janitorial cart down the hall, with mop handles sticking up and rags hanging from the side. They both retreated into the room.

"Hurry," Kelsey said.

Peter rushed back to the computer and scrolled through the rest of the autopsy. "There's more internal findings. Greater detail about the subdural hematoma." He spit out some facts about brain swelling and blood patterns. Stomach contents that helped narrow the time of the attack. Semen location in the upper vaginal canal indicated Becca never stood up after the attack. He clicked screens back to the toxicology report. He quickly read through some final notes, then stopped.

"Huh."

"What?" Kelsey asked, looking up from her notepad.

"Here's the toxicology report and blood work they did on Becca."

"What is it? Don't tell me she was doped up."

"No, not a trace of drugs in her system. Just human chorionic gonadotropin."

"What's that?"

"hCG."

Kelsey blinked her eyes. "The pregnancy hormone?"

Chapter 19

Becca Eckersley
George Washington University
April 7, 2011
Ten months before her death

Everyone in Milford Morton's class was required to retake the exam. The decision brought protests from the innocent students, and a few belligerent ones were allowed to skate quietly away. The faculty knew the ones who argued most and whose parents became involved were probably innocent, while the ones who protested least and kept their parents in the dark were guilty as sin.

For Jack, he was given a failing grade and not allowed to retake the exam. This, too, was a strategic decision by the faculty, since close scrutiny of his transcripts revealed Jack had taken more hours than required during his freshman and sophomore years, and a failing grade in Milford Morton's Business Law class would still leave him with the necessary requirements for graduation. The failing grade would dirty his transcripts and slash his grade point average, however, which might affect his life after graduation. Most importantly, it would demonstrate a visible punishment while allowing the university to graduate the status quo of low-income students and avoid unwanted attention from groups who would pounce and attack in a very public way if a poor kid from Wisconsin had been booted from the university months before graduation, when everyone knew most of the students cheated on the exam.

Jack wasn't sure exactly what the ordeal would do to his acceptance letter from Harvard, and for the first day or two after his verdict came he decided not to look into the matter. He came home from the library in the early evening, three weeks since his meeting with the dean, to find Brad at the kitchen table, a torn envelope in front of him along with a letter folded in thirds. Jack slowed as he entered the apartment. He knew from the look on Brad's face what it all meant, but had to ask.

"Well?"

Brad faked a smile. "Rejected!" Brad said in a strange voice meant to hide his sorrow, but which did just the opposite. "Just like everything else in my life," he mumbled to himself.

"Shit. Penn?"

Brad nodded.

"Screw Penn," Jack said. "You've got others out there."

Brad stood up with pursed lips. "No, Jackie Boy. That's the last of 'em. All the Ivies passed." His eyes widened in feigned excitement. "Oh, but I got into U of M. Can't wait for the 'Thatta Boy' from my old man on that one. He'll be real proud of his state-educated boy. I'll be a real hit at all his friggin' Who's Who parties, with all his friggin' judge friends."

Jack's voice was quiet. "Everyone passed?"

"It's a proud day in the Reynolds family."

"Why didn't you tell me?"

"You've been a little out of touch, Jack. You and Becca."

Jack didn't touch that comment. Or mention that swallowing the bullet for their little adventure had most likely cost Jack his own ride to Harvard. Instead he said, "So take a year off, find an internship." Jack's words hung in the air, untouched and unnoticed. "I thought U of M had a good program, that's why you applied."

"It was my backup, and I only applied because my counselor forced me into it." Brad slid his arm through the loop of his backpack. Then he looked at Jack. "It's actually a shitty school that would give my father a goddamned heart attack if I attended."

Jack watched him walk slowly out the door, not closing it as he left. He heard Brad's footsteps mechanically descend the stairs. Jack took out his phone and dialed Becca's number.

"Hey, major issues over here."

"What's wrong?" Becca asked.

"Apparently Brad got rejected from every law school he applied to, except Maryland. Never told anyone, unless you or Gail know."

"He hasn't talked to me in two months, and I'm sure Gail doesn't know anything about it." There was a pause. "Everywhere?"

"All the Ivies."

"And we were all just out celebrating our acceptances."

"He didn't seem too concerned that my acceptance will probably be rescinded. But either way, somebody's gotta talk to him, he's a mess."

"I'm coming over."

"He took off."

"Where?"

"No idea. Just threw on his backpack and left."

"I'll call his cell," Becca said. "And if he won't talk to me, I'll get Gail to call him."

"Let me know."

* * *

Gail and Becca sat on one side of the booth, Jack on the other. Burgers and sodas covered the table. It was a strategy meeting on how to help their friend, who they were sure felt like the world was falling on top of him.

"I say we just go to your place and wait for him," Gail said. "He has to come home eventually. Midnight, two in the morning, doesn't matter. We'll all just stay up and wait for him."

"He won't like the ambush," Jack said. "Has he been talking to you lately?" Jack asked Gail.

"Yeah."

"Doesn't screen your calls like he does to Becca and me?"

Gail smiled. "He's not pissed at me, and until today every time I've called him he's answered. He's been a little distant lately, and I guess I figured it had to do with . . . you know, you guys. But now I know it's because he's been shouldering this burden without telling anyone." Gail stirred her Coke. "I thought he had a contact at Penn, through his father or someone."

"I remember him saying something like that," Jack said. "Guess it didn't come through."

"Try him again," Becca said.

"I've texted him three times in the last hour. He knows I'm looking for him."

"Okay," Becca said. "So we wait at the apartment. Then what?"

"Then we get all this shit out on the table," Gail said. "This is so stupid. We were all best friends a few months ago, now no one talks to each other."

"That's not all our fault," Becca said.

"No," Jack agreed. "But some of it is. And Gail's right, we've got to get this stuff out there and talk about it. Then we've got to support Brad, who feels like his life just ended.

And most of that comes from his friggin' father, who puts more pressure on the kid than anyone. And it's so crazy that Brad hates the man one second and then can't stand the thought of disappointing him the next." Jack shook his head. "Whatever. Let's go wait for him."

They paid the bill and left the restaurant. It was a cool April night as they walked back to Jack's apartment, with winds blowing off the Potomac and carrying the scent of salmon and crabs. Jack's phone vibrated in his pocket from an incoming text message. They were at the base of the stairs to his apartment complex.

The girls started up the stairs as Jack fished the phone from his pocket. The text was from Brad.

You took her from me, Jack.
But I guess she was never really mine.

"Is it Brad?" Becca asked from the top of the stairs.

Jack hesitated for a second, then shook his head. "No, mass text from a professor about a paper due next week."

The girls stood at the top of the stairs as Jack read the message again. After a minute, the girls were restless.

"Hey, Jackie Boy," Gail said from the landing in front of his apartment. "Let's go, it's chilly out here."

Jack looked at the text one last time, studying it before sticking his phone in his pocket. He wanted to shoot a text back to his friend. Something to acknowledge Brad's pain, or his own presumed betrayal. He slowly climbed the stairs, thinking of how to respond. He stuck the key into the lock and pushed open the door. As he did, a fragmented series of images came to him, played in his head like a movie clip, black-and-white with static particles. The look in Brad's eyes earlier in the day as he left the apartment. Brad's rejection letter sitting on the table. His words . . . *Rejected! Just like everything else in my life.* Before the door was fully open, Jack knew what waited on the other side. A message back to his friend would not be possible.

Becca screamed. Jack stood like a statue in the doorway. He never looked at Brad's face, or if he had his brain blocked the blood-red, bloated image from his memory. But stained forever in Jack's mind was his friend's feet, limp and slowly twirling twelve inches off the ground, an overturned chair lying still on the floor.

PART III

HELLO, DETECTIVE

Chapter 20

Kelsey Castle
Summit Lake
March 12, 2012
Day 8

A cottony framework of snow-white clouds ripped and pulled their way across the sky, stretching over the lake and toward the horizon like a ceiling to the world. In the distance an opening formed, as though solvent spilled from heaven had burned a hole in the clouds, and through it shined vibrant yellow rays of morning sunlight that landed on the waterfall and ricocheted off the granite. The water glowed orange as it fell. Kelsey stared at the mysterious scene. The morning falls.

She woke early with Becca's pregnancy causing her imagination to run wild with possibilities. So many questions formed in her head that sleep was again elusive. Now she stood at the bottom of the falls with a good burn in her legs and all the questions about Becca Eckersley organized in her mind. Her gaze traveled to the origin of the falls, where two boulders stood on top of the cliff and flanked the water as it passed between them. The force of the water had probably eroded the rock face over time, Kelsey figured, until eventually the stream swelled and a small trickle sweated between the stones. Years later, the relentless pressure forced a gap in the rocks until finally the weakest portion fell away and allowed the stream to pour from the edge of the cliff. Over time, the endless flow rubbed smooth the rocks to create a shuttle through which the water passed freely before falling down the mountain. The evolution of such a magnificent setting was amazing. Kelsey stared at the falls and knew no matter how complex, all mysteries could be traced back to their genesis.

She was getting closer to the mystery here in Summit Lake, but stepping back the unknowns to reveal the truth about Becca Eckersley's death required Kelsey to span large gaps she couldn't fill on her own. Becca's parents were working to keep details of the case quiet, and now Kelsey confirmed that Becca, too, was keeping secrets. That she was married was one of them. That she was pregnant was another, and certainly enough to explain why Becca wanted her parents in the dark about her marriage.

After a few minutes, the orange glow ended. The water foamed and frothed in the area under the falls, then sat quiet and still a short distance away as the lagoon reflected the cotton-ball clouds. Mist coated the moss that clung to the side of the mountain.

"I see you've become a fan."

Kelsey turned and saw Rae standing behind her. Her face was red from her jog through the canopied forest.

Kelsey smiled. "Really beautiful here."

Almost before she could finish her sentence, Rae hugged her. Kelsey stood still for a few seconds and then slowly wrapped her arms around Rae. "You okay?"

Rae held her for a long time before she squeezed one last

time and let go. "I'm fine," Rae said. "But I should have given you that the other morning. It's what friends do when they tell each other personal, private stuff that's hard to talk about. They hug each other and support each other, and I wish I'd done it the other morning, but you caught me off guard when you told me about . . . what happened to you."

Kelsey swallowed hard, surprised to be so moved by the gesture. Perhaps it was because Rae was the first person—besides a brief and uncomfortable conversation with Penn Courtney—to acknowledge her situation and comfort her.

"Thank you," Kelsey said. Her eyes were watery and she blinked to contain the tears. "You're a good person, Rae. And a good friend. I'm really glad I met you."

Rae smiled. "Feeling's mutual. Come on, let's dunk our feet."

Kelsey followed Rae to the lagoon and they both sat at the water's edge, on top of large boulders embedded in the ground around the lagoon. They unlaced their running shoes and plunged their feet into the water.

"Why is the water so warm?" Kelsey asked.

"Natural springs. It bubbles up from deep underground where it's warmed. Without the waterfall, the lagoon would be too hot. The water from up top is ice-cold, mixes with the hot stuff, and this is the result. People swim here year-round, even when it's snowing and the surface is steaming." Rae leaned back to look up at the falls, stared for several seconds before she continued. "I walk down here sometimes after the morning rush. Kind of catch my breath and clear my head. Over time I've learned this is a great place to sort out my feelings. If I could look down on myself sometimes, I think my face might look like yours does now."

"How do I look?" Kelsey asked.

"Preoccupied," Rae said. "Those big brown eyes of yours

have a lot going on inside of them. I'm still convinced you're having boy issues."

Kelsey shook her head. "Sorry to disappoint. And once you hit a certain age, we stop calling them 'boys.'"

"What should I say? Adult male issues?"

Kelsey smiled. "I don't know. 'Guy' issues?"

"Fine," Rae said. "Your face looks like you're having *guy* issues. Dish."

"Dish what?" Kelsey said with a laugh. "There's nothing to dish."

"This doctor, have you seen him lately?"

"Yes," Kelsey said. "Last night, in fact."

"I knew it!"

"Knew what?" Kelsey continued to laugh. "He's helping me with the Eckersley article. He's got sources in town."

Rae stared at her with raised eyebrows and a suppressed smile.

"What's that look for?"

"I can tell you think I'm just some twenty-year-old kid who calls men 'boys' and wakes up before dawn to bake doughnuts. But I'm very intuitive."

"I don't doubt that."

"So what's going on with you two?"

Kelsey opened her eyes wide. "There's nothing going on between us. We're breaking into county buildings and looking at autopsy reports, not dating." Kelsey pointed at Rae. "And that's a secret, by the way. About breaking in. Not to be repeated to anyone."

"But do you like him?"

"Do I what?"

"I knew it!"

Kelsey shook her head. "Knew what?"

"Never answer a yes-or-no question with a question. It's a dead giveaway."

There was a pause before Kelsey said, "He called me and offered his help on something I was stuck on. Last night we went down to Eastgate and snuck into the Buchanan County Government Center to find Becca's autopsy report." Kelsey paused a minute. "I was moved that he was so willing to help me. That's it."

"Have you thought about him this morning?"

Kelsey shrugged. "Yeah."

Rae opened her arms wide. "And there it is. You're having *guy* issues. Why else would you be thinking about him? And that's not a bad thing. It's fun."

Kelsey squinted her eyes at the young girl's ability to drag her along to a point where she had no choice but to agree.

"But dish again," Rae said. "You find anything? With the autopsy?"

"Lots."

"Like what?"

Kelsey looked up at the falling water, then back to Rae. "We're friends?"

"Of course."

"You'd keep a secret if I asked you, right?"

"To my grave."

"Then I'm asking."

Rae nodded.

Kelsey stirred the water with her feet, then looked back to Rae. "Becca was pregnant when she died."

"Get out!"

Kelsey nodded. "Loaded up with hCG, a hormone produced during pregnancy. And when I talked to Millie Mays the other day, she told me Becca confessed to Livvy that she ran off and married some guy she was dating. So we've got a marriage no one knew about, a secret pregnancy, and a dead girl."

Rae slowly raised her chin. "And you think the guy she married killed her."

"He's leading the race of suspects, yes."

"Who is he?"

"No clue. So that puts me at a big fork in the road. I need to talk to people who knew Becca. Since her family is not about to tell me anything and I can't get to her sequestered Facebook postings or e-mails, I either have to go to DC and start asking around, find some of her friends who are willing to talk . . ."

"Or?"

"I find Becca's journal." Kelsey paused a moment. "You make any progress on that, by chance?"

"Maybe," Rae said. "I talked to Millie. She's old and sounds like she's losing it sometimes, but she knows more than she's letting on about the night Becca was killed. I told Millie the gossip group is in a frenzy about Becca keeping a journal. That's all they talk about. I asked Millie if she knew anything about it. If Livvy said anything about a journal."

"And?"

"She just shrugged, which means she knows all about it. I told her the police never found a journal at the stilt house, and you know what she said?"

Kelsey raised her eyebrows.

"*How could they have?* That's what she said to me. 'How could they have?' Said it right to my face and then got up and made sweet tea."

Kelsey shifted on the rock. "What's that mean?"

"Not sure, but it sounds like the old lady knows where that journal is."

"Yeah? How do we get our hands on it?"

Rae smiled. "I'm working on it."

They both pulled their feet from the water and slipped their socks on.

"Want a coffee?" Rae asked.

"I'm sweaty and gross," Kelsey said.

"Iced coffee, then."

"Done."

They jogged back through the canopied forest and cooled down as they walked along Maple Street to the coffeehouse. Inside, Kelsey took a spot at the bar while Rae prepared the drinks. Next to Kelsey, the gossip group was at it. The red-head was arguing with the heavyset lady when Kelsey sat down. But their conversation was interrupted by the forty-year-old guy, who held up a finger to quiet the group. Then he pointed at Kelsey.

"Aren't you Kelsey Castle?"

The whole group, six of them this morning, turned and stared with quizzical looks and wide eyes as though a movie star had just graced their presence.

Before Kelsey could answer, the guy said, "You're here because of Becca, right?" He looked around at his cohorts. "I told you she was here. This is crazy! Our little town has the attention of *Events* magazine?"

"All right," Rae said, setting the iced coffee in front of Kelsey and standing behind the mahogany bar. "Don't accost my other customers."

"Rae," the forty-year-old said, "you knew Kelsey Castle was in town and didn't tell us?"

"For a group of detectives like yourselves, you're not too observant. Kelsey's been here for a week, and has come in here almost every morning."

"Do you know who did it?" the heavyset woman asked, like a child begging for dessert.

Kelsey smiled. "I know probably as much as you all do."

"Why won't the police give any details?" the redhead asked with her eyes closed.

"Not sure about that, since they won't tell me anything either."

"When will your article run?" the forty-year-old asked.

"Not sure on that either. I don't have anything to write about yet."

"But you're not buying the random stranger argument?" he asked.

Kelsey shrugged. "About as much as you are."

The forty-year-old smiled and looked at his crowd, nodding. "I told you it was too random." He looked back at Kelsey. "So it was—I mean, you think it was someone Becca knew, right? Maybe someone she was close to?"

Kelsey smiled again. "I don't know what I think yet, I haven't gotten very far."

"Here's what we think," he said, then looked at the heavyset woman at the end of the bar. "At least what most of us think. Becca got mixed up with someone, like a lawyer at her father's firm or some other quasi high-profile attorney. Maybe to help her later in her career, maybe just because they fell in love. The affair turned into something, you know . . . illicit, secretive, scandalous. Whatever. Eventually either she wanted out or he wanted out. The other didn't." The forty-year-old slapped his hands together. "Boom. There's your motive!"

Kelsey puckered her lower lip. "Interesting theory. You guys have been busy working on this, huh?"

"Every morning," Red said. "They never stop."

"I mean, c'mon," the forty-year-old said. "Becca was young, gorgeous, and smart. This has to be a crime of passion, no?"

"Maybe," Kelsey said. "Go get me some suspects to interview, or something important to run with, and I'll put you in my article."

"Really?" the heavyset woman said, eyes wide and urgent.

"Did you tell her about the journal?" the forty-year-old asked Rae. He groomed his goatee with his hand, smiling like he held an unknown secret.

"I haven't told Kelsey *any* of your theories. She's pretty good at what she does without the gossip group's input."

"It's not a theory," he said to Kelsey. "I've heard it from more than one person. Becca kept a journal, and I bet the cops have it right now. That's probably why they're being so quiet about the case. Just ticking off each person in the journal until they hit pay dirt, but they don't want anyone knowing their play. Don't want to spook any of the suspects."

"Okay," Rae said. "Keep working on that one. I think you're almost there. We're drinking our coffee by the fire."

"Nice to meet you all," Kelsey said.

"If you need any statements or anything," the heavyset woman said, "just ask. You can quote any of us."

"Will do," Kelsey said before retreating with Rae to the thick-stuffed leather chairs by the fire.

"Sorry about that," Rae said. "I've heard it every morning for the last couple of weeks. The theories get more and more bizarre, and completely change based on what's printed in the paper each morning."

"I love it," Kelsey said. "A group of conspiracy theorists."

Rae smiled. "That's Summit Lake for you. Before they had Becca to gossip about it was something about the water being contaminated and every government official knowing about it but not wanting to spend money to fix it. Cancer and cover-ups and lawsuits. Always something."

"Morning gossip in coffeehouses around the world,

right?" Kelsey took a sip. She lowered her voice. "So dish yourself. They're actually on to something with the journal."

"I'm shocked. They've discovered something useful."

"And if a bunch of gossips are close, the cops are closer. We need a plan to find Becca's journal before anyone else does."

Rae smiled. "I told you. I'm working on it."

Chapter 21

Becca Eckersley
George Washington University
May 13, 2011
Nine months before her death

The campus began to fill on Thursday. By Friday afternoon traffic was tight as parents converged on campus and filled the walkways of George Washington University to see their sons and daughters graduate. There were rumors of Secret Service agents on campus as the vice president was due to deliver Saturday's commencement speech. It was an exciting time for the graduating students, who had mostly forgotten about their classmate who hanged himself the month before. To most he was just a statistic, but to Becca and Jack it was a much more tangible commodity. It was something they were both part of—an event they each felt they played a distinct role in producing. And because they were so close to it, ignoring it or letting it drift into the past was an impossible task.

Brad Reynolds hanged himself on April 7, five weeks before the ceremonial commencement day at GWU, and no one's life had been the same since. He sent Jack the text message just before he kicked the chair out from underneath himself, and he hung for sixty-three seconds before the kitchen door opened and Becca witnessed her friend dangling from the kitchen rafters.

The weeks leading to graduation were a quiet and isolated time for Becca and Jack, who spent most of their time together. They had trouble staying at Jack's apartment. Every time they opened the door they saw Brad's feet twirling and twitching over the kitchen floor. Sleeping there was simply not possible.

In the middle of April, Jack received a phone call from the admissions office at Harvard Law. A formal letter followed four days later, and Jack placed it ceremoniously next to his acceptance letter from months earlier. Becca placed her head on his shoulder and dabbed tears from her eyes as she hugged him. He wouldn't show any emotion. That was the way he handled things, Becca knew. And though Jack acted numb to the news, and detached from the reality that he would not be attending Harvard Law, or any other law program that fall, Becca knew eventually it would hit him.

"Well," Jack said to Becca. "Some kid on the waiting list just got the best news of his life."

Becca listened to Jack's philosophy about how life worked— one person's misfortune was another's dream come true, whether it was getting into law school or getting the girl of your dreams. She listened but didn't buy his bravado. She knew, despite all the talk about not wanting to practice law, he was hurt badly by the news, which was why she agreed without hesitation to go with him.

Becca finished packing Friday night. The graduation ceremony would be the next morning. Her parents had been up the weekend before to haul her possessions back to Greensboro for the summer. It was just before 10:00 p.m. when she entered Jack's apartment.

"Sure you want to skip it?" Jack asked.

Becca nodded. "I don't need the whispers and stares when they call our names."

"I don't think anyone will whisper and stare, but I don't want to find out anyway. Are your parents okay with it?"

Becca nodded. "They weren't thrilled, but they came last week to get my stuff so they're going along with it. They know this whole thing has been tough and we're just trying to figure out how to handle it."

"Didn't you think this year would be different?"

"That's a rhetorical question, right?"

"I guess," Jack said. He was sitting on the bed of his empty room. "When I trace it back, things were going really well until we stole that damn test, and nothing's really been the same since. I mean, follow Brad's life since we stole that test."

"Jack, we didn't do any of that to Brad, okay? Brad did it to himself. It sounds cold and terrible, and I miss him like I'd miss my brother. But you and I are not responsible for what happened to him. To protect us all, you took the blame for something *he* did, so that should absolve you of your guilt. Harvard was taken away from you, which I think is a lot worse than not getting in. And I know it was your thing, so I never got involved, but I think it was pretty shitty that Brad let you take the blame for the test."

Jack pulled his cell phone from his pocket and paged through his texts. "He sent this to me right before." Jack handed her his phone.

You took her from me, Jack.
But I guess she was never really mine.

Becca stared for a minute at the phone, her lips silently reading and rereading the message. "God, Jack." She sat on his bed. "Why didn't you tell me about this?"

"What's to tell? You knew he was pissed we were sneaking

around behind his back. This only adds a small element that he thinks I somehow stole you from him."

"It's almost . . . creepy. I'm starting to think of Brad in a different way." She shook her head. "I don't know. I just want to find a way to move on."

"I hear you," Jack said. He stood from the bed and grabbed his duffle bag. "Ready?"

"Let's go," she said.

Jack dragged the two duffle bags that represented everything he owned in the world down the stairs and crammed them into the trunk. He threw Becca's bag into the backseat and made one last pass through the apartment, taking the TV in his arms and leaving everything else that didn't stand a chance at fitting into his Volvo.

Last month, Brad's parents had been through the apartment to collect their son's belongings, leaving nothing but memories and an empty bedroom. Jack and Becca paused before backing out the doorway, TV cradled in his arms, and tears welled in Becca's eyes. They each looked up at the I-beam that ran the length of the kitchen. The last five weeks brought many scenarios into their minds of how things could have gone differently. Jack could have skipped his flight the day Brad confessed his love for Becca, stayed with his friend when Brad needed him most. Becca could have told Brad everything during one of their late-night talks and defused the bomb ticking in his mind. They could have told the truth from the beginning, when Gail and Brad returned for senior year. Jack could have taken that key from Brad and told him how stupid it was to steal a test, and together they could have weighed more seriously the consequences of getting caught. Maybe those things would have prevented the year from unfolding the way it had. Maybe nothing would have changed.

Becca and Jack finally walked down the steps, leaving the apartment door wide open. Jack tossed the television into the backseat and they each climbed in and waited for the old Volvo to turn over. The engine finally caught and they pulled slowly from the parking lot. Two hours later, Washington, DC, was an absent thing in the rearview mirror, and only dark highway was in front of them, like their lives, illuminated by the Volvo's headlights for only a short stretch, black and unknowing beyond the immediate. They drove without fatigue through the night, with very little conversation, until the sun filled the mirrors the next morning and stretched the Volvo into a long shadow that glided over the highway in front of them. About the time their names were being called back at graduation, they crossed the Mississippi River.

Two days after they left Washington, DC, Becca and Jack ended up in Wyoming. They purchased a tent and a campsite at the Yellowstone conservatory and found their lot in the Bay Bridge Campground where they pitched their tent and slept for twelve straight hours. They spent two days wandering small hiking trails under the high blue sky. That first night at their campsite Becca and Jack sat and stared into the orange flames of the fire, thinking of Brad and the way everything ended.

They talked until the sun set and darkness fell over the valley. They climbed into their tent and snuggled next to each other in the sleeping bag. Besides the things they couldn't control and were powerless to change, Becca and Jack decided the worst they had done was fall in love and keep it to themselves. They could live with that.

Becca would start her first year at George Washington Law in the fall, and she would meet new people and make new friends. Law school was off the table for Jack, and his future less certain. Word spread of the stolen exam and his rejection from Harvard Law, which did not bode well for his prospects of finding a job in DC. Though he had not dwelled on it much, being preoccupied with guilt and remorse, now under the starry night in Yellowstone National Park, Jack contemplated how his life had changed from a few short weeks ago. And when he allowed himself to consider his future, it sunk in that taking the blame for the stolen test may have affected his life more greatly than he originally considered.

The night grew cold and Becca and Jack pulled the sleeping bag over their heads and fell asleep.

Chapter 22

Kelsey Castle
Summit Lake
March 13, 2012
Day 9

"You told me to figure out why her secret was a secret. So I did," Kelsey said as she sat with Commander Ferguson in the small breakfast place on the lake. "I know why Becca got married."

They sat at the bar sipping bitter coffee while the commander picked at a stale donut.

"I'm listening."

"She was pregnant."

The commander stopped his picking, looked around the diner to make sure no one was paying attention to them. "Where did you come up with this theory?"

"It's not a theory," Kelsey said in a hushed voice. "According to Michelle Maddox, the county medical examiner who did the autopsy, it's a fact. Becca's blood work was positive for hCG, the hormone produced during pregnancy." Kelsey pulled a sheet of paper from her purse and laid it on the bar in front of Commander Ferguson. It was a printed page from the autopsy report describing the internal exam and Dr. Maddox's discovery of a female fetus presumed to be in the fifth gestational month.

"Son of a bitch," Commander Ferguson said, lifting the page from the bar and squinting at the words.

He looked at Kelsey with the droopy eyelids and congested face of a man who drank and smoked too much. "Should I bother asking how you got hold of an autopsy report I haven't seen yet?"

Kelsey sipped her coffee. "You should not."

The commander shook his head slightly and offered a hint of a smile. After a moment, his face relaxed in a stoic stare as he considered this new information. "So she got knocked up, then ran off and married the guy real quick?"

"It's plausible. Might explain why the family is trying to cover things up. A prominent father who is quasi-famous with his law firm and getting ready for a run at the bench doesn't want it known that his unmarried, pregnant daughter was raped?"

"I thought we were saying she *was* married."

"Secretly married. Maybe worse for a prominent attorney that his daughter ran off and eloped. But I need some help. These are all important parts of the puzzle, but alone they don't get me any closer to figuring out who broke into the Eckersleys' house that night."

"Well," the commander said, twisting his coffee cup on the bar. "First, you have to remember no one broke into that house. There was no sign of forced entry, which means a recent GWU graduate and current law student was either too ignorant to know not to open the door for a strange man while alone at her family's vacation home, or she knew the person and allowed him to freely enter the house."

"Okay," Kelsey said. "So Becca disengages the alarm and

opens the door. For whom? She was married and pregnant, but who the hell killed her?"

"Couple angles there off the top of my head." Commander Ferguson took a sip of coffee, then looked around again. The diner was mostly empty. "Maybe your source was wrong about the marriage. Or maybe the Eckersley girl was wrong about the guy's intentions. Maybe she *wanted* to get married and in her mind thought whoever got her pregnant wanted the same thing. She goes around telling people this, or at least tells your source. The only problem? The guy doesn't want to marry her. Doesn't want a kid either. And there's one way to fix that problem."

Kelsey lifted her chin. She'd thought of a similar scenario, although not phrased quite so bluntly. It was a good theory, but one with missing characters. And they were going about this backward. You typically find a suspect and then look for motive, not the other way around.

Commander Ferguson let out one of his horsey laughs as he watched her wrestle with possibilities. "No one said this stuff was easy to figure out. But as you move along on this case I want you to remember something."

"What's that?"

"In my experience, you can fit the person who does something this terrible to a beautiful young woman into two categories. The first is someone who hated the victim."

"I've considered that," Kelsey said. "And so far I've been unable to come up with anyone who might have hated Becca Eckersley. The girl had no enemies."

"So that brings us to the only other category of person who might do this."

"Which is?"

"Someone who loved her."

* * *

Later that night, after her visit with Commander Ferguson, Kelsey sat in her suite at the Winchester and tapped her computer. She was at the small dining table, which was covered with research material on the Eckersley case. A pegboard was propped on a chair and decorated with photos of the Eckersleys' house and Kelsey's handwritten flow charts of Becca's movements the day she died—from the campus of GWU in the morning, through the mountains to Summit Lake, to Millie's coffeehouse, and finally to the Eckersleys' stilt house. Times were written at each location to keep things straight in her mind.

She went back through the information she received from Commander Ferguson. Within an hour, the other chairs were covered with stacks of paper she organized in a system coherent only to herself. She came across travel information for Becca—an outline of her movements in the months leading up to her death. Becca started law school in August, six months before she was killed, and the police had tracked her to only three trips outside of DC in those months. The first was in November when she ventured to Greensboro, presumably going home for Thanksgiving. The next were airplane records to Green Bay, Wisconsin, over Christmas. The last trip out of DC was her drive to Summit Lake the day she was killed.

Kelsey started in Greensboro, cross-referencing credit card receipts and ATM records with the Eckersleys' home address. Definitely a trip home for Thanksgiving. Next she moved to the Green Bay trip. What was in Green Bay that would make Becca go there over Christmas break? A guy, Kelsey concluded. What else would take a twenty-two-year-old student away from her family over Christmas?

Kelsey spent another hour poring through Becca's phone records, looking for any calls made to Wisconsin area codes. None. Although over a three-day period that covered Christmas, Kelsey found one call per day to the Eckersleys' home number in Greensboro that routed through a cell tower in Green Bay. She was close, but she needed a name or phone number or address or something to track.

On her computer she pulled up the 1L class of GW Law—nearly one hundred names. She deleted the females and settled on fifty-two male students who attended law school with Becca Eckersley. Painstaking research told her only three were from Wisconsin, and none from Green Bay. She hunkered down for three more hours and looked into the other male students in the L2 and L3 classes. Not one was from Green Bay. She even looked briefly at profiles of the attorneys in William Eckersley's law firm, running briefly with the gossip group's theory that Becca might have been involved with one of her father's colleagues. It was a short run, though, since none was from Wisconsin.

She put her notes from GW Law to the side and looked further back in Commander Ferguson's records. During the summer after Becca graduated college, she was noted to have been on a private jet belonging to Milt Ward, a Maryland senator. Kelsey licked her finger and paged through some notes. Milt Ward was all over the news.

"Why was a senator from Maryland flying you around on his private jet?"

Feeling she was on to something, she grabbed another stack of papers and started to dig. But a knock on the door interrupted her research. She looked at the clock. 11:18 p.m.

Through the peephole she saw a man dressed in a suit with his tie loosened and crooked.

"Miss Castle," the man said, knocking again. "My name is Detective Madison. I saw your light on, so I figured you were up."

Kelsey pulled the door open as far as the chain would allow. "Yes?"

"Good," the detective said. "You're still awake. Can we talk?"

"About what?"

"Becca Eckersley."

"Can I see some ID?"

"Of course."

The detective removed his badge from his hip and handed it through the slot between the door and frame. He also offered his driver's license.

"I'd be happy to talk down in the lobby if you're more comfortable there."

Kelsey scrutinized the badge and knew it was legit. She'd talked to Commander Ferguson about this guy. Madison was one of the state detectives who had taken the case from the Summit Lake police force.

"What's so important that you're knocking at my door at eleven at night?"

"There's been an important development."

Kelsey closed the door and unlatched the chain. "Here," she said when she opened the door, handing the badge and ID back to the detective. "Something about Becca?"

"Can I come in?"

"Sure," Kelsey said. "The place is a mess."

Detective Madison walked into the suite and looked around at the cluttered research covering the table and chairs. "You *have* been busy."

"I'm here on assignment."

"So I've heard." He walked over to the table and flipped a finger through some pages.

"Please don't touch my property, Detective," Kelsey said. "Unless you have a warrant."

"I don't," the detective said, turning and facing Kelsey. "What are you trying to accomplish here?"

"I'm writing an article about Becca Eckersley."

He glanced back at the table and chairs covered in papers and outlines. "A magazine article or a book?"

Kelsey's face stayed stoic. "An article."

"Why so much digging for a simple article?"

"Becca's is a complicated story."

"That's for sure."

"So what's this development that has you out so late?"

The detective smiled. "I'd appreciate it if you'd stop poking around places you're not meant to poke around."

"I'm a journalist writing a story, Detective Madison. Poking around is what I do. And since you guys are so secretive about the details of this case, I've had to put things together by piecemeal research."

"Piece things together however you'd like, but if you break the law you'll pay the price."

"Asking questions in Summit Lake is hardly breaking the law."

"Agreed. But breaking into a government building is."

Kelsey didn't hesitate. "Who broke into any buildings?"

Detective Madison smiled again. "I'm working on that, trust me. But surveillance footage shows two individuals using a stolen access key to enter the Buchanan County Government Center the other night. The same card was then used to enter a private office and access classified documents."

Now Kelsey smiled. "Classified? Is Buchanan County, way up here in the mountains, responsible for some secret nuclear program?"

"That's cute. Where were you two nights ago?"

"Detective, please do not come to my hotel suite and try to intimidate me."

"I'm simply asking a question."

"Which carries the implication that I somehow broke into this building you're talking about."

"Did you?"

"If you'd like to interrogate me, then arrest me and do it at the police station."

Detective Madison puckered his lower lip in contemplation. "When are you going back to Miami?"

"When I finish my article."

"Oh," the detective laughed, shaking his head. "I don't think you'll make it that long. Once I know for sure it's you on that surveillance footage, I'm going to arrest you—if you're still in Summit Lake. And I'm going to arrest whomever you were with. Do you understand?"

"Not really, because I don't know what the hell you're talking about."

The detective put a thumb over his shoulder. "And I noticed some of your research material is stamped with a Summit Lake Police Department seal. You steal that, too?"

Kelsey didn't answer.

"No," the detective said. "I bet you didn't have to. Stan Ferguson probably gave it to you because he's being a pain in the ass since he was asked to step aside. Leaking information to the media about an active investigation is a big no-no." The detective shook his head as he walked to the door. "Have a good night, Miss Castle."

He closed the door behind him and Kelsey ran to the peephole to watch him walk down the hallway and enter the elevator. She grabbed her cell phone and called Penn Courtney. She got his voice mail and left a curt message to call back. She also texted him and left the same message on his home phone. She grabbed her jacket on the way out of her hotel room. She made fast work of the five blocks to the coffeehouse, which she knew was long closed. She looked up to the second story. The windows were dark. Around back, Kelsey climbed the stairs and knocked softly on the door. When there was no answer, she knocked harder and the kitchen light finally blinked on. The curtains moved to the side and then the door opened. "What's wrong?" Rae asked.

"I need your help."

"Come in," Rae said. Dressed in flannel pajama pants and a tank top, Rae shuffled through the kitchen with slippers covering her feet. "What's going on?"

"The lead detective in the Eckersley case just paid me a visit."

With sleepy eyes Rae squinted at the wall clock. "What time is it?"

"Almost midnight."

"Why were the police at your hotel room at midnight?"

"Because I think I'm in trouble. The guy's name is Madison and he wanted to know why I was poking around so much."

"So tell him you're writing a story. No crime there."

"Agreed. Except I illegally entered the county building the other night with Peter and looked at an autopsy report that was not made public."

"I thought that was a secret."

"Yeah, well, not quite," Kelsey said. "I'm on a surveillance camera in front of the building."

"Oh, boy."

"Yeah."

"The best journalists make the worst criminals. Isn't that how the saying goes?"

Kelsey shook her head.

"Okay. So don't freak out just yet. What's the guy want?"

"Me to leave Summit Lake."

"How close are you on Becca's article?"

"Really close." There was a long pause where Kelsey shrugged. "At least coming up with some ideas that don't match anything the police are looking at. I just need some time to work things out. Commander Ferguson says the state guys are stuck on the theory of a drifter strolling through town that night and randomly entering the Eckersleys' house."

"You obviously disagree."

"Completely. Becca was killed by someone she knew."

"Who?"

"I don't know. I'm right on the edge here, but I don't have the resources I need. Usually, I'd talk to the family to get a picture of her life. Get some personal insight into this girl. Find out who her friends were, who she dated. But there's no chance of talking to the family."

"How about her friends?"

"I don't know who her friends were. I don't have access to any of her e-mails, and her Facebook account is off-line. Subpoenaed by the DA and completely out of my reach. I could head to DC and start poking around GWU until someone tells me something useful, but I get the feeling from Detective Madison's visit that going to DC to poke around won't be an option for me."

"So what's your plan?"

Kelsey took a deep breath. "You and I go to Millie's and get that journal."

Rae laughed. "Let's not get ahead of ourselves."

"That's what you think, though. Right? Millie has that journal?"

"The thought's crossed my mind, but I don't know this for certain."

"So let's find out. I need to know about Becca's life. Then I can piece things together and come up with a theory of who killed her. I can't talk to her family and don't have the time to track down her friends. Right now, Becca's journal is my only hope. Otherwise, I lose the story." Kelsey stared at Rae, moved a little closer to her. "I need your help on this."

Rae shook her head and looked at the ceiling as she thought. "Okay. But if Millie somehow has the journal, and has kept it this long from the police, she's certainly not about to hand it over to us."

"Not a chance. So what's the plan?"

Rae smiled. "I don't have a plan. This was your idea."

"Stop it. You know we're on the same page."

Rae slowly nodded. "We are."

"So," Kelsey said. "How do we get our hands on that journal?"

"We get creative."

Chapter 23

Becca Eckersley
Yellowstone National Park
May 19, 2011
Nine months before her death

The senator's call, which woke Jack and Becca early Thursday morning, didn't save their lives—they weren't that dramatic—but it damn well changed them. The chirping phone was an unnatural sound that morning, interrupting the quiet and stillness that took precedence at Yellowstone. Jack rolled over, pushing Becca's arm off his chest as he sat up and searched his bag for the phone. He didn't recognize the number.

"Hello?"

"Jack?" a man asked in a cool Southern drawl.

"Yes?" Jack sat up in his tent, cleared his throat, and pushed the static-filled cell phone to his ear.

"Jack, it's Senator Milt Ward. I worked with you last year through an internship program at GWU."

Jack straightened his back. "Yes, sir. How are you?"

"In need of a young voice. As you know, I'm making a run next November and I need some help on my campaign."

"Sir? I'm not sure I heard you."

"I'm offering you a job, son. You'll be putting words in my mouth as one of my speechwriters."

There was dead air for a few seconds, then the senator said, "Son, you still there?"

"Yes, sir."

"I just offered you a job, Jack."

"Yes, sir. I'd be honored."

"Good. I'll let you talk to my campaign manager; she'll get you caught up on how things run here. And I'd like to meet tomorrow for dinner."

"Ah, sir. I'm out west at the moment and not exactly able to get back by tomorrow. I'm in Yellowstone Park with no way out for a few days."

"Next week work for you?"

"Yes, sir."

"I'll give you Shirley Wilson's number; she'll arrange for you to get back here."

"I drove out here, sir. Once I get out of the park it'll take a couple of days to get back to DC."

"Shirley will set things up. I'll have my plane meet you, it'll be much faster than driving and we need to meet sooner than later. See you in a few days."

"Senator, I, uh . . . you should probably know about . . ." Jack paused, not sure if he should offer so much. Becca sat up now, listening to Jack's end of the conversation. "I had some . . ." Jack searched for an appropriate word, "issues at school before I left." There was no reply from the other end, so Jack kept talking. "With a stolen test."

"I've heard Professor Morton is a ballbuster, son. I'd have stolen that test, too, given the opportunity." The senator laughed. "You've been vetted, Jack. I know more about you than you know about yourself. And there's nothing I don't like. Stealing a test to pass a class you couldn't otherwise handle is one thing. Stealing a test and not using it is quite another."

"How do you know I didn't use it?"

"Got ears in the right places, Jack. Take this number down."

Jack scribbled the number of Senator Ward's campaign manager on his hand.

"See you next week, son."

Jack closed his cell phone and looked at Becca. "Did that just happen?"

"Tell me!"

"Senator Ward. From my internship last summer."

"Yeah?"

"He's running for president."

"And?"

"He wants me to write for him."

Chapter 24

Kelsey Castle
Summit Lake
March 14, 2012
Day 10

She ate a banana as she walked down Maple Street. It was a cloudless morning with a hint of warmth in the air and the smell of spring all around. Kelsey needed to warn Commander Ferguson of the trouble that was heading his way. She turned on Minnehaha Avenue, walked up the steps and into the old police building. There was no one manning the front so she walked straight to the commander's office. She found him on his knees behind his desk, rummaging through the bottom drawer. A large cardboard box sat on top of the desk.

"Commander?"

He popped his head over the top of his desk. "Miss Castle, good morning."

"Sorry to drop by unannounced, but I need to talk to you."

He waved her over. "Come here a minute and help me off this bad knee."

Kelsey hurried around the desk and helped him stand.

"What are you doing?" She noticed now the office was in disarray. Papers were scattered behind the desk, and nails poked from bare walls where pictures once hung. As she continued to look around, she understood. "Are you cleaning out your office?"

The commander smiled. "It's time."

"Because of Madison?"

"Because of a lot of things."

"He came to my suite at the Winchester late last night to tell me to go back to Miami. He saw my research material, some of which had the Summit Lake seal on it."

The commander smiled again and shook his head. "Doesn't matter how he found out. And truthfully"—he pointed around his office—"my leaving isn't even a result of that. Retirement was inevitable. I hung in here as long as I could, but now I've gotta go. I was hoping to stick around long enough to figure out what happened to the Eckersley girl, but that isn't in the cards for me."

"So Madison is pushing you out?"

"Please. A kid who shaves three times a week doesn't have the authority to push me anywhere. The district attorney, however, does. His office asked me to take a leave, and I'm happy to."

"I feel awful, Commander."

"Young lady, don't blame yourself for my problems. The writing's been on the wall for some time, I'm finally getting around to reading it." He threw some more items into the stuffed box on his desk. "But do me a favor, will you?"

"Anything."

"Don't let them run you outta here like they did me. I've got politics and pensions to worry about. You follow a different set of rules. I know how close you are to break-

ing this case, so don't stop until you've got it wrapped,
hear me?"

"Yes, sir."

Commander Ferguson smiled. He looked around his office. "Well, I think that does it. Everything else can stay; I'll
leave it to the guys to decide what to do with the rest of this
junk."

"Who's taking your spot?"

"The Summit Lake Police Department will be in good
hands, whomever they give it to. Help me out to my car?"

"Of course."

Kelsey carried a box outside and dropped it into the back
of Ferguson's pickup.

The commander wiped his hands, looked up at the aging
brick building where he spent his entire career. "That's a
wrap."

"Where are you off to?" Kelsey asked.

"I've worked forty-three years and never took a sick day. I
know it's hard to believe looking at me, but it's true. I'm
going to relax a while."

"Where?"

"God only knows. But I'm ready, that's for sure." He
reached into his breast pocket and pulled out a package of cig-
arettes. "Do me a favor?" he said, handing Kelsey the pack.

Kelsey raised her eyebrows as she took it.

"Throw these away for me."

"Sure," Kelsey said.

He climbed into the pickup and pulled the door shut. His
left elbow hung through the open window. "Be careful,
Miss Castle. Madison's out for you, so get your work done
quickly and then get outta here." He handed Kelsey a card.
"My cell number. Call if you need anything. All you're
looking for is one or two more pieces to fall into place.

Everything will come together then." He started the truck and put it into gear. "Good luck."

Kelsey waved as he drove down the street and turned onto Maple. The diesel engine rumbled for a few seconds until it faded and he was gone.

Chapter 25

Becca Eckersley
George Washington University
August 4, 2011
Six months before her death

On a steamy day in early August, three months since their Yellowstone adventure, Becca moved into her new apartment in the Foggy Bottom neighborhood just west of the GW Law campus. It was, coincidentally, the same neighborhood where Jack settled earlier in the summer, and the two-block walk between their residences was easy to cover.

Law school orientation for 1L students started August 16. Classes began the 22nd, which gave them two weeks before Becca's schedule got crazy. Jack was already working long hours on Milt Ward's campaign but was granted the weekend to get Becca settled. He traveled intermittently, but the next two weeks would see him in DC, and the heavy lifting would not begin until late fall as they prepared for the Iowa caucus in January.

After breakfast and a tour of the law school campus, Becca's parents left Saturday morning. With their arms around each other, Jack and Becca waved as the Eckersleys drove away. Holding hands, they walked back through campus and imagined the coming year.

"You'll be in there a lot," Jack said, pointing to the law library.

"It's gonna be weird studying without you. I've been so used to you at the desk across from me. I'll either have to go it alone or find another guy to study with."

Jack smiled. "I think you're a loner."

"I guess I won't have time for boyfriends. I received the 1L curriculum in the mail and it looks intense."

"I'll take your word for it. The thought of studying long hours is too much for me to handle right now."

"That's because you got booted from Harvard, and now you're a hotshot speechwriter three months removed from the last time you'll ever take a written exam."

"Speechwriter, yes. Hotshot, far from it. More like rookie peon at the beck and call of Bill Myers, who writes almost everything himself. Except occasionally when he rewrites what I've written."

"You're making a salary and you have some job security—is anyone in his party even a legitimate opponent in the primaries?"

"Not at the moment. But so goes Iowa in January, so goes the rest of the campaign. And Iowa has produced some sleepers over the years. But if Ward wins the nomination, I'll be working around the clock on the way to the election next November. So we'll both be busy. I'll just be getting paid for my work, rather than the other way around."

Becca grabbed his arm as they walked away from the law library. "Don't rub it in." They headed off campus, toward Foggy Bottom. "Let's stop at the 19th for a beer," she said. "Like the old days."

Jack shook his head. "Let's find somewhere else. We need a new place, you and me. The 19th reminds me of college."

They walked down Providence and found a bar called O'Reilly's. They sat at a tall pub table by the window, ordered Guinness, and started their own tradition. The two weeks leading to the start of law school were special for Becca Eckersley. It was the first time, other than their brief rendezvous in Yellowstone Park, that she openly displayed her love for Jack. During her senior year, they walked together without holding hands, and kissed good-bye only in the abandoned hallways of campus buildings when both were sure they were alone. But after a summer of only seeing each other occasionally with Jack working on Senator Ward's campaign and Becca in North Carolina, their reunion represented a different time in their lives. They met for dinner without worry of being spotted, and stayed overnight without sneaking home the next morning.

On the Sunday before law school started—the unofficial end of summer—they sat at the window table in O'Reilly's for the fourth time in two weeks. They decided it was, indeed, their new place. The food was good, and Becca was learning to tolerate the Guinness. The music was pop and Top 40 at a volume that allowed conversation. A few undergrads were present, but mostly young professionals filled the booths and spent time at the bar.

Their pizza was delivered—green pepper and olives—and they dug in.

"I was thinking about our living arrangements," Becca said as she bit into a piece of pizza. She wore a sleeveless white blouse that showed off her tanned, toned arms.

Becca's eyes reflected a seductive essence that Jack noticed immediately. "Yes?" he said.

"It seems silly to have two places when you stay at my apartment every night."

Jack chewed his pizza. "What are you trying to say, Eckersley?"

"We should live together."

"Not a chance."

Becca opened her mouth in feigned surprise. "Why?"

"Let's see, where should I start? First, we both have twelve-month leases we can't get out of. And you should know that I'm not even the lawyer here. Second, this whole thing"—Jack pointed to himself and then the pizza and then Becca—"it's great. Going out to eat, staying up late and sleeping in. But school starts tomorrow, and soon you'll be studying like mad. I'll have to start working again, and when that happens we'll both be happy to have a place by ourselves." He looked up as if thinking of a final point. "Oh, yeah. Then there's that whole thing about your father and how he would rip the heart out of my chest if we lived together, so that's kind of a deterrent."

Becca took a sip of beer. "Okay. We'll keep our own places for now and talk again next year before we sign any leases."

"Deal."

They finished their pizza and beer and walked back to Becca's. Inside, Becca headed to the bedroom to change while Jack opened his MacBook and checked e-mails. There were a few from his bosses, asking Jack to draft something for the next week. He read the specifics and then checked the upcoming travel schedule.

"I've got to fly to California next week with Ward. Leaving Tuesday and coming back Friday." He was reading the itinerary from the screen, not looking at Becca, who walked out of the bedroom. When he got no answer he finally looked up. She was posed in the doorway of the bedroom, wearing nothing but her bikini bottoms. The bedroom light reflected off her toned thighs and smooth, olive skin.

"I just talked to my father," she said, holding her pose. "And he agrees with you about the living-together thing. And he added that he would prefer you not be in my apartment past ten o'clock on school nights, which this is." She turned around and sauntered into the bedroom. "Lock the door on your way out."

Jack shook his head, the image of her naked body burned in his mind. He wasn't sure if it was Southern girls in general who always found a way to get what they wanted, or Becca Eckersley in particular. Either way, he closed his laptop and walked quickly into her room where she had removed her bikini bottoms and he pretended to be startled.

"My father asked you to leave."

"Point taken," Jack said.

"Oh," Becca said, standing naked by the bed. "Was I making a point?"

Jack walked to her and put his hands on her slim waist. He kissed her as she unbuttoned his shirt. They fell onto the bed.

Chapter 26

Kelsey Castle
Summit Lake
March 14, 2012
Day 10

She didn't risk being picked up in front of the Winchester for fear that Detective Madison was watching from the shadows and would follow them. She was being paranoid, she knew. She also knew paranoia kept her out of trouble.

Kelsey pulled her leather coat closed as she walked out the back door of the Winchester and along a side street that led to the banks of Summit Lake. The sun was almost gone and the sky was a dying blue. As it sunk behind the mountains, the sun streaked thin clouds plum-purple and offered a pink glow to the lake. She pulled out her cell phone while she walked and tried Penn Courtney. It had been over a week since she arrived in Summit Lake, two since she took the Eckersley story. Penn answered on the first ring, and as Kelsey walked she brought him up to date on the most recent developments. He was not happy about the trouble she was getting herself into, but Kelsey knew the lure of a cover-up and the idea of *Events* beating everyone else to the Eckersley story was enough to placate him for the time being.

The real point of Kelsey's journey to Summit Lake was clear—this was a time for her to heal and recover. Take some time off and lay low. There was never any confusion about that. And after an initial protest, Kelsey was fully willing to kill a month under the ruse of chasing a story. The problem was, while sniffing for a story she thought didn't exist, she found one. And now she was neck-deep in it—possibly in some trouble and about to make things worse. She kept the details of her plan vague when Penn pressed her for specifics. When he requested something of substance from her—a draft or outline—Kelsey promised she'd get something to him soon.

"Tonight," Penn said.

"I'll try."

"Try? I just gave you a deadline. I want to see what you have."

"I've got something going on tonight, Penn. I'll get something out to you tomorrow. Promise."

"It better have some guts to it."

"Trust me," Kelsey said as she walked. "I'll be in touch."

"Before you go, remember one thing," Penn said.

"What's that?"

"I've allowed you to expense everything on this trip."

"You encouraged it, actually," Kelsey said.

"Okay, I'll go that far. But know this: Bail money is not included, so don't call me at 2 a.m. if this plan of yours breaks bad."

"Let's not get carried away."

"I'm serious, Kelsey."

"I know you are. I'll touch base when I know more."

"One more thing."

Kelsey waited. "Yes?"

"You're the best I've got and . . . just be careful, okay?"

"Always. Thanks, Penn."

She stuffed the phone in her purse as she approached the

corner of Spokane Avenue. She checked her watch: 5:53 p.m. She was about to sit on the corner bench when the SUV pulled up. The passenger side window rolled down.

"We've got to stop meeting this way," Peter said.

Kelsey shook her head and offered a nervous smile. She pulled open the door and climbed in. "Are you sure you're okay with this?"

"Not really, because I don't know exactly what I signed up for. Why couldn't I pick you up at the hotel?"

"Let's get out of here and I'll explain."

They drove fifteen minutes into the mountains and pulled over at a scenic overlook. The vastness of the lake was in front of them and the homes of Summit Lake were nestled in a neat pocket below, glowing in the evening darkness.

"Has anyone been around to talk to you?" Kelsey asked as they pulled to a stop.

"Anyone who?" Peter asked.

"Any police? To talk to you about breaking into the county building the other night."

"No. Why? What's happening?"

"One of the detectives on the Eckersley case paid me a visit last night. Told me to stop snooping around and go back to Miami."

"Really? Not sure he has the authority to kick you out of town."

"Normally, I'd agree with you. But he started asking questions about stolen documents from the county building, and where I was that night."

"What did you tell him?"

"I acted like I didn't know what he was talking about, but I don't think it was a very good bluff. He told me they're reviewing surveillance tapes that show two individuals entering the building after business hours with a stolen access card."

"Uh-oh."

"Yeah, we're in trouble. I wanted to give you a heads-up. You might also mention to your friend who got you the card that some heat might come down on him."

"So with all this 'heat,' as you call it, about to come down on us, you thought it was a good idea to pull another B and E?"

Kelsey smiled at his sarcasm. "Not a good idea, but my only shot at finishing what I started here."

"What's with this case?" Peter asked. "Why is it so important to you?"

Kelsey stared out the windshield, where the dying sun laid a cherry runway quivering across Summit Lake. In her heart was empathy toward Becca—who, like Kelsey, had undergone a brutal assault. That no one ever paid the price for this crime was something Kelsey could not turn her back on. She was hungry for closure, and she couldn't leave Summit Lake without it.

"I'm not sure," she finally said. "But I know too much about this girl to leave with all these questions floating around." She shrugged. "Just not enough to find the answers."

"Which is why you asked me to help you break into some woman's house tonight?"

"Correct. I know you're sticking your neck out again for me, something you don't have to do. I'm nervous to try this by myself. And I hope to hell you don't get in any trouble for what we did the other night."

Peter smiled. "You're worth a little trouble."

Kelsey's cell phone buzzed. She looked down and read the text message. "Okay. Rae's got her out of the house—they're headed to dinner. We've got about an hour. Hour and a half tops."

"Let's go," Peter said, backing out of the parking spot and starting down the mountain road. "Where does the old lady live?"

* * *

Ten minutes later, they pulled to the front of Millie's house. Peter parked in the driveway and turned off his headlights. They sat in darkness and stared at the house, lighted now only by two porch lights and a stray living room lamp.

"Okay," Peter said. "Now what? You've got a key?"

"It's not that complicated," Kelsey said. "Come on."

They slowly moved up the front walk, making sure no neighbors were watching. When they reached the front door, Kelsey simply turned the knob and pushed.

"You've got to be kidding me," Peter said.

"Rae said she'd make sure the door was unlocked." She handed Peter a small flashlight. "Let's go."

Inside, they closed the door behind them.

"No lights, just in case the neighbors saw her leave. A blazing house will draw suspicion."

"Got it," Peter said. "What is it again I'm looking for?"

"A journal, like a diary."

"Description?"

"That's it. Let's go upstairs first."

In Millie's bedroom they carefully took fifteen minutes to look through dresser drawers and nightstands and under mattresses and in old boxes in the closet.

"If I find something inappropriate," Peter said, pulling open the nightstand drawer, "I swear to God I'll scream."

Kelsey laughed. "She's in her eighties."

"Then I'll scream louder."

"Hurry up," Kelsey said, laughing as she entered the closet.

"Nothing out here," Peter finally said.

"Yeah," Kelsey said, walking out of the closet a minute later. "Nothing in there either."

They headed to the second bedroom and went through the same routine, taking painstaking efforts to leave everything they touched and looked under in the exact position they found it. Another fifteen minutes passed. They took a quick tour of the hallway closet. Nothing.

They were in the house for thirty minutes when they walked down the stairs to the first floor and picked their way through the dining room armoire. Kelsey thought they were on to something when she stumbled across a bound book in the bottom cabinet, but it turned out to be Millie's wedding album. Another ten minutes were spent in the dining room, and ten more fruitlessly in the living room.

Kelsey started to sweat, and her palms became clammy. They'd been at it for nearly an hour. They set in on the kitchen, flashlight beams floating through cabinets and pantries, over baking goods and plastic jars of cereal. Finally, Kelsey placed the flashlight on the kitchen table, its beam still now as it came to rest against the backsplash. She took a defeated breath. With no journal, she was stuck. A stale plan of tracking down Livvy Houston and asking about the journal formed in Kelsey's mind, but she knew it would be difficult. She'd have to find Livvy first and then convince her to talk. No guarantee of that. And even if Livvy agreed to meet, she might not know a thing. This was all assuming Detective Madison hadn't already paid Livvy a visit himself. Kelsey ran a hand over her face and shook her head.

Peter walked over to her. "Hey."

She looked up at him.

"I'm sorry. I wish I could find it for you."

Kelsey nodded and closed her eyes. Peter moved closer and wrapped his arms around her. She rested her cheek on his chest and surprised herself by returning the gesture and locking her fingers behind his back. She thought briefly of the self-help books that suggested she may not be able to tolerate a man's touch for some time, but she felt good in Peter's arms. Safe, even.

"I wish I could do more for you," Peter said into her ear.

"It's okay. I was reaching, I know. For something to help me with this story. For something that will provide the information I can't find on my own. Becca's journal was all I had left."

"Some secrets are meant to be kept," Peter said.

She adjusted her position and looked up at him. Their faces were close. His eyes, in the dimly lit kitchen of Millie's house, were caring and genuine. He smelled from aftershave and lotion. She looked at his full lips, thought of what it would feel like to kiss him and if she was ready and if she could handle it, and whether this was the place to do it or if they should just get the hell out of there.

As these thoughts passed through her mind, Peter's head tilted just a bit and his face came toward hers.

Kelsey blinked a few times before her eyes widened. She moved her hands to his face and smiled. "Say that again."

Peter shook his head. "Say what?"

"What you just said."

"I wish I could do more to help you?"

"No, no. After that."

Peter thought for a second. "Some secrets are meant to be kept?"

"Yes!"

With her hands still on his face, Kelsey tilted her head back and laughed. She remembered her time in this kitchen a couple days before, when she sat with Millie and drank sweet tea and listened to the old lady reveal things about the night Becca was killed. About the night her daughter, Livvy Houston, sat with Becca at the cafe and talked with her just hours before she died. There was something about that conversation that stuck with her, something Kelsey couldn't define until she heard Peter say it.

She looked at the flashlight, which was resting on the table and shining across the room, illuminating the kitchen countertop and backsplash. Captured in its beam was a row of cook-books. Kelsey recognized one of them as Millie's secret recipe binder.

Kelsey remembered Millie standing at the counter mixing her sweet tea.

"Is your recipe available to the public?" Kelsey had asked.

"Oh, no, sweetheart. This book is strictly off-limits. If I let people know what was in here, all my secrets would be revealed. I'm eighty-six years old. My secrets are all I have left."

Kelsey broke free from Peter's embrace, grabbed the flashlight, and walked quickly to the binder. She pulled it out of the row and dropped it flat on the counter. She opened the cover, flipped through dozens of laminated recipes until there were no more pages to turn. And there it was. In the back pocket of the recipe binder a small hard-covered journal rested. In a girl's cursive was scrawled: *Becca Eckersley.*

Chapter 27

Becca Eckersley
George Washington University
October 12, 2011
Four months before her death

It only became an amazing thing later. At first it was complete shock and disbelief.

Law school began on a muggy day at the end of August where the humidity hung still in the air and stuck to her face when she walked from the cool air-conditioning of the campus buildings. September was more merciful and by the time October rolled through, the dog days were gone and everyone had their eyes set on the cold and brutal winters DC knew well. Becca was putting in twelve- and fifteen-hour days between classes and study. Jack was gone much of September, either traveling or working late at Senator Ward's office. She hadn't bothered to tell him about the vomiting, since it came only in the mornings and was mostly cleared up by the time she was into her day. For the first week she accused influenza, but when day fourteen approached she got suspicious. School—Civil Procedure and Contracts, in particular—had her so preoccupied she couldn't remember the details of her period the previous month, but she was definitely late now.

She bought a pregnancy test at the corner pharmacy on the way home, and now sat on the lid of the closed toilet as she waited for the results. When they came she tried again. After five more minutes her perfect little life and the next ten years, which were planned out and lined up like a precise set of dominos, toppled. She tried Jack's cell phone and got his voice mail, where she left a frantic message asking for a call back. She texted him five minutes later, then finally jumped into her car and drove downtown to his office.

She'd been there before, during Senator Ward's courting phase in the summer, when she tagged along with Jack on the grand tour. This was her first visit during working hours and her first while Jack was a true employee of "Milt Ward for President." Senator Ward maintained an official office at the Dirksen Senate Office Building, and that was where Jack spent most of his time when he was not on the road. She parked in employee parking off Constitutional Avenue and walked inside.

"Hi," she said to the secretary, in the best calmed-down voice she could find. She asked for Jack. "I'm his . . ." She paused a moment as she tried to figure out what, exactly, she was. A friend? A girlfriend? It didn't matter, because she wasn't his wife and that meant pure hell when it came time to discuss this with her parents. "I just need to talk with him," she finally said.

"He was with Senator Ward on Capitol Hill earlier today, but let me see where he is now." The secretary picked up the phone. "Oh, you're back," she said. "There's a young woman here to see you." She covered the receiver with her hand and looked at Becca with an expression that begged for a name.

"Becca . . . Eckersley."

"Becca Eckersley," the secretary said slowly. "Okay." She replaced the phone. "Through security, then down the hallway. Left at the T and then the second door on the right."

Becca smiled and headed through the metal detectors. Once through, she started down the hall. Before she could reach the aforementioned T, Jack appeared with a broad smile, wearing the tie she'd given him when he officially accepted the position.

"Can you believe I wore this tie the first time you're at the office?"

Becca forced a smile. "Looks good. We need to talk."

He raised his eyebrows. "Okay, come into my office."

They walked around the corner into Jack's office. His isolated laptop sat on the desk with shallow stacks of papers in a semicircle. He closed the door and offered Becca a chair.

"What's up?"

She took a deep breath. "I'm pregnant."

Jack's lips stayed sealed together and his forehead wrinkled.

"I know," Becca said.

"Well," Jack said. "The clichéd response is, 'How did this happen?' but I'll start with, 'Are you sure?' "

"I've taken two pregnancy tests."

"I didn't even know this was a suspicion."

"I didn't either, until today. I haven't felt well and with school and the hectic schedule I thought it was the flu."

"Okay," Jack said, sitting behind his desk. After a few seconds, he said, "Holy shit. Let's not freak out here."

"But here's the problem—there's so much to freak out about! I'm a pregnant 1L student at GW Law. That might be a first. I mean, how do you finish law school when you have a baby? Then there's my parents. Holy shit is right, Jack! I can't imagine telling my father. And finally there's you and me, and what this means to us and each other and our future." Becca was on the verge of tears.

"All right," Jack said. "So there's lots to think about. Even if we were married and you were out of law school there'd be a lot to think about. First of all, if we do the math, you're due when? Summer?"

Becca nodded, she'd already gotten that far. "Not sure, but probably May or June."

"So that shouldn't affect your first year of school, other than the obvious. But you can finish year one. Then we either hire help or think about taking a year off—if we talk to the right people, a year off is possible and I'm sure Milt knows a few people."

Becca stared out the window as Jack talked. There were many reasons to come here and talk to him, but the main reason was because he always calmed her down when she faced something she couldn't handle on her own. So far, what he said was correct, and for the first time since this morning she considered that she still one day might be a lawyer.

"Second," Jack went on, "I'll sit right next to you when you tell your parents, so we'll have that to look forward to together. And lastly, this does nothing to us—nothing bad, anyways. At least according to me."

She knew she loved him, knew it the previous summer when they said it to each other for the first time, and she knew throughout her senior year as their relationship grew. It was confirmed on their trip to Yellowstone when they skipped graduation and shared a week together under the blue Wyoming sky. But here, today, Becca loved him more for being a man and for never thinking of anything other than how to get through this situation together.

"There is one other problem, though," Jack said.

"What's that?" Becca asked.

"We've got to figure out how to get married, and very quickly."

Chapter 28

Kelsey Castle
Summit Lake
March 15, 2012
Day 11

The sun was an orange ball just above the horizon, its edges sharp and visible at such a young hour, and its reflection spread like marmalade across Summit Lake. The light peeked through the curtains of Peter's living room window and fell softly on Kelsey's face. She tried to open her eyes, but the sunlight was too intense. Her neck ached from the awkward position she was in, and when she sat up she realized where she was. Peter was asleep next to her, his arm draped behind her neck and his leg propped up on the coffee table.

They came back to Peter's house the night before, after finding Becca's journal in Millie's recipe book. Together they read it, cover to cover, learning the names of Becca's friends and the dynamics of her relationships. Becca was in love with Jack, and Kelsey suspected there was a problem with her relationship with Jack's best friend, Brad. Kelsey read the neat cursive writing for three hours, taking notes along the way, details coming together in her mind, until her eyes drooped and the journal fell softly onto her chest. Peter sat next to her and soon they were both asleep.

Now, with the sun bright in her eyes, Kelsey sat up. She had been sleeping with her head on Peter's chest while they both slouched on the living room couch. Denying the pain in her neck, she surveyed her surroundings. "Sorry." She rubbed her face. "I fell asleep."

"Me too," Peter said in a groggy, morning voice. "Ouch." He pulled his stiff leg off the coffee table.

Kelsey stood up and ran a hand through her hair. "What time is it?"

Peter checked his watch. "Just after six."

"I must've crashed."

"Me too. It happens after an adrenaline rush like we had."

"Can I . . . use the bathroom?"

"Of course," Peter said. He pointed to the door down the hall. "There's a package of toothbrushes in the top drawer, so help yourself."

"Thank you." Kelsey headed to the bathroom and shut the door. "Dear God!" she said when she saw her image in the mirror. The left side of her head was a bird's nest of tangled hair, and her cheek was covered in a red road map of wrinkles with a prominent depression from the button on Peter's breast pocket.

She washed her face, brushed her teeth, and ran a comb through her hair. Her mind played tug-of-war, one part wanting to reminisce about the almost-kiss she shared with Peter; the other, more analytical part, wanting to get back to Becca's journal and sift through the cast of characters who were in it.

She finally emerged from the bathroom a few minutes later, looking more put together. Her hair was pulled into a ponytail and her teeth minty with fluoride. They switched places, smiling awkwardly at each other as they passed. Peter closed the door; then she shook her head. "What the hell am I doing?" she asked herself.

Peter popped his head out of the bathroom door. "What's that?"

She waved him back in. "Nothing."

She went to the couch and paged through Becca's journal. A few minutes later, Peter walked out of the bathroom, also looking more presentable.

"Wanna get breakfast?" he asked her.

"Sure." Kelsey smiled.

Outside, the sky sponged up the colors of the rising sun. Buds on the trees looked to have blossomed into leaves overnight. The air was crisp and fresh, and the temperature rising with the sun. The smell from wood-burning fireplaces mixed with the pine of the forest. It was spring in Summit Lake.

They walked down Maple Street and turned on Nokomis Avenue, where they found a breakfast place. They ordered pancakes and eggs. Sipping coffee, the awkwardness of waking next to each other quickly faded as they recalled the previous night's journey.

"So I fell asleep right about when Becca headed home for Christmas with Jack."

"I finished it," Kelsey said.

"And?"

"Becca was an interesting girl, for sure. She was clearly in love with Jack and we know she married him after she found out she was pregnant. But there were other men in her life."

"Brad, right. One of her college friends?"

"Yes, and if I read between the lines, I can imagine Brad

maybe believing his relationship with Becca was more than platonic. But that's not all. There were other men Becca wrote about. A professor she had a somewhat secretive relationship with."

"She was sleeping with him?"

"No, at least Becca didn't come out and say as much in her journal. But he's mentioned enough to make him a worthwhile candidate to track down. And there was also an ex-boyfriend in the picture. A guy from high school who made frequent trips to the GWU campus from Harvard. Also someone I'd like to talk to."

"How about the husband? Jack? Shouldn't you talk to him first?"

"Talk to him, for sure. But not first. I want to find out who these other guys are, see if they can provide any insight into Becca and their relationships with her. Then see what they know about Jack. Once I've got all that, I'll pay him a visit."

"You don't think the police have already found these guys?"

"I'm not sure what the police have found. According to Commander Ferguson, the state investigators are stuck on the theory of a simple burglary turned ugly."

"But that theory has to be based on something. Some evidence they found."

"Becca's purse was missing. That's it. At least that's all Commander Ferguson knows about why they're running so hard with the burglary angle."

"And you're not buying that theory?"

"Not even close. With some help from Commander Ferguson, it looks like the person who killed Becca not only knew her well, but quite possibly was close to her."

"Like someone who loved her?"

"Maybe. But my first move is to track these guys down and talk to them. And I've got to do it quickly."

"So where do we start? I want to help."

"You sure about that?"

"Absolutely. Whatever you need."

"I get the feeling from Detective Madison's visit the other night that we don't have a lot of time. The first thing we have to do is identify the people in Becca's journal. I went back through it last night and couldn't find a single last name attached to any of her friends. So let's start there." Kelsey pulled out her notes. "Jack lives in Green Bay, Brad in Maryland. At least that's where they're from. Who knows where they are now. It sounds like the roommate, Gail, lives in Florida but goes to school at Stanford."

Kelsey wrote block letters on a napkin: *JACK AND GAIL*. She slid the napkin across the table. "If you want to help," she said, looking Peter in the eye. "And you're not worried about the trouble we might be headed for from the county building, then I'd ask you to find out who Gail is and track her down. Talk to her. Find out what she knows about Becca and Jack. Get me Jack's last name and any information Gail is willing to provide. If you're feeling it with her, if you have a good rapport, tell her my theory of what might have transpired between Becca and Jack and get her reaction."

Peter put his hand on the napkin and began to pull it toward him. Kelsey put her hand over his and stopped the napkin's progress. "If you're worried, Peter, about getting in trouble for any of this, then you should back out now. I'm sure you can hide behind some sort of physician immunity about looking at that autopsy and using that card to get into the building. Currently, as we sit here, you're likely in less trouble than I am. I'm okay with it if you want to keep it that way."

Peter maintained eye contact and pulled his hand, and the

napkin, from her grip. "I'll find Becca's roommate and talk to her. I'll let you know what I find out."

"Thank you."

"You're welcome. And what's *your* plan. Track down the other guys in her life?"

"Absolutely."

"Let's get going," Peter said. "We've got work to do."

Chapter 29

Becca Eckersley
George Washington University
December 21, 2011
Two months before her death

The plan was to wait until the second trimester to tell their parents, under the ruse of making sure the pregnancy was without complication and the baby was healthy. In reality, it gave them a little breathing room. They had nearly two months to figure things out and lay some groundwork that might help them look less crazy. If all went according to their flimsy strategy, Jack and Becca would sit down in Greensboro for Thanksgiving dinner and tell the Eckersleys they were going to be grandparents.

Jack worked hard to hold it together, but Becca wasn't buying his eternal optimism that all would work out or that her parents, after the dust settled, would be thrilled. Becca played the scenario in her mind of the moment she dropped the bomb, and no matter how hard she tried, she could not realistically see her father being excited about his twenty-two-year-old daughter being pregnant and unmarried. Her father was a powerful man in North Carolina. He carried influence and a persona. He was getting ready to hand over his firm to her brother and the other partners as he transitioned to being a judge. And Becca knew such a move required a clean background. Not only for her father, but for his family. A pregnant, unmarried daughter who dropped out of law school was not the family portrait with which her father could win the bench.

That thought was what brought them to the courthouse in DC.

Becca understood the logistics of a formal wedding, and the impossibility of it occurring in her current situation. Instead, a justice of the peace married them in a very informal ceremony. It was not how they planned things or how the narrative of their lives was meant to go. But if she and Jack learned anything over the last year it was that the road of life has detours, and the long-way-around can sometimes be a shortcut.

After the justice pronounced them married, they kissed and then sat behind a desk in the processor's office and filled out forms. They were told they needed to get their marriage certificate finalized, and took a copy of instructions on how to do so.

They spent a single night at the Four Seasons in downtown DC, where they celebrated with an expensive dinner and a nice bottle of wine from which Becca sneaked two or three sips. Saturday was a quiet day shared at Becca's apartment before Jack flew to New York on Sunday and Becca hit the books for an exam. They started the weekend as boyfriend and girlfriend and ended it as husband and wife.

For the next few weeks, they settled into a routine of being a secretly married couple with a baby on the way whom no one knew about. And when Thanksgiving finally rolled around, the time they originally agreed to tell Becca's parents, they choked. Neither could settle on the right approach, and so the two nights spent at the Eckersleys' house in Greensboro were filled with anxiety and whispered conversations. They headed back to DC on the Saturday after Thanksgiving. Jack had a busy schedule until Christmas, then a week off that coincided with part of Becca's break. They planned to head to Green Bay for Becca to meet Jack's parents. That Jack would be introducing his wife, and explaining that his mom and dad would soon be grandparents, was sure to make this Christmas one to remember.

Becca finished her final exam week with back-to-back exams of Civil Procedure and Contracts and never felt more relief. She sent a text to Jack when she was done.

Just finished! Celebrating by myself at O'Reilly's. I'll have one for you.

It was midafternoon and O'Reilly's was moderately crowded with law students and business people at the end of their week and the end of their semester. Jack was traveling with Senator Ward and not due back until the day before Christmas Eve—two days from now.

The doctor completed the calculations and it was determined that they conceived at the beginning of the school year, when they shared time together at the end of summer and forgot about the world. The due date was officially stamped as May 18, which was two weeks after final exams. The timing was not perfect, but she knew it could be worse—and still could be if the baby came early and caused her to miss finals. But Becca was staying optimistic for delivering in a narrow window of time that would allow her not only to finish her first year, but also get things together enough to possibly return on schedule the following fall. They discussed the other options of either taking a year off and then returning full-time, or switching to part-time and graduating later than planned. Either way, after four months of pregnancy, Becca had options.

Under close scrutiny in the bathroom mirror, her belly had not yet betrayed that a baby was growing there, even from a profile view. For now, she kept her secret to herself. Besides a few study buddies, Becca made no close friends during her first semester of law school and with Gail on the other side of the country, she wasn't concerned with anyone discovering her secret before she decided to reveal it.

At O'Reilly's she ordered a salad and a Sprite and felt the weight of her first semester rise from her shoulders. She had two weeks to relax. She pulled her iPhone from her purse and scrolled through her e-mails, hoping to see one from Gail. They promised to let each other know when they finished their finals. She just opened her in-box when the stool on the other side of the table dragged across the ground and someone sat down with her.

Becca looked up, shocked at first and then happy to see her old friend, Thom Jorgensen, her old logic professor who left GWU for a position at Cornell.

"Thom! What are you doing here?"

"Hello, Becca Eckersley," he said.

"Look at you." Becca ran a hand over her face. "You've grown an Ivy Leaguer. I'm surprised Cornell allows facial hair on professors. I thought they were only for students."

Thom Jorgensen smiled. "They're encouraged, actually. What do you think?"

Becca puckered her lips. "Very handsome. How's the new gig?"

"Good. Could be better."

"Better? You don't like being at the top of the food chain?"

"No, no. The job's great, university is top-notch and I've never been part of a better institution."

Becca squinted her eyes. "So what's wrong?"

Thom shrugged. "I guess I don't understand why you turned Cornell down."

Becca sat silent for a few seconds. "How did you know I turned them down?"

"Becca, I pulled a lot of strings to get you accepted to their law program. Stuck my neck out like I've never done before, in a position where I haven't yet fully found my footing. I told all the people with decision-making abilities what a great asset you'd be. And you returned the favor by saying no."

"Thom, I didn't know you did any of that for me. I heard from GW first, and it's my dad's alma mater. I never really considered going anywhere else unless GW was a no."

"What happened to the discussion we had about finally being able to spend time with each other?"

"Well," Becca said. "I think becoming a student at the university in which you work would put us in the same situation."

"So why haven't I heard from you?"

"I've been busy with law school and we live hundreds of miles from each other."

"Okay. So I'm just an idiot who misread our friendship."

"No, you didn't misread anything. But logistically, it's hard to get together for coffee when we live in different states."

"I just wish you'd have considered Cornell more closely. It's a great opportunity and we'd be closer."

Becca stared at her old professor, feeling confused and sad for him. Before she could respond, a woman walked through the door and directly over to their table.

"You are a son of a bitch!"

Thom Jorgensen looked up, then closed his eyes. "Jesus Christ, what are you doing, Elaine?"

"What am *I* doing? You don't have the right to ask me questions, not anymore." She looked at Becca. "How old are you?"

Becca opened her palms. "Who are you?"

"Oh, I'm sorry. I'm Elaine Jorgensen. Thom's wife."

Becca looked at Thom. "What the hell?"

"Elaine," Thom said. "Let's go outside."

"Of course, now that I caught you, you finally want to talk to me."

"Listen," Becca said. "He never told me he was married, and nothing's going on between us. I haven't seen him for a year, since he was at George Washington."

"But now you're conveniently having lunch with my husband."

"No, I was having lunch by myself and he interrupted me."

"Thom," she said. "Stand up. We're leaving."

Professor Jorgensen stood like a dog following a command.

Elaine looked at Becca and pointed a finger at her face. "Stay away from my husband."

She grabbed Thom by the arm and pushed him out the door.

Becca swallowed hard and, without moving her head, glanced around the bar and absorbed the stares. Slowly, people got back to the business of eating and drinking.

"Damn, Eckersley. You sure know how to make a scene."

Becca looked over her shoulder. Richard Walker, her high school boyfriend, stood next to her.

"First a cheesehead and now some slimy dude cheating on his lady?"

Still rattled, her hands shook. Becca quickly stood and hugged Richard. The last time she saw him was a year before when she and Jack spent Christmas in Summit Lake.

"Good to see you, too," Richard said, holding her tight. "What's wrong?"

Becca shook her head and released her grip around his shoulders. "Oh, just a little disturbed. That's all."

"By Professor Numbnuts?" Richard pointed to the door. "What's his story? Do I need to kick someone's ass?"

"He's an old professor of mine who was a little needy. I never knew he was married and now—" Becca shook her head. "His wife actually thinks we're involved."

Richard made an ugly face and shook his head. "Has that school gone completely nuts? First no-nothings from Wisconsin, and now stalker professors?" Richard cocked his head sideways. "So you're not sleeping with him?"

Becca slapped his shoulder. "No, the whole thing's just creepy. Keep me company while I eat. What are you doing here?"

"Just got done with finals. Heading home for two weeks. You too, right?"

Becca nodded. "Tomorrow, yeah." They sat down.

"Haven't seen you for a while," Richard said.

"Yeah, it's been a long time."

There was a pause.

"You still seeing that guy?"

Becca nodded again.

"That's too bad."

"Stop it."

"Is it serious?"

"Yes."

Richard stared at her a minute. "Like, he's-the-one serious?"

Becca looked into his eyes. "He's the one, Richard."

He took a deep breath. "I should have tried harder," he said.

"What are you talking about?"

"To get you back. I visited you a couple times freshman

year, but I was too dumb back then to know what I was losing. I should have worked harder. Maybe you and I would be
celebrating the end of finals together now."

Becca motioned back and forth. "We are."

"Only by accident."

Becca smiled. "I need a friend right now, okay? Not a lecture and not sobbing."

"Wow," Richard said. "You're going to be a good lawyer.
Completely heartless."

Becca rubbed his hand in apology.

"Fine," Richard said. "Just friends. Tell me how bad your
first semester sucked."

Chapter 30

Kelsey Castle
Summit Lake
March 15, 2012
Day 11

After leaving the restaurant, Kelsey and Peter took off in opposite directions. Peter headed home to start his research into Becca's roommate, while Kelsey walked to the Winchester in hopes of a shower and change of clothes before starting the next leg of the Eckersley journey. With her purse over her shoulder and Becca's journal nestled inside, Kelsey made her way along the lakefront until she reached Tahoma Avenue, where she headed west toward Maple Street and the entrance to the Winchester. Halfway down the block she stopped. Ahead, in the semicircle drive in front of the hotel, three state police cars sat with rolling red and blue lights. A single officer stood in front of the building talking into the radio on his shoulder and occasionally looking up at the top-floor rooms.

Kelsey stepped into the alcove of an art gallery and took a deep breath. She peeked out and then reminded herself that hiding in the shadows gathered more attention than simply walking down the street. She gathered her wits, stepped out of the gallery, and quickly walked the other way, back toward the lakefront and then south along Shore Drive. With her heart pounding, she kept her eyes on the steeple of St. Patrick's Church as she walked. She passed the docks of stilt row. When she reached Tomahawk Avenue she turned right and walked to the corner of Maple. Across the street was Millie's Coffee House. A few cars drove past before Kelsey crossed. She snuck a peek to her right and saw the flashing squad cars a few blocks away at the Winchester. Pulling open the door to the cafe, Kelsey walked in and saw Rae behind the counter. It didn't take much—just Rae's quick eye contact and subtle headshake—for Kelsey to know something was wrong. Before she could retreat out the door, though, Detective Madison appeared from the back of the cafe.

"Actually, Detective," Rae said just as he emerged from the back hallway where the restrooms were located. It was enough to take his attention away from the front of the cafe where Kelsey stood. "I think I *do* know who you're talking about. Brown-haired girl? Real pretty. With, like, caramel eyes? Writes for that magazine?"

"Yeah, that's her," Madison said, resting his elbows on the bar and turning his back to the front of the cafe. "You seen her around here?"

"Yeah," Rae said, running a hand through her hair. "She's come in a couple of times for coffee."

"She been in recently?"

"Couple days ago. Let me get you a coffee. It's on the house."

"I appreciate it."

Detective Madison grabbed his cell phone from his breast pocket and scrolled through e-mails. While his eyes were on his phone, Rae looked at Kelsey and gestured upstairs with her thumb.

"There you go, Detective."

"Thanks. You talk to her at all while she was here?"

Kelsey slowly backed away, turned, and snaked through the front door just as a couple was entering the cafe. Outside, Kelsey now recognized the unmarked state cruiser parked around the corner. She walked quickly to the alley behind the cafe and turned in just as a state trooper pulled off Maple Street and crept along Tomahawk.

"What the hell?" Kelsey muttered to herself. She looked down the alley and then up the stairs that led to Rae's apartment. She took the stairs two at a time, twisted the handle, and ducked inside the apartment just as the state trooper turned and slowly crawled down the alley.

She dumped her purse on the kitchen table and slumped into a chair. She couldn't go back to the hotel, her rental car was probably impounded, and she was sure Peter's house was infested with police by now. She pulled out her cell and called him, then hung up when she got his voice mail. She texted him that police were outside her hotel, Madison was looking for her, and state detectives were likely to pay Peter a visit soon. Then she sat at Rae's kitchen table, pulled her MacBook from her purse, and started writing. The police didn't want Becca Eckersley's story told, that much was obvious. At least, they didn't want a reporter to tell it.

Kelsey pictured herself on the phone in the police station asking Penn for the bail money he promised not to give her. She wasn't sure she'd make it out of Summit Lake, but as much as she knew about Becca sure as hell would. In an hour she turned out 2,000 words for her article. Besides quick sentences and short paragraphs scribbled on her notepad over the past ten days, the pages she produced while hiding in Rae's apartment were the first she had written on the Eckersley case. There was no style to the writing, mostly bullet points. She began with the murder itself, reviewing the details she gained from Commander Ferguson and from the medical records, then covered some of Becca's past and her time at George Washington University. She jumped ahead and made sure to get on paper that Becca was likely married and was definitely pregnant at the time she died. She included as many details as she could remember about the autopsy and toxicology report, then wrote down the names of Becca's friends from college, and also the other men who were swarming her at the time of her death.

Her efforts resulted in ten pages of cluttered mess, but at least it was a start and something for Penn to work from if she were unable to continue the story. She attached it to an e-mail and sent it to Penn's in-box just as she heard footsteps climbing the stairs outside.

Rae pushed open the door and quickly closed it behind her. She pulled the curtains to the side, looked down at the alley for a minute to make sure no one was behind her, then turned to Kelsey.

"Holy cow, girl. You shook the wrong beehive."

Chapter 31

Becca Eckersley
George Washington University
December 31, 2011
One month before her death

Becca and Jack returned from Green Bay the day after Christmas. The days passed in Green Bay without the big reveal they both planned. Becca was introduced as his girl-friend, not his wife, and her pregnancy remained a secret. The idea of their marriage and a baby only a few months away had become such a giant cover-up that it was getting too big to unload. Becca was nervous about telling Jack's parents such intimate details about herself the first time she met them and before her own mother knew. Christmas came and went, and their families were no closer to knowing the truth about them.

More than a week had passed since her encounter with Thom Jorgensen, and Becca still held such mixed emotions that she never told Jack about it. That she spent an hour consoled by Richard Walker was also something she left out of the description of her celebratory trip to O'Reilly's. Becca decided to put Thom and Richard out of her mind as she headed to Summit Lake to spend five quiet days with Jack before he started his travels again the day after New Year's. The primaries kicked off with the Iowa caucus in January and could go on intensely until summer before a nominee was determined, although no one really thought Milt Ward would have to fight long after Super Tuesday in March before he was crowned the presidential nominee. Even with a quick wrap of the primaries, Jack would still be on the road for over a month. And though not in play, the other states would need to be visited, rallies attended, and speeches given. Jack would have an occasional night or two when he was not traveling, but a straight week together was something Jack and Becca would not see for some time.

Becca's parents handed over the keys to the stilt house before they headed to Venice, Florida, for the week. Mr. and Mrs. Eckersley's original plans to ski in Summit Lake over New Year's were trumped by a client who needed immediate attention down in Florida.

The days in Summit Lake between Christmas and New Year's were a quiet time for Becca. She and Jack ventured out only for dinner or a movie before scurrying back home to light a fire and climb under thick cotton blankets on the couch. There had been heavy snow over Christmas, and the sidewalks and streets were a mess of salt and slush. The mountains looked inviting with so much white powder covering them, and Becca told Jack stories about how great the skiing was. In no condition to ski, Becca was happy to stash her textbooks for a couple of weeks, content to sit and relax while Jack typed on his computer and asked her to proof his work.

On New Year's Eve they had a late lunch in town and beat the crowds. They rented three movies and spent the night on the couch by the fire. At five to midnight, they turned on the countdown in Times Square and watched as a million people froze in the streets of New York. Jack was on his side on the couch with Becca on her back, her head under his left arm. He kissed her at New Year's as "Auld Lang Syne" played in the background.

"I want you to know that even though none of this was planned, I only think of it as a fast-forward," Jack said. "I was going to marry you someday, and we were going to have kids someday, too. It's just all happening sooner than we expected. But I don't have any regrets. I'm excited for us to be parents this year, and I'm proud to be your husband."

"Well, shucks," Becca said, tears spilling from the corner of her eyes. "You sure know how to make a knocked-up girl feel special."

"I love you," he said.

"I know you do. And I'm going to miss you like crazy while you're gone."

"It's just until the middle of February, and I'll be home sporadically in between. For a night or two, but I'll be home."

"Tell me the truth, okay?"

"Sure."

"Do you think a baby is going to mess up your career?"

"How will our baby mess up my career?"

"Your boss will be running for president and he'll need you by his side. What if this really happens, Jack? What if Milt Ward wins the election in a year from now? We've both heard the horror stories of what a president's staff goes through. The hours they work make first-year associates in New York look like slackers."

"So I work long hours. If I need time off, I'll ask for it."

"Come on, Jack. Everyone will want more time with their family, but you'll have an infant and you'll be working twenty hours a day."

"I don't think it'll be that bad."

"Still. What are you going to do? You'll have to see the baby. And I'll need some help. I can't do it all by myself."

"I'll help."

"But will that cause stress at your job?"

"Maybe. I don't know yet. But I'm going to see my kid."

"That's what I mean. What if taking time for your family causes you to lose your place with Milt's team."

"He's not like that. Milt's a family man, he'll understand."

"And if he doesn't?"

"I'll figure it out."

Becca took a deep breath. "I know this job is your dream. I don't want to be the one to spoil it."

"You're not spoiling anything. You're part of my dream. Now listen, it's a new year and we've got tons to look forward to."

He kissed her. They watched New York celebrate for a while, then returned to their movie. They both fell asleep on the couch. It was a new year.

Chapter 32

Kelsey Castle
Summit Lake
March 15, 2012
Day 11

"This town is buzzing with state police," Rae said as she walked through the kitchen. She went to the front of the apartment and looked down on Maple Street. "I mean, they're all over the place. There's another one parked across the street."

"This is all for me?" Kelsey asked.

"And your doctor friend."

"What did Detective Madison tell you downstairs?"

"Not much. I asked why he was looking for you and he told me it was a police matter. Asked if I knew Dr. Ambrose."

"What did you say?"

"No, because I don't technically know him, I only know about him. So I figured I wasn't really lying to a cop, right?" Rae thought for a moment. "Where's your car?"

"At the Winchester."

"I'm sure they've found it by now, so they know you're still in town. Can't walk off this mountain. And there are only so many places to hide in this little town."

Kelsey opened her palms. "I'm writing a magazine article, what the hell?" She joined Rae at the front window and through the curtains watched the activity below. Uniformed officers walked along Maple Street, in and out of establishments. "They should have been this concerned when Becca was killed. Maybe they'd have figured things out by now."

"Did you find the journal, by the way?"

Kelsey forgot she had Becca's journal in her purse. She nodded. "In Millie's recipe book."

"Figures. Read any of it?"

"Yes, all of it. Last night, before I fell asleep."

"Where? After I dropped Millie off and sucked down a sweet tea in her kitchen—I wanted to make sure you didn't make a mess that she'd call the police about—I came over to the Winchester, but you didn't answer."

"Oh, I went to Peter's place and . . . stayed the night."

"Really?"

"I fell asleep on his couch."

"Anything else going on?"

"I've got police at every corner of this town looking for me and you're concerned about my love life?"

"I'm concerned about everyone's love life. You'd be shocked what people tell me over coffee."

Kelsey just looked at her and shook her head. "Currently, I'm concerned with keeping the two of us out of jail." Kelsey turned her back to Rae and looked out the front window again. "I need to make sure he's okay."

"Call him."

"He didn't answer." She closed the curtains. "How am I going to get out of here?"

"You broke into a building. That doesn't carry a life sentence. Or *any* jail time, I bet."

"So what's all this for?" Kelsey said, gesturing toward the window.

"Becca, for sure. Like you suspected, Becca's father wants the details of her death to emerge on his terms. Not yours. What did you find in the journal?"

"Names of Becca's friends. Including the guy she married. Plus a few other guys who were part of her life."

"How so?"

"It turns out Becca was quite a social butterfly. Maybe a bit of a manipulator of men. It's hard to tell just from journal entries. But she had lots of relationships with lots of men when she was killed."

"I could see why her father wouldn't want that coming out. So what's the plan?"

"There are no last names in the journal, so I've got some fieldwork to do to ID the men who were part of Becca's life. Peter is tracking down Becca's old roommate to see what she knows about Becca and the guy she married. I was going to start looking into the other men in Becca's life." Kelsey looked out the window one last time at the police activity. "I'm not sure I'll have the time to find them all."

"That's BS," Rae said. "You didn't get this far to give up now. We've got two computers here, Internet access, and coffee. It's all we need to track down some frat boys and law students."

Kelsey smiled. She picked up her MacBook and headed to the bedroom with Rae. Rae sat at her computer, Kelsey next to her with her laptop. She put Becca's journal on the desk between them and pulled out her notes. "Three guys. Brad, Richard, Thom. College friend, high school boyfriend, GWU professor."

Rae tapped at her keyboard. "Let's do some creeping. I'll take Brad. You take the professor."

Chapter 33

Becca Eckersley
George Washington University
February 15, 2012
Two days before her death

January in the nation's capital was bitter cold with winds off the Potomac that rattled teeth and sent people scurrying for shelter. The first month of the year also marked the official beginning of the election season, and Milt Ward stormed into Iowa and took the caucus as if it were his birthright. With an incumbent president in office there were no meaningful primaries for the other side, and as January unfolded and Super Tuesday approached, the talking heads pitted the sitting president's ideas against those of Milt Ward. Everyone agreed the showdown in November would be fierce. Ward was on every cable news program, and Jack let Becca know over the phone which speeches he had written for the senator. It was an exciting time.

By the beginning of February, Becca was deluged with keeping up with her classes and managing the end-of-the-day fatigue that came with her pregnancy. She learned to get her work completed by seven or eight at night since she was rarely seeing a minute later. She fell asleep too many times on her couch—with notes around her and her textbook on her chest—to realistically think she could comprehend material during the evening hours. Instead, she packed her books away and climbed into bed each night around 8:30 and was gone to the world.

On the second Tuesday in February, Milt Ward's only serious contender dropped out of the race and ended his campaign. One month before Super Tuesday, Becca watched Milt Ward and his campaign race around the country campaigning for votes. By the end of the night his bid as the nominee for his party was inevitable. It was early and unprecedented. The country buzzed with the news, and the party celebrated as it got behind their candidate. Jack called at just past 10:00 p.m. to tell her the official news. They shared a quick conversation before he was off to prepare an acceptance speech. Jack was writing speeches for a man running for president, he reminded her, and potentially someone who would occupy the White House by the end of the year. It was a historic moment, and they shared it from hundreds of miles away.

The next day, Becca lay on the table of her doctor's office while the technician ran a cold probe over her stomach.

"Strong kid," the male technician said. "Bigger than normal for twenty-three weeks."

"Really?" Becca said. "Is that good or bad?"

"Neither, really," the tech said. "Has a good heart rate, and everything looks perfect. Just a little bigger than usual. Maybe we've got the dates off by a couple of weeks. No big deal."

"A couple of weeks *are* a big deal. I need this baby to hang out in my womb until sometime after May 4th." Becca saw the tech squint his eyes. "I'm in law school and I need to finish finals before this kid makes an appearance."

The technician smiled as he logged information from the ultrasound into her chart. Without looking at her, he said, "If

I were a betting man, I'd say this kid's not gonna wait until the middle of May. But talk to the doctor about it. She'll be right in and should be able to give you a better idea of the date."

An hour later, Becca was bundled in her wool coat with a scarf wrapped around her face as she headed to her car. The doctor had determined all was normal and that the baby was just bigger than usual for twenty-three weeks. Still, she moved Becca's due date up a week based on today's testing and explained the details of inducement if there were no signs of labor by the beginning of May.

Becca fought hard to figure out how she might successfully complete her 1L year with a baby arriving in the middle of finals week. It was time to tell her parents. It was well past the time, really. They waited longer than they should, and with the due date a week earlier it was time to come clean. It was looking more certain that to get through the year, especially with the recent campaign developments and the fact that Jack would be traveling, Becca would need to rely on her mom to get through her first year of school.

She started her car and cranked the heat. She dialed Jack's cell phone and he answered on the first ring.

"What did the doctor say?"

"We have a very healthy baby, and one who will arrive a week earlier than expected."

"Why is that?"

"The baby's totally healthy, just big. It's making Dr. Shepherd rethink the due date, which she now pushed up a week. And even if the baby doesn't want to come out until the due date, she won't let me go that long if the baby continues to grow at this pace. Delivery would be too difficult, and possibly dangerous because I'm small and our baby is big. So I'm having a baby right around finals, Jack. I don't know how we're going to do this."

"Okay," Jack said. "We'll figure it out."

"I've got to tell my parents. I don't know what we're thinking. They're going to find out, so I want to tell them. About the baby and about us being married. Everything. I know you keep saying we should wait, but I don't want to wait anymore."

"You're right," Jack said. "We're idiots for waiting this long."

"What are we doing, Jack? You're traveling all over the country, I'm barely keeping pace this semester, we've got this huge secret sitting on our shoulders, and we haven't even filed our marriage certificate yet."

"Yeah," Jack said. "Sorry. Things are crazy here. But it'll calm down in a week or so."

"I just feel like, I don't know. Is this whole thing real? Nobody knows about us being married or about the baby. It feels wrong. Like we're trying to hide it forever. I know this is going to screw up law school for me, and probably interfere with your job, but we've got to do something. This baby has to start taking precedence instead of being something we keep trying to work around."

Becca listened to Jack breathing through the phone. As he thought things over, she heard him rub his face, which was covered now with heavy scruff from working nonstop.

"Jack! I'm freaking out here."

"Yeah, I'm just thinking. You're right, Becca."

"Listen," she said. "I need to get out of here for a while. I've got a test next week I've barely studied for because I can't stay awake past eight o'clock. I'm going to ask my parents if I can use the stilt house for a long weekend of studying."

"Good idea," Jack said. "Head up to Summit Lake. I'll meet you there on Saturday."

"How?"

"I'll talk to Ward. Tell him I need some time. Simple as

that. He'll understand. And if he doesn't, I'll quit. Either way, I'll meet you this weekend to collect our thoughts. Get things straight between us. Then we'll take a day next week to drive to Greensboro and tell your parents."

"For real this time."

"Absolutely."

"They're going to freak out."

"Probably," Jack said. "They have a right to freak out— we're idiots. But guess what? They'll get over it because in a few months they'll have a grandkid they're going to love, and after a while we'll all get over how we handled this. Let me talk to Ward and I'll call you back. Don't tell your parents anything without me."

"Okay."

"Promise me," Jack said.

Silence.

"Promise me you won't say anything to your parents until we see each other."

"I promise," Becca finally said. "I won't talk to my parents."

"I love you."

"Me too," Becca said.

She clicked her phone off and held it to her forehead, thinking of sitting in her parents' living room and telling them she had run off and gotten married and they would soon be grandparents and she might not finish law school. She shook her head and wiped the tears from her eyes. After her car warmed up, she drove to her apartment in Foggy Bottom. With an oversized purse on her shoulder and a bag of Baked Ruffles in her hand, she shuffled from her car. It was almost 6:00 p.m. and the cold winter days pulled darkness over the city before five each night. She jogged through the parking lot under the yellow glow of halogen while a wicked wind worked to prevent her progress. She struggled with the key as her frozen fingers stabbed at the lock. The frantic nature in which she ran from her car and now grappled with the deadbolt put a sense of urgency and fear into her. There was something else, too—an eerie feeling of another's presence. All of this transcended onto her in the seconds it took to fight the door open, which she finally did, and then quickly slammed it behind her, reengaging the deadbolt as soon as the door hit the frame.

She dropped her purse on the kitchen floor and threw the Ruffles on the table, running her hand over her frozen cheeks and wiping away the tears the cold night brought to her eyes. Her hands were shaking from the panic of wrestling her apartment door open.

"You're losing it," Becca said out loud.

She looked through the peephole and into the dark evening. She needed Jack. That was all. She needed his rational thinking to get her past her fear of attempting to make it through finals with an infant, and his reassuring nature that was able to conquer any obstacle. She found solace in the idea that they would spend the weekend together.

Two hours before fatigue would steal her motivation to do anything but lay in bed, she needed to read three chapters of ConLaw and get caught up on Torts. She jumped in the shower to rejuvenate and warm herself. The panic that overcame her earlier faded as the hot water flowed over her body.

Alone in the bathroom, her eyes closed and the roar of the shower filling her ears, she never heard the front door as the knob was tried from the outside. The deadbolt held and after three attempts, the door went quiet.

Chapter 34

Kelsey Castle
Summit Lake
March 15, 2012
Day 11

"Here," Kelsey said. "Got it!" She was tapping the Mac-Book with efficiency, staring at the screen.

"Let me hear it," Rae said. She, too, was staring at her computer, working hard.

"Brad Reynolds. Lives in Maryland. At least his parents do. Father is a big league tort guy. Attended GWU, part of Becca's freshman year enrollment. But out of all the Brads we've looked at, this is most likely the one mentioned in the journal. I found an internship program Becca was part of her sophomore year. Brad Reynolds participated in the same program. He also lived in the same coed dorm as Becca freshman year. No Facebook presence, but this has to be him."

"Where is he now?" Rae asked.

"No idea. But I have an address and phone number in Maryland. I'll start there."

"Okay," Rae said. "I've got two for you. The professor is Thom Jorgensen. Former GWU professor of logic and critical thinking. Becca took his course sophomore year, got an A. Now he's on staff at Cornell University. Made the change during Becca's senior year. Phone number is no problem. We can reach him through the university."

"Easy," Kelsey said.

"There's a catch, though," Rae said.

"What's that?"

"You say he and Becca had a relationship?"

"Of some sort. He's mentioned in her journal quite a bit. More in the earlier entries. Why?"

"Professor Jorgensen is married with two kids. So if he was involved with Becca . . ."

Kelsey stared at Rae, then scribbled on her notepad. "Okay. What else?"

"High school boyfriend, I'm almost sure, is Richard Walker. He went to Northwest Guilford High, same age as Becca. Harvard undergrad and now Harvard Law. Which, obviously, you said Becca mentioned in her journal. An old Facebook posting shows him at the prom with Becca. He's our man."

"Contact info?" Kelsey asked.

Rae went back to the computer. "Shouldn't be hard. We can get his phone number at Harvard. I'll look."

Kelsey grabbed the phone. "I'll start with Brad Reynolds." Kelsey dialed the Reynoldses' home number in Maryland and held the phone to her ear.

"Check this out," Rae said, still working the keyboard. "Richard Walker's family owns a vacation home right here in the foothills."

Kelsey momentarily dropped the phone from her ear, eyes squinted. "Here? The foothills of Summit Lake?"

"Yep," Rae said with a smile. "So we might not have to go far to find him. Plus . . ."

"It puts him in the vicinity the night Becca died."

"Possibly."

A faint voice captured Kelsey's attention, and she realized someone had answered the phone at the Reynolds household. She quickly put the phone back to her ear.

"Hello, Mr. Reynolds? Yes, my name is Kelsey Castle. I'm a reporter for *Events* magazine, writing a story about Becca Eckersley. She was murdered a couple weeks back . . . uh-huh . . . well, I know she attended school with your son, Brad, and I was hoping to talk with him to get some information about Becca."

There was silence for several seconds as Kelsey listened to Mr. Reynolds. "Oh," Kelsey finally said, looking at Rae. "I'm sorry to hear that."

PART IV

THREE KNOCKS

Chapter 35

Becca Eckersley
Summit Lake
February 17, 2012
The day of her death

She skipped her Friday morning class and didn't worry about her afternoon study session. With the car packed the night before with anything that wouldn't freeze, Becca was on the road by 8:00 a.m. It was a five-hour ride to the mountains and another hour or so to Summit Lake. She talked to Jack before she left. Milt Ward offered Jack all the time he needed, and Jack was arranging a flight for Saturday morning that would get him there by late afternoon. He settled on four days off, which were closely plotted to include two days in Summit Lake—Saturday and Sunday—one day in Greensboro for the long overdue talk with Becca's parents, and one day to get back to DC before he hit the road again with Senator Ward. That was the plan he offered, and Becca hungrily ate it up.

She called her parents on the way up to let them know her progress and promised to call again when she arrived. With the extra bathroom stops, the trip took seven hours. It was almost 3:00 p.m. when she pulled into the small drive at the front of the stilt house. She dragged her bag from the trunk and dumped it in the bedroom, then ran out and brought in the groceries she bought the night before. Once she settled in the house and had the thermostat adjusted to a comfortable level, she pulled on her heavy coat, threw her backpack over her shoulder, and headed to one of her favorite spots. By the time she came back, the house would be warm and cozy.

She set the alarm and locked the door behind her, then headed into town. It was a two-block walk to Millie's Coffee House. Livvy Houston was a family friend, and over the years Becca grew to love the café, the coffee, and especially the sweet tea—a secret recipe Livvy said was passed down from her mother. It was Friday afternoon and the café was mostly empty when Becca found a table by the window, not too far from the warmth of the fireplace. Though a latte would keep her alert, she had been off caffeine for four months and instead settled on a sweet tea, which she was sure had enough sugar to compete with the coffee. Pulling out her textbook and notes, it was not half an hour before Becca was lost in ConLaw and the intricacies of various Supreme Court rulings. The more she read, the more notes she produced. She pulled other research materials from her bag and soon the little table at Millie's was a cluttered mess. Even the chair next to her contained dog-eared notes and a soft-back research book.

Becca logged two hours and a couple of sweet teas, along with multiple trips to the bathroom, before she leaned back in her chair and stretched. She needed a break. From her purse she produced a small, hardcover journal. She wasn't always a diary girl. The thoughts and desires and fears that found the pages of her journal were private things shared with no one. Not even Gail, and certainly not published on the journal blogs she often read. Becca hadn't chronicled her entire life, like many of the girls who took to the Internet to share their entries, but she was very consistent since freshman year. She made daily entries, sometimes every other day. Some were long descriptions of her life and feelings, others short quips about love and the goings-on of a college student. This afternoon at Millie's Coffee House, she chronicled the last days of her life—her recent trip to the doctor, her fears of an early delivery, and the way Jack had talked her through and calmed her down—the way he always did. She wrote about her impromptu trip to Summit Lake and of the weekend she hoped to spend with the man she loved. She filled two pages before Livvy Houston appeared from the back of the cafe.

"Hello, Becca," Livvy said.

Becca looked up from her journal with a large smile. She stood and hugged her old babysitter.

"What are you doing up here?" Livvy asked as she sat down at the table across from Becca.

"Studying, unfortunately." Becca sat also. "I have a big test next week and needed to get away to make sure I absorbed it all."

Nervous that Livvy would ask about her journal, Becca slipped it under the table and onto the empty chair next to her.

"Are your parents with you?"

"No, my dad starts a trial next week so he's been super busy. They said I could have the house to myself."

"So you have a great big, quiet house to study in, and you're here?"

Becca smiled. "I love this place. It's perfect for studying. But I'm about to head back to the house, I'm almost done."

"How's school going?"

"Good." Becca nodded. "You know, it's law school. Some things are interesting, some things are terribly boring."

Livvy pointed to the papers on the table. "This?"

Becca shrugged. "Constitutional Law? It's okay, not my favorite. I guess that's why I'm up here. Making sure I get it straight."

"I talked to your mother a week back and she said you're dating a bright and polite young man. Works for a senator."

Becca smiled. Her mom and Livvy were good friends and Becca remembered spending many hours at the Houston household while growing up. Becca and Jenny Houston were one grade apart and close friends during grade school. But it was with Livvy that Becca always felt closest. The two had a special relationship, and Becca supposed it started with the day—as a ten-year-old—she wet her pants while at the zoo with the Houston family. The ride was almost an hour and by the time she told Livvy of the emergency that was brewing, there was not enough time to get to the bathroom. A potentially mortifying experience was handled with such swiftness by Livvy—who brought Becca to the parking lot and changed her into an extra pair of jeans she had in the minivan, then concealed the evidence until it was washed and folded the next day—that not only did none of the kids find out, but Becca never had to tell her parents.

Small cover-ups continued through her childhood and into adolescence. A broken lamppost was fixed without alerting the Eckersleys, trash cans run over when Becca was first conquering the steep angle of her driveway were replaced overnight, empty beer cans found in Jenny Houston's bedroom the night after Becca slept over were properly confronted but never snitched to her parents. So it was not odd, after thirty minutes of talking with Livvy, that Becca felt comfortable dishing a few secrets about Jack. Hell, all the secrets of her life sat silently in the journal next to her, and Becca was tempted to open to page one and start reading. She hungered to tell someone about the man she loved, about her marriage, and about the baby growing in her womb. Becca wanted to spill her secrets—so securely kept over the past year that she sometimes wondered if they were real. Wanted to open her mouth and let them all flow from her vocal cords and lighten the anchor they were on her life.

"It sounds serious, you and this young man," Livvy said.

"It is serious. We're not just dating, you know?"

Livvy paused. "Not really. What do you mean? You two are exclusive?"

Becca shook her head. "More than that."

Livvy's eyes grew wide. "Becca Eckersley, are you engaged?"

Becca smiled, swallowed hard, and shook her head.

"Then what? You two are about to get engaged?"

Becca took a deep breath and slowly exhaled. "Remember when I peed my pants at the zoo when I was a kid?"

Livvy thought for a second, then nodded.

"Remember how you kept that a secret?"

Another nod.

"This is the same thing, okay?" Becca said. "You can't tell anybody."

"What is it?"

Another deep breath. "I'm married."

"Well, Rebecca Alice Eckersley! Your mother didn't mention a word about it when I talked to her."

Becca took on a sheepish grin. "That's 'cause she doesn't know yet."

Chapter 36

Peter Ambrose
Summit Lake
March 15, 2012
Day 11

After breakfast with Kelsey, Peter headed to the hospital. He dropped his wallet and phone onto the top shelf of his locker and showered in the staff locker room. Donning blue scrubs and a long coat twenty minutes later, he attached his hospital ID to his breast pocket and rounded on patients for an hour and a half. An elderly man was having difficulty with a drainage tube Peter had placed after removing the man's gallbladder two days prior. It took Peter another hour to prep the patient and replace the failing stent. By the time he finished, it was close to 3:00 p.m.

He entered his office and sat behind his desk. This was not his forte, tracking people down. He pulled out the information he had on Becca Eckersley's old roommate and got to work. After an hour of searching he realized locating someone with only their first name was harder than he imagined. It was past 4:00 p.m. when he discovered a first-year Stanford law student named Gail Moss. Some more digging confirmed she attended George Washington University and roomed with Becca Eckersley freshman year. A solid hit.

Peter wrote down three phone numbers he found from a search site online before he noticed the commotion in the hallway. Sticking the phone numbers in the breast pocket of his scrubs, he walked to the doorway of his office and saw uniformed police officers at the nurses' station. He left his office and slipped back into the staff locker room. From his locker he grabbed his wallet and phone, noticing several missed calls and texts from Kelsey. A partial text was displayed. Peter caught only a sentence of it.

Entire police force looking for us. Detective Madison was

Before he could swipe his phone and read the full text, the locker room door slowly swung open. In the mirror, Peter saw an officer walk through the door. Ducking below the row of lockers, he hurried into the shower area without being noticed. Entering a shower stall, Peter pulled the curtain closed and started the water, adjusting the showerhead away from him. He stood close to the wall and tried not to get soaked.

A full minute passed.

"Dr. Ambrose?" the officer called into the showers with an authoritative voice.

Peter ducked down a bit. "No, Dr. Ledger," he yelled over the rush of water. "Ambrose is in the ER. Is there a problem with a patient?"

"No, Doc. No problems."

Peter waited, the minutes dragging by, until he finally peeked around the shower curtain. When he was sure he was alone, he walked out of the stall with the shower still running. In the back of the locker room was a service elevator. He climbed in and pressed the button for the basement. The elevator dropped into the bowels of the hospital and Peter pulled open the accordion-like metal grate when he landed. He walked into a storage area filled with cleaning supplies stacked on tall shelves. Mops and buckets and electric floor polishers lined the walls, as did five-gallon buckets filled with chemicals meant to rid the place of the many diseases that circulate and percolate and otherwise infest hospitals.

Past the supply room, Peter entered the laundry area. Industrial washers and dryers rumbled with bedsheets and blankets. Towels and linens were stacked tall on large carts that employees pushed around. He caught more than one glance from the hospital employees who likely wondered what a physician, dressed in scrubs and a long coat trailing him like a cape, was doing in the basement.

When Peter made it through the laundry room, he found himself in the delivery bays. Three large garage doors were pulled open. The trailer of a semitruck filled one bay. A forklift hummed as it lifted crated supplies from inside the trailer. At the second bay, a big rig was just arriving and backing into the spot, the *beep beep beep* filling Peter's ears as the truck was set in reverse. The third bay was open, and Peter walked to the edge and jumped down to the pavement. He pulled off his coat and dumped it, along with his hospital ID, into a garbage can. Then he walked from the back of the hospital and off campus. When he reached the lake, he headed south toward town. Far enough away now, he stole a glance back. The front of the hospital was filled with police cars parked at odd angles and lights flashing. A similar scene was present in front of the ER entrance.

He knew he wouldn't get far in blue surgical scrubs, and he didn't consider going home. Instead, he headed into town. There, too, he noticed heavy police presence. He took back streets and deserted alleys until he found a lakefront pub. He ducked in and found a booth in the corner. There were only two people in the establishment, both bellied up to the bar and not at all interested in Dr. Peter Ambrose.

He ordered a Coke from the waitress and pulled out his phone. There were four text messages from Kelsey. The first warned that police would likely pay him a visit at his house or the hospital. The second told him she was holed up in Rae's apartment writing a draft of the Eckersley article to send to her editor. The third was a request for a call back to let her know he was okay. And the final text told him that she and Rae had made a break in the case and were heading into the foothills to talk to one of the men from Becca's journal, whose family owned a cabin there.

Peter dialed Kelsey's number, but the phone went straight to voice mail. The waitress delivered his soda and Peter declined the menu she offered. He looked around the empty pub, keeping his eye on the front door. Finally, he pulled Gail Moss's contact info from his breast pocket. The first two numbers were misses, but on the third call he convinced a pleasant young lady to connect him to Gail's dorm room.

She answered on the third ring.

"Hi. Is this Gail Moss?"

"Yes, who's this?"

"Hi, Gail. My name is Peter Ambrose. I'm a physician in Summit Lake and I'm working on Becca Eckersley's case."

"Are you with the police?"

"No, not exactly. But I'm trying to help them figure out what exactly happened that night. To Becca. I was hoping to ask you a few questions."

"No one's talked to me yet. The police, I mean. They haven't asked me any questions."

"Really? I'm sure they will soon. Things, as you can imagine, are still a little hectic up here. Gail, you knew Becca well, correct? You were roommates?"

"Yes, we were best friends."

"I see. Do you know who Becca was dating?"

"Sure. Jack Covington."

Peter scribbled down the name. "Did you know Jack?"

"Of course, we all went to school together. We were close friends."

Peter collected his thoughts. He originally imagined having more time for this conversation. "Gail, do you know anything about Becca and Jack getting married?"

"Married? No, Becca wasn't married. I mean, I'm sure someday they would have gotten married. They were really in love. But, no, she and Jack weren't married."

A pause. "Do you know anything about Becca being pregnant?"

"What? No, no. You've got things mixed up, sir. Becca wasn't married, and she sure wasn't pregnant. That's ridiculous."

"Did Becca and Jack have any problems?"

"Like what?"

"Like, was their relationship volatile or strained in any way?"

"No, they were totally in love. What are you getting at?"

"I know this will be confusing to hear, but there is a suspicion that Jack might have had something to do with Becca's death."

"Jack? No, sir. You're on the wrong track."

"I know it's hard to hear. You being friends with him and all."

"It's not hard to hear. It's impossible."

"Listen, Gail. There are some things developing here in Summit Lake that point to Jack being a strong suspect in this. There's evidence developing that suggests Becca and Jack married privately. Just before she was killed. And it's been confirmed by one of my colleagues that Becca was pregnant the night she died."

"Dr. Ambrose, I don't know anything about the evidence—

that Becca got married or that she was pregnant. I can only tell you that if those things are true, she never told me. And that would be very shocking. But one thing I'm certain about is that Jack Covington had nothing to do with Becca's death. He certainly didn't kill her."

"Like I said, I know it's hard to hear, but I just need to get an idea—"

"You're not listening to me. It's not hard for me to hear, it's simply not possible."

"No matter how unlikely it seems that Jack—"

"Sir!" Gail said with force. "It's not unlikely. It's *impossible.*"

"If you let me explain, I might be able to change your mind."

"You'll never change my mind."

"Why is that?"

"Because Jack died the same day Becca did."

Chapter 37

Becca Eckersley
Summit Lake
February 17, 2012
The night of her death

"Thanks a lot for this, Milt," Jack said as he settled into the small jet. It sat fourteen passengers, was owned by Milt Ward Industries, and was scheduled to leave Denver, Colorado, at two in the afternoon and arrive in DC three hours later. From there, Jack would drive to Summit Lake and surprise Becca, who didn't expect him until the following evening. If things went well, he figured he would pull into Summit Lake about 10:00 p.m.

When Milt Ward heard Jack's predicament, he told Jack to cancel his commercial flight for Saturday afternoon and jump on with the senator, who was heading back to DC Friday afternoon and was happy to help Jack out.

"It's no problem," Ward said. "Family always comes first. Before work. Before a campaign. Before everything. Understand?"

"Yes, sir."

Jack pulled out his laptop and tweaked a speech the senator was giving over the weekend to a group of coal miners. Thirty minutes after takeoff, the small jet began to rumble with turbulence. Jack had never been on a plane until his first trip to George Washington University, but since joining Milt Ward's campaign he logged many hours in the air. The turbulence went unnoticed until it grew strong enough to rattle his laptop and spill his soda. He looked around the small plane and noticed a few other concerned faces and fake smiles. A sudden dip of a hundred feet sent screams through the cabin. Jack slapped his computer closed and secured it next to him, quickly folding the tray table closed and forgetting about the spilled soda.

Another deep dip and more screams. Then a thud, like the jet hit something solid. The turbulence continued. One more dive and the oxygen masks fell from the ceiling and dangled in erratic fashion around the cabin. Jack gripped the elbow rests while a strange cold filled the cabin.

Then another dip. Unlike the others. This was a continuous dive. One that never ended, until four minutes later when the small jet crashed in a prairie outside Omaha, Nebraska. There were no survivors.

Thirty minutes after Becca left Millie's Coffee House, with hair still warm from the hair dryer and wearing cozy sweatpants and heavy wool socks, she sat at the kitchen island of the stilt house. She felt light and free, the heavy burden she carried for so long was finally lifted from her shoulders when she told Livvy Houston about her and Jack's marriage. To get it out and off her chest, to simply tell someone—even if it was only her fifty-year-old former babysitter whom she talked with twice a year—was a relief. Becca considered it practice for when she and Jack would soon have a similar discussion with her parents.

Before diving back into ConLaw, Becca pulled the ultrasound photographs from her purse. There were eight pictures, black and white, spaced one on top of the other on a long piece of paper the technician printed during her last appointment. Becca looked at them now, studying the small baby growing in her womb. The tech showed her what she was looking at, and now Becca recognized the baby's hands and feet. She smiled when she thought of herself as a mother; then she laughed out loud. What a crazy road.

Folding the photos, she stuck them in a white, business-size envelope. Then she pulled out a clean sheet of paper and laid it in front of her. She didn't know where the inspiration came from, or what prompted her to write a letter to her unborn child, but somewhere in her heart Becca wanted to communicate with the child growing in her womb. She wrote for ten minutes before she signed the bottom with her initials, folded it in thirds, and slid the letter into the envelope along with the ultrasound photos. She wrote *To My Daughter* across the front and placed the envelope on the corner of the kitchen island. She might have tucked the envelope into a private place had the thought come to her, maybe slipping it into the back pocket of her journal. But Becca was unaware—perhaps intoxicated by the freedom from her conversation with Livvy Houston—that she had left her journal on the chair at Millie's Coffee House.

Chapter 38

Kelsey Castle
Summit Lake
March 15, 2012
Day 11

They walked down the back stairs to the alley behind the café.

"Wait here," Rae told her. "Under the stairs so nobody sees you. I'll get my car."

Kelsey hid in the shadows of the stairs to Rae's apartment. Things had broken for them, and heading into the foothills to interview one of Becca's friends who might provide insight into Becca and her relationship with Jack was the best lead she had. That this young man might have been in Summit Lake the night of the murder was also an intriguing angle. Kelsey had to chase it. Getting out of town was not a bad idea either.

As she took cover, with tiger stripes of late-afternoon sunlight finding their way through the deck stairs and painting her face, an uneasiness set in. It felt like a lifetime since she decided to come to Summit Lake. In reality, it had only been two weeks since she fled Miami and her house and the office and the demons that hid along her once-safe running path where this whole thing started. Commander Ferguson was gone, fired because he offered her information about an unsolved murder in his small town. Peter was unreachable and surely in a world of trouble for helping her. The town was teeming with police, and her hopes of escaping Summit Lake were placed in the hands of a twenty-year-old girl she met a week and a half ago. If there was a picture of losing control, this was it.

A car pulled around the corner and into the alley. The passenger side door swung open and Rae leaned over the seats. "Get in."

Kelsey quickly climbed in, and they drove down the alley and turned right when they reached the end.

"Stay down," Rae said. "They're on every corner. Maple Street is a traffic jam of police, this is crazy."

"Do you know where you're going? How to get out to this house?"

"She called it a cabin. I know the area, so I'll get us in the vicinity. She left directions, so when we're close I'll have you navigate."

With Kelsey slouched in the passenger seat, Rae drove through town and turned to avoid the congested main drag where squad cars lined the streets. The Winchester was their hub, with police milling around the entrance and on the street out front. Rae looked in her rearview when they got to the edge of town. She saw the WELCOME TO SUMMIT LAKE sign behind her, and a few minutes later Kelsey sat up. Thirty minutes after that, they entered the foothills to chase their lead.

Chapter 39

Becca Eckersley
Summit Lake
February 17, 2012
The night of her death

Becca stared at the letter to her daughter a moment longer, then opened her textbook and got back to work. Had she not been secluded in the mountains with the television off, Becca would have seen the news story that percolated across the country over the last few hours. Had she decided to take a break from studying and distract herself by clicking the browser on her laptop, she would surely have seen the story that was hot across the Internet—a small jet owned by Senator Milt Ward had crashed not long after takeoff from Denver. Emergency crews were on-site, as were federal investigators, but looking at the fiery wreckage there were certainly no survivors. Twelve members of the senator's campaign were on-board.

Instead, though, she was holed up in her parents' stilt house in the Blue Ridge Mountains, reading for an exam and waiting for the man she loved to arrive the following day. Organizing herself at the kitchen island, she picked up where she left off at Millie's Coffee House. Her iPod played subtle tunes, too low for her to catch the lyrics but just enough to erase the still of the house.

A half hour into studying, a noise outside the mudroom door overwhelmed the music. She stopped to listen. Too vague to identify, the noise held the ring of keys rattling, or maybe the door vibrating in the lake breeze. She turned the music down and listened more closely. Only silence followed. She clicked her iPod back on and returned to her textbook. It was twenty minutes later when three loud knocks came from the mudroom door.

Startled, she jumped off the kitchen stool. She knew Jack was trying to get an earlier flight, and there was a remote chance Milt Ward would invite him to take a spot on his private jet. If he could make it happen, Becca knew it was possible that Jack could arrive tonight to surprise her. She didn't expect it, though. Wouldn't allow her mind to venture to the thought of sleeping in his arms tonight, since lying alone in the giant king bed would become a disappointment if Jack couldn't get in until tomorrow.

But now, the three knocks on the door burst open the dam she had used to stymie her emotions. Jack managed to pull it off. He came a day early to spend time with her. To plan their conversation with her parents. To comfort her and love her and hold her in his arms and tell her it would all work out. Becca ran to the door, feeling foolish for worrying that Jack's job was beginning to overshadow their relationship. Jogging through the mudroom, a giddy feeling of anticipation filled her chest.

Chapter 40

Kelsey Castle
Summit Lake
March 15, 2012
Day 11

It was approaching evening as they drove into the foothills, with a dusky blue sky settling over the mountains and casting a teal shade to the narrow road they were following.

"Here's the fork she was talking about," Rae said.

"Okay," Kelsey said. A map was unfolded on her lap and her finger was marking their location. "Stay to the right."

Rae maneuvered her car along the gravel road. The bush was thick on either side of them, with barely any clearance between the just-budded leaves and the car's windows. They drove more slowly now that the paved road was gone and gravel crunched under their tires. After fifteen minutes, they came to the final T.

"Play it again," Rae said. "Make sure we're going the right way."

Kelsey pulled out her cell phone and replayed the message. On it was a female's voice that gave them directions to the cabin they were looking for: "Turn left at the final T and you'll run into it in ten minutes."

Rae swung the wheel to the left and a few minutes later they saw an isolated cabin in the distance. They slowed when they pulled to the front of the property.

"Who lives out here?" Kelsey asked.

"No one," Rae said. "These are hunting cabins. No electricity, just propane generators and outhouses." She stopped at the front of the cabin and put the car in park. "Well? Now what?"

Kelsey opened the passenger side door. "Now we go talk to him. See what he knows about Becca. And if he can give us any insight into who she married."

Chapter 41

Becca Eckersley
Summit Lake
February 17, 2012
The night of her death

Becca headed to the mudroom door, a smile coming to her face. She flicked on the outside light and pulled the curtains to the side. What she saw confused her. She looked more closely, squinted her eyes, and then smiled again, laughing.

"Oh. My. God!"

Brad Reynolds stood on the landing outside the door. He had a heavy wool cap pulled to his eyebrows and his bearded face offered a white fog of vapor into the cold night. She barely recognized him.

Becca wondered many times over the past several months if she'd ever see her old friend again. The last image she had of him was when he was hanging from the rafters of Jack's apartment. That night, Jack rushed in to lift Brad by the waist and take the pressure off his neck after a full minute without oxygen. It took another minute to wrestle the noose free, and when the paramedics arrived Brad was conscious and talking. Terribly emotional about his failed suicide attempt, he spent the night in the hospital until his parents took him home the next morning. Becca tried several times to contact him, but Brad was well-buffered by his mother and father, who were not subtle about blaming Becca and Jack for what happened to their son.

So shocked and excited to see him now, Becca tapped the alarm code and waited for the red light to turn green, then turned the deadbolt, unlatched the chain, and finally pulled open the door. Brad slipped in immediately. He had changed since she saw him last, almost one year ago. His hair was long and on the greasy side, which was odd since he always kept it short and manicured and still with gel. And he wore a beard that was thick and bushy, like a nonconformist college student so similar to everyone else that the hope of a beard and long hair might make him stand out.

"What are you doing here?" Becca said. She wrapped her arms around him.

Brad held her tight. "I came to see you," he said.

She stood back from him, keeping her hands on his shoulders. "You look . . . good, but different." Becca smiled. "You've gone backwoods on me." Brad's face was stoic. "So what've you been up to?" she asked. "You know I tried to reach you a bunch of times? Your mom kind of told me to . . . you know, back off until you were ready to talk."

"Yeah," Brad said, staring over her head with lost eyes. "She told me you called. I was just upset and embarrassed and . . . just didn't want to talk to anyone."

"I was thinking of calling you again, but I didn't want to push. Here, come in out of the cold."

He walked farther into the mudroom and she closed the door.

"Come into the kitchen," Becca said. "I heard through the grapevine that GW said you could finish your last semester."

Brad shook his head. "Nah, I'm done with school."

Becca raised her eyebrows. "Well, give it some time. You might change your mind." They were both in the kitchen now, the iPod barely audible in the background. "I can't believe you're here. This is crazy. What are you doing up here? I mean, how did you know I was here?"

"I've been staying at my dad's hunting cabin, I don't know, for like a year now."

Becca paused. "In the foothills?"

"Yeah, needed to get away."

"Really? For the entire year? There's no electricity out there, right?"

"No, there is. Propane generator."

"This is the cabin where your dad hosted that attorney convention? My dad went a couple of years ago?"

"Yeah, that's the one. The old man canceled the convention this year. Didn't want to make me leave, I guess. Probably thought I'd move back in with him." He let out an awkward laugh.

Becca smiled and stared at her old friend, so different from what she remembered. "Sometimes it's good to get away."

There was a long pause as they both stood in the kitchen of the stilt house.

"Well," Becca said. "Come on in, stranger. Let's get caught up on our lives."

Chapter 42

Peter sat in the dark pub and listened to Gail Moss tell her story. He knew, of course, about Senator Ward's plane crash. In the middle of the presidential primary race, it was the biggest news story around. That Becca's husband was on the plane was a development that destroyed Kelsey's theory about what happened that night.

"And I would never tell you this," Gail said over the phone. "But under the circumstances, I think it's important."

Peter cleared his throat. "What's that?"

"Becca liked a lot of attention. From guys, I mean."

"Yeah? How so?"

"Don't get me wrong. I loved her. She was my best friend. But she sort of had this character flaw she wasn't aware of. At least she always seemed oblivious to it."

"To what?"

"The way she led guys on. She was just one of those girls who had a lot of boyfriends. I mean, friends who were boys.

Way more than she had girlfriends. And, you know, guys hang around girls when they like them. Girls are different. They can see a guy as just a friend. But guys, you know. They always want more."

"And why do you think this is important?"

"Because there was one guy who had a really serious relationship with Becca, and she sort of broke his heart. Not on purpose. Like I said, she didn't really know she was doing anything wrong. And I'm not saying she did—"

"Gail," Peter said. "Who are you talking about? Whose heart did she break?"

"One of our friends from college. His name is Brad Reynolds. After Becca and Jack got together, he sort of freaked out. Tried to kill himself, then dropped out of school and fell off the grid. I heard he was living in his father's hunting cabin in the mountains."

"Where?"

"There. In Summit Lake. Or, you know, the foothills. Way out. Like with nothing around. He told me once that it was like an hour from Becca's place. And I just think it would make sense for the police to at least talk to him. I'm not saying he had anything—"

"I'll call you back."

Peter ended the call and scrolled through Kelsey's texts.

Heading into the foothills to talk to one of Becca's friends.

He scrambled with the keypad and tried Kelsey again, but her phone went straight to voice mail. He knew she was already too far into the mountains for cell reception. Peter pulled out his wallet and ripped through it until he found the business card. Then he dialed the number and hoped for someone to pick up.

Chapter 43

Becca Eckersley
Summit Lake
February 17, 2012
The night of her death

Becca stood in her kitchen with Brad in front of her. "So what's going on with your dad? You guys on any better terms?"

Brad closed his eyes and shook his head. Becca could tell he was about to cry.

"What's wrong?" She moved closer to him and placed her hand on his cheek, feeling the thick, coarse beard that covered his face.

Brad took her by the wrist and pressed her hand harder to his cheek. Keeping his eyes closed, he asked, "You and Jack still together?"

Becca nodded her head slowly. "Yeah."

Brad opened his eyes and stared at her. "So, I've just gotta know, because it's been killing me. Was there ever a chance for you and me?"

Becca slowly pulled her hand away from his face. "Brad, I'm really sorry for what happened. I'm still upset that I kept my relationship with Jack a secret for so long. A lot happened our senior year. Things that changed all our lives forever. If I could go back and undo some of it, I would. But the thing is, I'm not sure I'd change the relationship I had with you. You were one of my best friends. I never knew you considered me anything other than the same."

She looked at him for a long time.

"That's so hard for me to handle," Brad finally said. "I just don't know how I read this whole thing so differently than you. I can't stop thinking that maybe I was just your backup plan."

"My what?"

"Keep me around and interested in case nothing better came along."

"Brad, that's ridiculous—"

"But then I guess Jack was different than me. The mysterious Jack Covington—not really interested in law school, just for the résumé. Never going to practice law, sort of a rebel. Not really our crowd, you know? Gonna be a writer someday."

"Brad, come on. What you're saying isn't close to the truth."

"I just." Brad ran a hand through his disheveled hair, pulling the cap from his head. "Were you really going to get a C in Business Law?"

Becca squinted her eyes. "What?"

"See, I stole that test to help you because you convinced me that without it you'd mess up your transcripts. Screw up your chance at law school. Jack thought you were just playing the situation for attention. And I still don't know. Maybe you were manipulating the whole thing and would have done fine without the test. Just like you manipulated me and our relationship when you used to sleep in my bed all night."

"I'm so sorry I hurt you. It was never my intention."

After another moment, he began to cry.

"What can I do for you?"

"You can get me the girl I fell in love with. The same one who told me she loved me, too." There was a long stretch of silence filled by the subtle rhythm of the iPod. "This is where you broke my heart," Brad finally said. "When I came up here after Christmas? Found you with him."

Becca nodded. "I'm sorry."

Brad looked around the house for an instant, then back to Becca. "Where is he, anyway?"

The question, and the way it was posed, put a scare into Becca's chest. A quick synapse fired in her mind, triggering an awareness that the sound she heard earlier was the handle of the mudroom door being tried from the outside. Her brain registered again and she thought back to a few evenings before in Foggy Bottom when she struggled to unlock her apartment door and panicked that someone was behind her. The same feeling came to her now as Brad stood in her kitchen.

"He's with the senator, right? Running all over the country thinking he's some kind of hotshot. It's so funny, Becca. You can't see what's so obvious." Brad laughed, a frantic, fake wheeze. "It's freezing outside. What if the heat went out tonight? Or the water lines froze? What if you needed him tonight? He's not here for you. I would never do that! Leave you all alone. Or let you come up to the mountains by yourself."

The volume of his voice was elevating with each sentence, and Becca heard a slur in his words.

"I would never leave you alone! Why did he?" His voice softened. "It's because he doesn't appreciate you."

"It's his job, Brad. He—"

"Don't make excuses for him!"

The sudden outburst sent Becca's adrenaline flowing. She still had her cell phone in her hand and was tempted to dial 911, but she wasn't sure what was happening, or if she could call the police on her friend.

"Brad," she said, trying to calm the situation and figure a way to get him out of the house. It was all she wanted. To be alone. To call Jack and tell him to come home. "I'm fine," she said, forcing away tears and smiling to hide her fear. "Okay? I don't need Jack tonight. I don't need anything tonight. Let's talk about this tomorrow." She walked back into the mudroom.

"No, I'm done talking. I've talked to myself about this for a year."

When she turned around he was close to her. His eyes rattled in their sockets. Becca noticed the strange vibration, his irises twitching in fast-forward. She remembered reading somewhere of the way narcotics cause the muscles of the eyes to fire as the central nervous system is altered by their impact.

"You know what?" she said, sliding past him so she was in the doorway of the mudroom, trying to get him to commit to the side door. "Let's have lunch tomorrow and then we can have a long—"

He grabbed her by the shoulders and in a violent surge yanked her through the mudroom and into the kitchen, pinning her to the wall. Startled by the sudden onslaught, Becca dropped her cell phone and put her hands on his wrists.

"Didn't it mean anything to you? When we kissed?" His teeth were gritted. "Or is that just what you do with every guy you meet? Tease him and pull him along until you have a couple to choose from and then run off with one of them."

"Brad, don't hurt me."

"Hurt you? I love you, why don't you understand!" He tightened his grip on her shoulders and pinned her harder against the wall.

"Brad, I'm pregnant! Don't hurt my baby."

A disgusted look came across his face. "That's why you've

been to the doctor so much. So classy that you let him knock you up?"

"Brad. We got married. Privately, we just decided—"

"Yeah, you guys do everything privately."

There was something in his eyes she couldn't name. Some combination of shock and resignation. For an instant his arms went slack, his shoulders drooped, and his grip on her shoulders loosened. But as soon as Becca pushed him away, Brad's eyes went wide with rage, like a bolt of lightning had hit him. Unprepared for his onslaught, she felt her heels skid and drag across the tile floor until he slammed her against the adjacent wall.

Clutching her shoulders, then a fistful of hair at the base of her skull, he wrestled her around the kitchen. Panic wiped her mind blank—all the ideas and images there just seconds before, erased now—allowing her fight-or-flight instincts to take over. As he dragged her violently through the house, Becca fought for her life. Grasping and kicking at anything that might help her, she saw her textbook and laptop scatter to the floor. The envelope containing the letter to her unborn child sailed through the air and landed in the corner of the kitchen as her wool-stockinged feet struggled for traction on the cold tile. As he jerked her through the room, Becca's legs scissored back and forth. A wild kick met the kitchen hutch, sending dishes shattering across the floor.

With the chaos in the kitchen still settling—bowls rolling, stools bouncing—she felt the carpet of the family room under her feet. It gave her leverage and Becca used every bit of it to push him away, but her resistance only fueled Brad's rage. He wrenched her head backward, ripping a clump of hair from her scalp as her feet left the ground and her body went horizontal. As she fell, Becca felt her head crack against the wood frame of the couch as he heaved himself on top of her. The pain in her head vibrated down her spine. Her vision blurred and the noise of the world began to fade, until his ice-cold hands thrust into her sweatpants. This snapped her back to consciousness. As the weight of his body pinned her down, she punched and clawed until her knuckles broke and her nails became thick with skin and blood.

When she felt her underwear rip away, she screamed a piercing, shrill cry. But it lasted only a few seconds, until his hands found her throat and crushed her voice into raspy gasps. He was vicious and possessed as he silenced her, his hands clamping with a powerful rage around her neck. She sucked for air, but it would not come, and soon her arms fell like deflated balloons to her sides. And though her body could no longer respond to the panicked calls from her mind, she still resisted by never breaking eye contact with him. Until her vision faded like her voice.

Broken and bleeding, she lay there, her chest barely rising with shallow breaths. She drifted in and out, waking each time he brutalized her in angry, violent waves. It went on for an eternity before he left her. Before he fled through the sliding glass door of the family room, leaving it wide open. As the cold night air filled the room and crept over her naked body, Becca's eyelids fell to slivers. All that was left now was white halogen glowing in the doorframe, bright against the dark night. Becca lay motionless, unable to blink or look away had the desire come to her. It did not. She was strangely content in her paralysis. Tears slid down her cheeks and climbed the curve of her earlobes before dripping silently to the floor. The worst was over. The pain was gone. He was no longer on top of her, and his absence was all the freedom she wanted. His fists no longer pummeled her, and her throat was finally free from his crushing grip. His hairy thighs had stopped rubbing over her, and his hot breath was gone from her face.

On the floor with her legs splayed and arms like two broken tree limbs attached to her sides, she faced the wide-open patio door. The lighthouse in the distance—with its bright beacon calling out to lost boats in the night—was all she knew and all she needed. It was life and she clung to its swaying image.

Far away a siren bounced through the night, low at first, then gathering strength. Help was coming, although she knew it was too late. Still, she welcomed the siren and the aid it would bring. It was not herself she was hoping to save.

Chapter 44

Kelsey Castle
Summit Lake Foothills
March 15, 2012
Day 11

The cabin sat at the edge of the forest, and the dying evening light cast it in an ominous glow. A creek curled around from the back and cascaded over three tiers of staircase rocks before trickling into a large pond to the side of the cabin. Cattails swayed in a gentle breeze, and other than the gurgle of the water and a few bird calls, it was quiet and still this far out.

"It looks empty," Rae said, staring through the windshield.

There were no lights on and no vehicles parked near the cabin.

With the passenger side door open, Kelsey shook her head, tapped her phone, and played the message one more time. She put her phone on speaker. Back in Rae's apartment, Kelsey had spoken with Brad Reynolds's father, who told her he and his son were not on speaking terms, and that Brad was no longer part of his life. But soon after Kelsey ended the call, and while she was attempting to reach Richard Walker, Brad's mother had called and left a message. Kelsey and Rae listened to it again now.

"Hello? This is Diane Reynolds, Brad's mother. You just spoke with my husband. Sorry for his rudeness. He and Brad are going through a rough time, that's all. Brad is still very much part of our family. And he did know the girl who died. They went to school together, and I'm sure he'd be willing to talk to you about Becca. He's staying at our hunting cabin about an hour outside of Summit Lake. If you see him, tell him we love him very much and that we asked him to call home."

Kelsey and Rae listened once more to Mrs. Reynolds's directions. They were sure this was the cabin. They climbed out and walked to the front porch. Kelsey took the three steps slowly. Dried and crumbled leaves, once bright and colorful, were now black and brittle and accumulating in the corners of the porch.

"Brad Reynolds?" Kelsey called out. "Are you home?"

Kelsey walked across the porch and noticed the front door was open. She squinted her eyes and peeked inside.

"Hello?"

When she got no answer she pushed the door open. Blue, dusky light spilled through the windows and cast the interior in a grainy hue. The cabin was a cluttered mess. A couch by a fireplace and an ancient, makeshift television with bunny-ear antennae. A desk and a chair covered with scattered papers. Newspapers stacked everywhere. Kelsey cocked her head slightly when she saw it. The purse resting on the end table, with its Coach insignia and smooth leather, looked out of place in the dingy cabin.

Her instincts kicked in and Kelsey walked through the doorway and into the dark cabin.

Chapter 45

Brad Reynolds
Summit Lake
February 17, 2012
The night of Becca's death

Brad stood over Becca's motionless body, his chest heaving like an asthmatic. He stood while minutes passed, chasing his breath, not sure exactly what he had just done or what he should do next. He quickly looked around the stilt house, which was trashed from the mudroom to the kitchen to the family room, where he stood, like a mini tornado had spun its way through the house.

He ran to the kitchen and picked up Becca's Coach purse from the floor. An envelope was next to it and he grabbed that also. There were other things he should do—unlock a door or break a window or go upstairs and take her mother's jewelry—but the thoughts descended on him in an avalanche of panic. Instead, he ran with Becca's purse to the sliding glass door, looking at her still, naked body once more before pulling the door open and running into the night. The cold winter air entered his lungs and stung his eyes.

He had parked his truck on a side street off Maple. After he ran the length of the dock, past all the stilt houses, he pulled up and began to walk. The last thing he needed was someone to remember a man running through the streets tonight. When he reached his truck, he grabbed the handle and looked up and down the street. He was alone. He pulled the door open and climbed in, throwing the purse on the passenger seat next to him.

Bringing his breathing under control, he started the truck and put it in gear. Five minutes later, he pulled out of the town center and drove the dark mountain roads that would take him back to his father's hunting cabin. He turned on his high beams and his mind went blank. Before he was aware of his actions, and without being able to recall anything about the hour's drive, Brad was taking the final switchback, the headlights illuminating the cabin as he approached.

His eyes were unblinking when he killed the engine. He sat for many minutes as the truck cooled in the night air, ticking every so often. Finally, he grabbed Becca's purse from the passenger seat and walked through the beams of the headlights and into the cabin. Leaving the door open, the truck's headlights spilled through the doorframe as he sat on the couch.

He held the purse close to his chest, clutching it like a child's teddy bear. He blinked just in time for tears to roll down his cheeks. In front of him, on the wooden coffee table, were the items he had doted over before deciding to drive into town and see her. Pictures of Becca from school, when she wore cutoff jeans and a GWU T-shirt bunched and held with a rubber band at her side. A photo of the two of them at an Orioles game when Becca visited the summer after freshman year. The notes she used to leave on his nightstand when she stayed the night and left before he woke. There were dozens of them.

B— See you tonight at the 19th. You're cute when you snore. —B

The stolen Business Law test also rested on the table. In so many ways, that test was what sent his life spiraling. He had to know the truth. If she really needed him to steal it for her or if it was all a play. He had gone to the stilt house tonight to ask that one simple question. No more. He just wanted the truth.

He finally released his grip on Becca's purse, unzipping it and looking inside. It was her, this purse and its belongings. It was Becca. A piece of her. It carried her smell and her being. He pushed the contents around with his hand and found her lip balm on the bottom. Uncapping the tube, he closed his eyes and inhaled. He could still conjure in his mind the taste of this lip balm from the night he and Becca kissed. He pulled out her law school ID. Staring at Becca's image, he wanted to ask this girl he loved a thousand more questions. Wanted to rewind time and visit her again, make it a different ending.

Finally, he threw the lip balm and ID back into the purse and dropped it onto the end table. Ripping open the envelope he had taken from the stilt house, Brad unfolded the single page and immediately recognized her cursive. The letter was to Becca's unborn child. Brad's breaths were labored again as he read, his chest anvil-like. His eyes teared up as he sat on the couch and read the letter. The truck's headlights continued to pour through the open cabin door while he sat rocking on the couch. Back and forth. Back and forth.

Chapter 46

Kelsey Castle
Summit Lake Foothills
March 15, 2012
Day 11

Rae grabbed Kelsey's wrist as she started into the cabin. "Where are you going?"

Kelsey pointed with her other hand at the purse. "Come on. Something's not right here."

Together, the two walked into the cabin. Without the evening light they were both cast in shadows. Kelsey picked up the purse from the end table and looked inside. She pulled out an ID badge and there she was: Becca Eckersley, staring back at her. Kelsey could feel the stare, as though the photo taken long ago was a portal through which Becca spoke to her. She was asking for help and Kelsey would not deny her.

Rae was crouched over the coffee table now, staring at the scattered mess of photos and notes and school papers. Rae had seen Becca's face plastered in the paper and on television often enough to recognize her instantly.

"Hey," Rae said, pointing at the table. She looked quickly around the cabin. "This is freaking me out."

Kelsey glanced at the photos on the table, then held up

Becca's law school ID. They both nodded at each other, not having to speak to let the other know her thoughts. Kelsey pulled out her phone and began to dial Commander Ferguson's number. She stopped mid-dial and looked at her phone.

"What?" Rae said, whispering suddenly.

"No service."

"Let's get the hell out of here."

Kelsey nodded, but then she saw the cellar door, cracked open and covered with photos. "Wait," she said. "Look."

Against Rae's protests, Kelsey walked deeper into the cabin. An investigator to her marrow, Kelsey could not allow herself to leave. With the morbid fascination when one stares at a car wreck, Kelsey walked to the cellar door and pulled it open, marveling at the shrine that was there.

Stuck to the back of the door and to the wall that followed the stairs to the basement were hundreds of photos of Becca, all pinned dutifully with a single thumbtack and curled at the edges. Most appeared to be from college, with campus or dorm room paraphernalia in the background. Some were staged photos from yearbooks. Others were cut and pasted, zoomed in to isolate Becca's face. A few were rectangles of only her eyes, staring out at nothing. Until now. Kelsey felt the stare again. Accepted it.

The notes were here, too, farther down the wall. The short notes that started with a single "B" and ended the same way. Scores of them tacked to the wall in a descending path that led to the basement. The stairs creaked as Kelsey took them, one at a time, staring at the photos and the notes as she descended into the basement. Halfway down the stairs, the dying light that spilled through the cabin's windows was gone, so Kelsey used her phone to highlight the wall. The flash reflected off the glossy photos. As Kelsey scanned the shrine, the pictures became hypnotic. Toward the bottom of the staircase, she came across more disturbing photos. Not of a young student posing and smiling for the camera, but of a young woman unaware she was being photographed. In these shots, taken paparazzi-style, Becca was walking through campus, removing items from her car, leaving a doctor's office. In several photos, Becca's image was blurred as she jogged with headphones dangling, hair in a ponytail.

Kelsey stopped on these frames, the ones of Becca jogging. She ran her finger over one of the images, blocking from her mind those thoughts that tried to trespass.

"Jesus Christ," Rae said, staring at the wall from several steps above Kelsey. She had come across several close-up prints of Becca sleeping. Eyes closed, hair matted. Some were full-body shots of Becca in bed, covers pulled down to her feet, wearing a tank top and shorts. "Let's get the hell out of here."

But Kelsey was too far gone. From her years on the beat, she understood the work of a disturbed man. More than that, she was fascinated by it. Kelsey tapped her phone and took pictures of the wall. Of the photos and the notes. Of the purse she still carried and the ID badge. Of the cabin stairs and the way a deranged killer lives. She saw the privileged life of Brad Reynolds deteriorating before her, and in her mind she wrote the story.

"See," Kelsey said aloud, but she was clearly talking to herself. "He's an organized asocial."

"Oh, really?" Rae said. "He's also a psychopath stalker. Now let's go."

Kelsey was still snapping photos. "Stalker, yes. Psychopath, no." Kelsey slowly took the last two steps into the basement, videoing now as she moved slowly, trying to capture everything she could. "I see it all now. It's all come together in my mind. See, Brad loved Becca, but she didn't love him back. Becca loved Jack instead. Brad became obsessed."

"Obviously."

"No, it's more than that. It's more than an obsession. It's

called organized asocial. It's the pattern of a killer. A particular type of killer. He's smart. High IQ smart. Can be very personable and charismatic, but withdraws from society. Holes himself up out here in the foothills, where no one will bother him. Breaks bonds with his family so he can concentrate on his prize. Then, with nothing else to distract him, his obsession grows. It happened right here in this cabin. Grew until it overtook him. Until an image of Becca formed in his mind that never really existed. And this false image of her became his reality. These types of killers are unaware of their growing obsession. Until one day, with Becca's image constantly surrounding him and all the memories of their time together eating away at him, he decides to see her. To talk to her. That's what he told himself. He only went to talk. Went into that stilt house to ask her a question. But in reality, he went to kill her. To take her life so no one else could have her."

Rae stayed in the middle of the stairway, refusing to venture beyond the safety of the open door a few steps away and the scant light that was there. Kelsey, still videoing, walked into the basement. Her phone like a lone star in the dark sky. The beam lit up a workbench covered with tools Brad had used to create his shrine. Scissors and straight-edged paper cutters. Photos of Becca waiting to be cut and pasted. A Nikon camera resting in an open case, various lenses set to the side. Newspapers, too, were stacked on the workbench. Some were discarded on the floor, large squares missing from them. To the side of the workbench, Kelsey found the isolated articles. They chronicled Senator Milt Ward's plane crash. She snapped photos of them but failed to make a connection.

Against the adjacent wall was a small desk and chair. Kelsey played the light over the surface to find handwritten letters. She picked one up and held it close. *Dear Becca,* was the heading, then a page filled with incoherent sentences and half thoughts. It was signed by Brad. There were ten sealed envelopes, all addressed to Becca. Stamped and ready to be dropped in the mail—had Brad ever mustered the courage to do so, Kelsey guessed.

Above the desk, tacked to the wall, were formal letters addressed to Brad. Kelsey took a closer look and realized they were rejection letters from Penn, Columbia, and Yale. She snapped photos of the letters. Then something else. Positioned perfectly in the middle of the desk was a white piece of paper. In ugly, block lettering a message was scrawled.

TO THOSE WHO COME FOR ME: MAY YOU KNOW MY HELL, AND NEVER ESCAPE THIS PLACE AND WHAT WAITS FOR YOU HERE.

Kelsey came back from that investigative place in her mind where she spent the last several minutes writing her article, seeing it clearly in the full arc from Becca's acceptance to GWU through her death, and all the events in between that brought her to the stilt house just four weeks before.

"Rae?"

"Yes?"

"We should get out of here."

"Thank God. Come on," she called from the stairs.

Before the words were out of her mouth, headlights from a truck flashed through the cabin's windows as it came down the narrow road out front. The lights spilled into the basement stairwell and lighted Rae's face.

"Shit!" Rae said. It came out like a scream.

"What's wrong?" Kelsey asked, running to the stairs.

"He's here."

"Come down here!" Kelsey said, grabbing Rae by the wrist and pulling her into the basement.

Outside, the truck skidded to a stop on the gravel.

Chapter 47

Brad Reynolds
Summit Lake Foothills
February 17, 2012
Just after Becca's death

The night's events finally crashed down on him as he sat reading Becca's letter to her unborn child. Brad was helpless to stop his mind from replaying the image of his hands around her neck. Why had she thrown it in his face? Her pregnancy. It was as though she couldn't wait to destroy him with it. God, he wanted to do it all again. Go back and talk to her. Ask her about the Business Law test, that was all.

He sat for hours with these thoughts spinning in his head. Considering different scenarios of how things could have gone, of how it all could have worked out between him and Becca. But in the end, his visit to the stilt house backfired. He had more questions now about the girl he loved than before he went. Married and pregnant and nothing like the girl he loved.

The rising sun caught him by surprise. It appeared suddenly, draining the blackness from the cabin windows and replacing it with a subtle glow. In one deep breath, Brad looked around the cabin and knew what he needed to do. It wouldn't be long. Someone would come for him. The police, maybe. His father, he hoped. And if it was his father, God help him. The man would finally get what he deserved.

He took the entire day to prepare the cabin, spending most of it in the basement. He added final additions to his shrine, then set the cabin up so that anyone who entered would not soon leave. He set a trail of clues starting at the front door. They were unmistakable, with Becca's purse as the first lure. It was sure to draw whoever came for him into the cabin. And if the purse pulled them in, the rest of the items would keep their attention.

When he was finished, he climbed into his truck. It was early evening and the sun was just starting to fade. He remembered the last year of his life. For nine full months he had been at his family's hunting cabin, alone and isolated the way he wanted it. But every day was not the same. Yes, there was a routine he adopted. It allowed him to stay warm and full and bathed. He gathered wood, chopped it, and fed the fireplace. He went to town when he needed food or supplies or propane. As the months passed, he developed an unwritten schedule to take care of his basic needs. But there was something else inside of him that needed tending. The temptation to see her could not always be contained, and when his longings spilled over he took to the road. It was good to get away from the cabin. Therapeutic to see her. Of course, he always meant to confront her. To talk to her. But the sight of her always held him off. Instead, he became satisfied with simply photographing her. Stealing her image and keeping it for himself. He had done this before—jokingly, he told himself—when she slept in his bed. He always meant to share those photos with her. Explain how beautiful she looked when she slept. But she broke his heart before this could happen.

Becca, too, had a routine during the week, he found.

Studying at the law library was one of them. And he knew when his cravings became too great, he could perch on a campus bench and wait for her to walk the path that led up the steps of the library. The photos he took then were easy, he simply blended in as another student. The ones he shot when she entered her apartment were more difficult since these were through the windshield of his truck. And one night, not long ago, he was so close. Waiting for her around the corner of her apartment, hidden in darkness, he had almost earned the courage to step from the shadows and embrace her. Maybe things would have ended differently had he comforted her that cold, dark night. He had wanted so badly to hold her in his arms when she returned from the doctor. He was sure back then that she had fallen ill. And to think now about how worried he was by her frequent trips to the medical clinic. Only to find she was pregnant. He thought again of the disgusting way she blurted it in his face.

The sun was dying now as he sat in the truck, draining the cobalt from the sky as it melted again to black. It was irony, Brad thought, that such a beautiful day ended by turning to darkness. Staring at the fading sky, he knew no one would understand him. He could explain what he'd been through. Tell the cops or his parents or the shrinks what Becca did to him. About Jack's betrayal. His law school rejections. He could detail it all, piece by piece, and still no one would understand him.

He started his truck, put it in gear. He was finally ready to leave his cabin. Leave it for those who would come for him. He pulled away, knowing he still had much to do to prepare. Knowing that when he came back to this place, he would never leave.

Chapter 48

The truck's lights were bright on the landing as Kelsey and Rae ran into the basement. Her phone was soon the only light in the darkened space. They searched for a place to hide, and were ready to settle on a dingy closet before Kelsey saw it.

"There!" she said, pointing to the corner.

She and Rae ran to the back of the basement, where three stairs led to a crawlspace. Ten feet farther were coffin-like doors in the ceiling. They climbed the stairs and on all fours crawled through the cobweb-infested space. They both groaned as the silky webs broke across their faces. A truck door slammed outside and footsteps pounded up the outside porch.

"Go!" Kelsey whispered, pushing Rae from behind. When they reached the doors, Kelsey held her phone while Rae fumbled with the sliding lock. She finally released it and they both pushed open the double doors, finding themselves at the back of the cabin. They clambered out of the crawlspace and into the dying evening light.

As soon as they did, a rancid smell settled all around them. A sound, too, unidentified at first but after a few seconds recognized as the buzzing of flies. Thousands of them circling the shed at the edge of the property.

"What is it?" Rae asked, covering her mouth.

Inside the cabin, the front door burst open.

"Go!" Kelsey said, and they both ran for the dark woods behind the property, shielding their noses from the rotten odor. Rae let out a short screech as their feet pounded gravel. As they approached the shed, the doors were wide open. The flies were heavy here, accumulating in dense swarms. The air was thick with rot. Kelsey slowed to a jog, Rae heading off in front of her. After a few strides, Kelsey stopped and stared. In the fading light she saw the dark silhouette of a limp body hanging in the shed, the head propped up and slumped to the side like a twisty straw. Finally she stopped, changed direction, and headed for the shed. Rae slowed also.

"Kelsey! Come on!" Rae was crying now, wanting to run and hide and get away from this haunted place.

"Wait," Kelsey said, as she organized her thoughts and pieced together what she was witnessing.

As she approached the shed Kelsey realized what it all was and what it all meant. The cellar and the photos and his cryptic message. In front of her, Brad Reynolds's bloated and decaying body hung, unmoving, from the rafters. The noose cinched so tight around his neck that his eyes bulged like a thyroid patient from his sockets. His tongue fat and stiff, like a dried baguette had been shoved in his mouth. Flies feasting, maggots burrowing.

Rae screamed when she saw the body. Kelsey quickly turned and hugged her, shielding her from the gore.

"Kelsey!" a man yelled from the cabin. She recognized the

voice. When she turned from the shed she saw both Peter and Commander Ferguson, with his revolver drawn, bounding through the cabin's back door.

"Here!" Kelsey yelled.

Rae bent over and put her hands on her knees.

Peter and the commander ran across the back lawn. Peter grabbed Kelsey in a tight hug.

"You okay?" he asked.

"I'm fine. Just shaken up."

As Peter let go of her, Kelsey pointed to the shed.

"Oh God," Peter said as he looked at the grisly scene.

Still hunched over, Rae gagged and dry heaved. Peter crouched beside her. "Breathe. In and out."

"Mr. Reynolds, I presume?" Commander Ferguson replaced his gun with a flashlight that he played over the body and through the shed.

"That's my guess," Kelsey said, covering her nose as she left Rae to Peter's attention. "And pretty ripe. Wait until you see the basement of that cabin. Disturbing."

The beam of Commander Ferguson's flashlight fell to Brad Reynolds's feet and highlighted a note that rested on the ground. The commander reached into his pocket and produced a pair of thin rubber gloves, which he stretched over his fingers. He carefully lifted the note, thumb and index finger, and held it up to read. It hung sideways and he tilted his head. It was three sentences:

I only went to talk. I loved her. Despite everything she did.

Chapter 49

Kelsey Castle
Summit Lake
March 18, 2012
Day 14

She spent her last three days in Summit Lake holed up in her third-story room at the Winchester. She gave one morning to Detective Madison, answering questions and giving details. Madison's boss had made his way to Summit Lake by then, the case having broken so fast and messy and without the slick case-solver having anything to do with it. Madison's questions, at first asked in a forceful and abrupt manner, soon mellowed. Especially after his boss arrived. Every question Madison asked was one he himself had no answer to. The more he asked, the more clueless he looked. Kelsey gave a quiet smile and quick wink to Commander Ferguson when she left the station. He had been asked back as a special "consultant" to wrap up the Eckersley case.

After the questioning, Kelsey stopped to see Rae at the coffeehouse. Still reeling from the night at the cabin and the scene in the shed, Rae was not her usual self.

"You going to be okay?" Kelsey asked, as they sat in the overstuffed leather chairs and sipped lattes.

Rae forced a smile. "Just have to scrub that image from my mind, that's all."

"I'm sorry I dragged you to that cabin, Rae. I had no idea what we'd find."

"It's not your fault. I wanted to go, and be part of this thing." Another smile. "Got more than I bargained for, right?"

Kelsey smiled. "Me too." She stared at her friend and confidante. "I consider you a good friend, Rae. I hope you know that."

"I do. And I feel the same about you."

"Good. Once I get home and settled, I hope you'll come see me. Spend a weekend. I'll show you Miami."

"That'd be nice."

Kelsey stood up. "I've got to get going. I should write this up before it all leaks from my head."

"Yeah," Rae said, standing also. "I've got to get back to work myself. It helps to stay busy."

They looked at each other, then embraced in a long hug. Kelsey whispered into her ear, "Thank you, Rae. For everything."

Kelsey wrote the three-piece article in long stretches where time floated by without notice. Hunger never bothered her, and only occasionally did she have the urge to use the washroom. Kelsey never had trouble writing. Throughout her career she was quite prolific with her articles and her book. She had zip drives full of ideas and outlines and stories that would likely never be published in any form of media. Putting words on paper was never a problem for her, but the three days spent at the Winchester after discovering Brad Reynolds's body were unique. She found herself in a zone she had only previously read about or heard about from snobby writers she knew who wrote novels and considered themselves elite. But now Kelsey finally understood that nirvana. She barely needed to think as she wrote Becca's story. The ugly draft she whipped up in Rae's apartment was trashed and she started anew.

After a beginning hook, capturing the essence of Becca's death and the terrible way this beautiful girl was killed, Kelsey captured Becca's early high school days in a short jaunt. George Washington University followed and, with permission from Jack Covington's parents, Becca and Jack's love story found the page. Her friendship with Brad came next, and all the highs and lows of the group's senior year of college. She quoted Gail Moss extensively. The article followed Becca into law school and Jack onto Milt Ward's campaign. That the two stories were related was astounding and "great luck," Penn Courtney had said. Kelsey chastised him for such a comment, but knew it was the truth.

Kelsey chronicled Becca's secrets, as she knew she had to. They were, after all, the essence of the story. Her pregnancy, her relationships, her marriage. Kelsey wrapped things so tightly in the first two segments that anyone who read them would surely be waiting anxiously for the final installment. That third part, written in one sitting, covered Becca's impromptu visit to her family's stilt house in Summit Lake to study for her exam. There was some speculation, of course, but Kelsey was pretty sure she had things straight. She still had in her possession, after all, Becca's journal. Detective Madison didn't need to know everything. In fact, didn't deserve to.

The town, so special to her now, was covered in a beautiful opening to her third piece. Kelsey even managed to quote two members of the gossip group—the heavyset woman and the forty-year-old. Then, the beginning of the end for Becca, the girl she felt so connected to. From Becca's arrival in Summit Lake to her visit with Livvy Houston to her return home,

Kelsey plotted her path to death. And from the other side, Brad's presence in the shadows, his life in the foothills, and his arrival at stilt row late that night. Of course there was no forced entry. Of course Becca allowed him into the house. They were once close friends, reunited on February 17 in a sad and tragic ending.

The final night of Becca Eckersley's life flowed from her fingertips with no effort at all. Kelsey then chronicled her own two weeks in Summit Lake, concluding with her trek into the foothills and the morbid discovery at the hunting cabin. The photos from her cell phone were an added touch that would make the story.

At 2:15 a.m., she stuck the entire three days of writing on a flash drive and e-mailed a copy to Penn Courtney. She pulled the cork from a bottle of chardonnay and poured a glass, wandering out to the balcony. Summit Lake was asleep, dark but for the light posts on the corners and St. Patrick's Church five blocks away, with its V-shaped lights blazing up its façade. She sat for half an hour, drinking wine and remembering the life of Becca Eckersley.

Chapter 50

Kelsey Castle
Greensboro, NC
April 28, 2012
Two and a half months after Becca's death

He pulled into Raleigh-Durham International Airport at 4:18 p.m. She had landed nineteen minutes earlier and the timing was perfect. He took the lanes to arrivals, pulling to a stop at the United terminal. Only a single loop around the airport was necessary to free himself from the traffic nazi who hounded him. When he circled the second time, he saw her standing at the curb with her suitcase next to her.

Peter rolled down the passenger side window as he approached. "Welcome back to North Carolina," he said.

Kelsey smiled. "Look at you. I literally just walked out here."

He shrugged. "We've got good synergy, what do you want me to say?"

Peter climbed out, walked around the car, and engulfed her in a giant hug, then leaned back and kissed her cheek. Awkwardly, Kelsey turned in the middle of the gesture and their noses touched. She quickly kissed his lips.

"Hi," she said. "Thanks for picking me up."

"I'm glad you came."

"Me too. You sure you don't mind a road trip?"

"Not at all. I like that you're including me."

Kelsey shrugged. "I couldn't have written the article without you; figured I'd include you in this final adventure. Plus, I don't know how this will turn out, so I might need some muscle."

Peter put her bag in the back.

"Mind if I drive?" Kelsey asked.

Peter wrinkled his brow. "I guess not."

She held up the folder in hand. "I won't make you wait until it's printed. The whole story's here. I thought you could read it on the way."

Peter took the folder. "For sure."

The Eckersley article comprised twenty-five pages of white computer paper. As Kelsey drove, Peter read slowly and deliberately for forty straight minutes, licking his finger with each page turn. Interruptions came only occasionally from Kelsey, who inquired about his facial expressions. She was always jittery watching someone read her work. When he finished, they discussed the article until they were on the outskirts of Greensboro. The road trip was Kelsey's final hurrah on the Eckersley article, and the very last bit of money Penn Courtney was going to allow Kelsey to expense. She had no qualms about taking advantage of it. This trip had everything to do with Becca Eckersley.

They pulled into the parking lot of the Marriott in downtown Greensboro. At the front desk they checked into separate rooms and wheeled their bags to the elevator. Peter pressed the button for the fifth floor, then looked at Kelsey.

"Three," she said.

They stood in silence until the doors opened again on the third floor. Kelsey pulled her bag behind her as she exited the elevator, then turned around. "How long do you need?"

"Thirty minutes, maybe."

"Meet you down there at seven?"

"See you then."

Kelsey took half an hour to clean up. She fixed her make-up and primped her hair, changed into a casual dress, and swiped a streak of perfume across her neck. She took the elevator down to the lobby, where she found Peter waiting for her at the entrance of the hotel restaurant. He, too, had changed from his jeans and T-shirt into slacks and a sport coat with an open collar.

Seated at a table in the back of the restaurant, they ordered a bottle of wine.

"I read your book," Peter said.

"Yeah?"

"Of course. You're a very talented writer."

"Hold on," Kelsey said, pretending to dial her phone. "Will you talk to my editor?"

"Please," Peter said. "I sense he feels the same way."

Without the pressure of the case over them, they talked easily for two hours. It was what they had hoped to achieve in Summit Lake but never were able to. Now, sipping the last of the wine long after the table was cleared, they talked until they were the only ones left in the restaurant. Finally noticing the waitress waiting in the corner, Peter paid the bill and they walked to the lobby elevator. A big day awaited tomorrow.

As the elevator doors closed, Peter pressed the button for the fifth floor. "Where are you again?" he asked.

Kelsey smiled. "Same."

The next morning they had breakfast at a diner down the street and were back on the road by 9:00 a.m. It was approaching 10:00 a.m. when they reached the Greensboro suburbs and pulled to the large house with a manicured lawn. Tall trees in the front yard did not sprout branches until they were far above the roof, like southern pillars of protection.

Kelsey sat with the manila envelope on her lap and stared at the intimidating front door. Peter rubbed her knee as she took deep breaths. Finally, she climbed from the car and walked up the steps. Rang the bell.

A petite, middle-aged woman answered the door.

"Mrs. Eckersley?" Kelsey asked.

"Yes." The woman wore a serious expression. "I'm Mary Eckersley."

"My name's Kelsey Castle. I'm from *Events* magazine."

There was a moment of silence between them.

Mary Eckersley finally said, "I know who you are."

"Sorry to show up unannounced, but I wanted to see you before my article runs."

"And when will that be?"

"Two weeks."

"We're not going to give you any statements for the article."

"I understand. But that's not why I came."

Mrs. Eckersley waited.

"I wanted you and your husband to know that this case . . . this thing, horrible thing, that happened to your daughter has touched me in a way that no other story has. I know this will sound intrusive, but I feel connected in some small way to her. And it's important for you to know everything I wrote was with Becca in mind. With what she went through on the forefront of my thoughts as I wrote about her life and . . . her death."

Kelsey had a prepared speech. Two full paragraphs she had written and rewritten. Spoken aloud in the bathroom mirror and committed to memory. It covered her own struggle with having been raped. Her questions about life and death, and why one person lives through such a horrible event while another dies. It was beautiful and poignant, meant to disarm the Eckersleys and bring them safely onto her side. It was sincere, too. Meant to show that there was nothing vindictive in what Kelsey had written. But when she saw William Eckersley walk up behind his wife, the entire speech leaked from her mind leaving a giant black void that prevented thought. Kelsey smiled at him awkwardly. No introductions were needed.

"Anyway," Kelsey finally said. "I came here to give you this."

She handed Becca's mother a manila envelope. "I think Becca would want you to have it."

Kelsey slowly backed away from the front door, finally turning and walking down the steps. As Peter backed down the long driveway, Kelsey watched Mr. and Mrs. Eckersley handle the envelope, turn it over for any clues about what might be inside. Finally, they opened it and pulled out Becca's journal and the letter she wrote to her daughter.

Kelsey caught Mrs. Eckersley's eyes as she looked up from the journal. Peter shifted the car into drive and they pulled away.

Chapter 51

Kelsey Castle
Miami, FL
May 11, 2012
Three months after Becca's death

The morning sky was patchy with clouds as Kelsey left her house. She wore an Under Armor tank top and shorts. Tight ankle socks were invisible under her green running shoes. Jogging along the beach for a mile, she smelled the salty air as her body glistened from the humidity. It took ten minutes until she came to her old turnoff, which she followed for another quarter mile to the edge of the forest. Her heart was racing. The mile run responsible for some of it, anxiety doing the rest.

Staring into the forest, the path was shadowed and poked with sunlight trickling through the foliage. There were no other runners or bikers present. The thought of turning around crossed her mind, of taking the beach path back home. It would be a sufficient two-and-a-half-mile run, but would completely defeat the purpose of this morning. It had been months since she ran this trail. Four long months since she was last here, showing the police *where* it happened and *how* it happened. A lifetime since this journey began. And finally, with Becca's article debuting today, Kelsey was ready to end this chapter of her life. Type the last sentence and ship it off.

She felt a few raindrops splash her shoulders, then looked up to the sky. It was a mix of distant sun and overhead clouds. The rain grew heavier. She put in her earphones and took off along the shaded forest path, the thick foliage protecting her from the drizzle after a few strides. Seven minutes in, she passed The Spot. She refused to look into the woods. Refused to let her mind run wild. Instead, she ran right past. Her long, muscular legs propelling her beyond this part of the forest and her life, one foot in front of the other, until The Spot was far behind her.

Two miles went by before she saw the exit up ahead, a curved doorway out of the forest. It was bright and alluring. Calling her. She picked up her pace, lifted her knees in a high runner's gait, touching the path with just the balls of her feet. Her arms swung in a tight, controlled motion as sweat rolled down her wrists and across her open palms and flew from her fingertips. As Kelsey grew closer to the forest exit she saw the pavement outside was covered in sunlight, reflecting off the puddles that had formed. Highlighting the dripping trees.

A sunny rainstorm.

In this gripping new thriller from #1 international best-selling author Charlie Donlea, a TV news host sets out to uncover the truth behind a brutal, decades-old murder . . .

Avery Mason, host of *American Events*, knows the subjects that grab a TV audience's attention. Her latest story—a murder mystery laced with kinky sex, tragedy, and betrayal—is guaranteed to be ratings gold. New DNA technology has allowed the New York medical examiner's office to make its first successful identification of a 9/11 victim in years. The twist: the victim, Victoria Ford, had been accused of the gruesome murder of her married lover. In a chilling last phone call to her sister, Victoria begged her to prove her innocence.

Emma Ford has waited twenty years to put her sister to rest, but closure won't be complete until she can clear Victoria's name. Alone she's had no luck, but she's convinced that Avery's connections and fame will help. Avery, hoping to negotiate a more lucrative network contract, goes into investigative overdrive. Victoria had been having an affair with a successful novelist, found hanging from the balcony of his Catskills mansion. The rope, the bedroom, and the entire crime scene was covered in Victoria's DNA.

But the twisted puzzle of Victoria's private life belies a much darker mystery. And what Avery doesn't realize is that there are other players in the game who are interested in Avery's own secret past—one she has kept hidden from both the network executives and her television audience. A secret she thought was dead and buried . . .

Please turn the page for an exciting sneak peek of
Charlie Donlea's newest thriller
TWENTY YEARS LATER
now on sale wherever print and e-books are sold!

Catskill Mountains
July 15, 2001
Two Months Before 9/11

D eath was in the air.
He smelled it as soon as he ducked under the crime scene tape and stepped foot onto the lawn of the palatial estate. The Catskill Mountains rose above the roofline as the early morning sun stretched shadows of trees across the yard. The breeze rolled down from the foothills and carried the smell of decay, causing his upper lip to involuntarily twitch when it reached his nostrils. He wasn't sure if it was because this was his first case as a newly minted homicide detective or if it was because of some perverse fetish he had never known he possessed, but the odor filled him with a sense of purpose.

A uniformed police officer led him across the lawn and around to the back of the property where he found the source of the foul odor. The victim was hanging from a second story balcony, his feet suspended at eye level. The detective looked up to the terrace. A white rope stretched over the railing, tight and challenged by the man's weight. The twine disappeared through French doors that led, he presumed, into the bedroom. Walking closer to the victim he noticed the man's pants sagged on his left hip, exposing part of the buttocks. That the man wore no underwear was his first observation. The thin bruise marks that started at the waistline and surely covered the man's right buttock was the second. The contusions flared a faint lilac against the liver mortis blue hue of the dead man's skin and looked to the detective a lot like whip marks.

A spiraled bundle of rope wrapped around the man's ankles. Rigor mortis had bent his bloated feet at ninety-degree angles to his shins. The detective reached into his breast pocket and removed a pair of latex gloves that he slipped his hands into. He walked around to the back of the body. The man's right arm was swollen and stiffened at his side, wanting but unable to extend further due to the rope that bound the man's wrists together. The left arm was bent behind the man's back with a bundle of rope wrapped multiple times around each wrist. The length of twine connecting the wrists was stretched tight as rigor mortis attempted to bloat the man's arms away from his sides. Cut this rope, the detective imagined, and the guy would unfold to like a scarecrow.

He gestured for the crime scene photographer, who waited at the periphery of the lawn.

"Get close-ups of the wrists and ankles."

"Yes sir," the photographer said.

The crime scene unit had already been through the property, taking photos and video to log as the *before* evidence. This second time through would be during and after the detective had his first look. The photographer raised his camera and peered through the viewfinder.

"So what's the initial thought here?" the photographer asked as the camera's shutter clicked redundantly as he snapped a series of photos. "Someone tied this guy up and threw him over the balcony?"

The detective looked back up the second story. "Maybe. Or he tied himself up and jumped."

The photographer stopped shooting and slowly took his face away from the camera.

"Happens more than you'd think," the detective said. "That way, if they have second thoughts they can't save themselves." The detective pointed at the dead man's face. "Get some clicks of that gag in his mouth."

The photographer squinted as he walked to the front of the body and looked at the dead man's mouth. "Is that a ball gag? As in S&M bondage?"

"It would certainly go hand-in-hand with the whip marks on this guy's ass. I'm heading upstairs to see what's holding this guy in place."

Latex gloves covered the detective's hands and plastic wraps enclosed his shoes as he walked into the bedroom. The balcony doors opened inward and allowed the same breeze that had earlier filled his nostrils with the smell of death to gust through the bedroom. The pungent odor was less noticeable here, one story above where death hung in the morning air. He stood in the doorframe and moved his gaze around. This was clearly the master suite. A king-sized four-poster bed stood in the middle of the room with night tables on either side. A dresser sat against the far wall, its mirror reflecting his image back at him. Through the open balcony doors, the white rope curved up over the railing and ran at waist height across the room and into the closet.

He stepped into the room and followed the rope. The closet had no door, just an arched entryway. When he reached it, he saw a spacious walk-in filled with neatly organized clothes hanging from scores of identical hangers. Shoes filled the thick pine cubbyholes that covered the back wall. Against the far wall, amid the cubbies, was a black safe about five feet tall, likely weighing close to a ton. With an ornate knot, the end of the rope was tied to a handle on the side of the safe. The other end, the detective knew, was attached to the man's neck, and whether he jumped off the balcony or was pushed, the safe had done its job. It had not budged an inch—the four legs indented the carpeting with no adjacent depression marks to suggest the safe had moved from the weight of the man's body.

A large kitchen knife lay on the floor next to the safe. He pulled a flashlight from his pocket and shined it at the carpeting. Morning sunlight spilled through the balcony doors and trickled into the walk-in closet, painting his shadow across the floor and up the far wall. He was interested in the small fibers next to the knife. He crouched down and examined them in the bright glow of his flashlight. They appeared to be bits of frayed nylon from when the rope had been cut. Within the carpet fibers were three small drops of blood, and a fourth on the handle of the knife. He placed a triangle-shaped yellow evidence placard over the blood droppings and fibers, and another next to the knife.

He turned and walked out of the closet, noticing a nearly empty wine glass on the night table. He was careful not to disturb it as he placed another yellow evidence marker next to it, noting the lipstick that smeared the rim. High stepping over the taut rope, he walked past the mirrored dresser and into the bathroom. He slowly looked around and saw nothing out of place. Soon, the forensics team would be in here with luminal and black lights looking for hidden blood evidence. At the moment, the detective was interested in his first impression of the place. The toilet lid was open but the seat was down. The toilet water held a yellow color, and the faint smell of urine registering now as his nose caught up with his eyes. Someone had used the toilet but failed to flush. The lid was up but the toilet seat was down, and dry. A lone segment of toilet paper floated in the bowl. Another evidence placard found the toilet.

He walked from the bathroom and into the main area, once again surveying the room. He slipped his suit coat off his shoulders and draped it over the chair next to the dresser, and then followed the rope out to the balcony. He looked down at the dead man hanging from the other end. In the distance, the Catskill Mountains were cloaked by early morning fog. This was the house of a very wealthy man, and the detective had been tasked with figuring out what had happened to him. In just a few minutes he had identified blood evidence, DNA from the lipstick on the wine glass, and a urine sample that likely belonged to the killer.

He had no idea at the time that all of it would be matched to Victoria Ford. And the detective could have no idea that in two short months, just as he had all his evidence organized and a conviction all but certain, commercial airliners—American Airlines Flight 11 and United Airlines Flight 175—would fly into the Twin Towers of the World Trade Center. In a single sun-filled, blue sky morning, three thousand men and women would die, and the detective's case would go up in smoke.

The New York City Medical Examiner's office was located in a nondescript, six-story white brick building in Kips Bay on East 26th Street and First Avenue. If offices had occupied the top two floors they would provide views of the East River and the north end of Brooklyn. But the upper floors were not meant for the scientists and doctors who roamed the building. They were instead reserved for water and air purification systems. The circulated air within the world's largest crime lab was clean, pure, and dry. Very, very dry since humidity was bad for DNA, and DNA extraction was one of the crime lab's fortes.

In the cold, damp basement was the bone-processing laboratory. A technician opened the airtight seal of the cryo tank, releasing liquid nitrogen fog into the air. A triple layer of latex gloves protected the technician's hands. His face was safe behind a plastic shield. He reached into the tank with a pair of forceps and lifted the test tube from the fog. It was filled with a white powder that had minutes earlier been a small bone fragment specimen. The liquid nitrogen had been used to freeze the bone, and then the frozen specimen was shaken violently in the bulletproof test tube. The result was total pulverization of the original bone sample into fine powder. The technique allowed scientists to access the innermost portion of the bone, which made the chance of extracting usable DNA more likely. The concept was remarkably simple and had been developed based on two of the basic concepts of physics—the law of motion, and thermodynamics. If an apple were thrown at a wall, it would break into many pieces. But if the same apple were frozen solid by liquid nitrogen and *then* hurled at the wall, it would shatter into millions of pieces. When it came to extracting DNA from bone, the more pieces the bone could be broken into, the better. The finer the powder, better still.

The tech placed the test tube into a rack with a dozen others containing pulverized bone. With the nitrogen fog still spiraling from the latest tube, he dipped a titrating syringe into a beaker of fluid, drew ten ccs into the chamber, and added the extraction products to the pulverized bone. The next day, instead of bone powder, a pink liquid would fill the tubes. It was from this liquid that a genetic code would be procured—a sequence of twenty-three numbers unique to every human on the planet.

In the room next to the bone-processing lab, a continuous bank of computers lined all four walls. It was here where scientists took the DNA profiles generated from the original bone fragments and attempted to match them to profiles stored in the Combined DNA Index System databank known as CODIS. But this was not the national databank the FBI utilized to match DNA profiles gathered from crime scenes to previously convicted criminals. The databank searched here was a standalone archive of DNA profiles provided by the families of 9/11 victims who were never identified after the towers fell.

Greg Norton had worked at the Office of the Chief Medical Examiner for three years. Most of those years were spent in the computer lab. Each morning he was met with a stack of DNA profiles recently sequenced from bone fragments that had been collected from the rubble of the twin towers. He entered each sequence into the CODIS databank and searched for matches. In three years of employment he had never made a single match. But this morning, just as he sat down with his second cup of coffee and pecked away at the keyboard, a green indicator light blinked at the bottom of the screen.

Green?

A red light meant no matches had been found on sequences entered, and Greg had become so accustomed to misses that the red light was all he ever expected. He'd never seen a green indicator light during his tenure at the OCME. He clicked on the icon and two DNA profiles popped up onto the monitor—white numbers against a black background. They were identical.

"Hey boss?" he said in a careful tone, keeping his eye on the set of twenty-three numbers in front of him to make sure they didn't change.

"What's up?" Dr. Trudeau asked as he worked his fingers over a keyboard on the other side of the room.

As the head of Forensic Biology, Arthur Trudeau was in charge of identifying the remains of mass casualties from across the sate of New York. For nearly twenty years it had been his mission to identify every specimen collected from those killed in the World Trade Center attack.

"We got a hit."

Trudeau's fingers stopped tapping the keyboard and he slowly glanced over at Greg Norton's station. "Say that again."

The tech nodded and smiled as he continued to stare at the numbers on his screen. "We got a hit. We got a fickin' hit!"

Dr. Trudeau stood up at his desk and walked across the lab. "Patient?"

"One one four five zero."

Trudeau pulled the keyboard from a standing computer station toward him and typed the numbers.

"Who is it?" Greg asked.

Other technicians had heard the news of a confirmed identification and gathered around. Trudeau stared at the monitor and the small hourglass that spun as the computer searched. Finally, a name appeared on the screen.

"Victory Ford," he said.

"Next of kin?" Greg asked.

Trudeau shook his head. "Parents, but they're deceased."

"Any other contacts?"

"Yes," Trudeau said, scrolling down the page. "A sister. Address in New York State."

"Want me to make the call?"

"No. Let's run it one more time to be sure. Start to finish. If it hits a second time, I'll give her a call."

"First one in how long, boss?"

Dr. Trudeau looked over at the young technician. "Years. Now run it again."

Connect with Us

Visit us online at
KensingtonBooks.com
to read more from your favorite authors, see books
by series, view reading group guides, and more.

Join us on social media

for sneak peeks, chances to win books and prize packs,
and to share your thoughts with other readers.

facebook.com/kensingtonpublishing
twitter.com/kensingtonbooks

Tell us what you think!

To share your thoughts, submit a review,
or sign up for our eNewsletters, please visit:
KensingtonBooks.com/TellUs.